Deadly Crush

DEADLY CRUSH

Deadly Trilogy Book 1

Ashley Stoyanoff

Ashley Stoyanoff Books

London, Ontario

Also by Ashley Stoyanoff

Dedication

For my sister, Jonel, because you are awesome!

CHAPTER 1

JADE

I should have taken my own advice.

It was good advice. Simple advice. Advice that I had lived by for two full years. All I had to do was stay clear of the pack. They were just a bunch of dogs. That was it. Nothing special. Just dogs with a superiority complex. Nothing good ever happened by getting mixed up with them. I had seen the proof of their destruction over and over, and what had I done? I had let one of them help me. *Stupid. Stupid. Stupid.*

The thing was, it wasn't easy to avoid them. The pack had been a part of Dog Mountain since, well, forever. I was pretty sure that the town was even named after them. Why else would they have called it Dog Mountain? Anyway, they were everywhere; in school, on the streets, at the stores; you couldn't go anywhere without running into one of them. Everyone knew about them. That would have freaked people out in most towns, but not here. Here, everyone welcomed the werewolves, well, everyone but me.

Personally, I couldn't stand them. They walked around as if they owned everything. I guessed they

1

kind of did, or their families did. But that wasn't the point. They were possessive, territorial, and a serious pain in the butt. Especially the *she-wolves*. The *she-wolves* were the worst.

And it was because of one of those nasty *she-wolves* that I was trapped in the girls' locker room in my underwear.

I should have figured something like this would have happened. Erika and her little gang of dogs had been on my back ever since Dominic — the alpha's beta — drove me home last week. It had been completely innocent. It had been pouring rain, my car had broken down, and he had stopped to help. That was it. But Erika, well, Erika wanted him all to herself, and she couldn't seem to get it through her thick head that it had only been a ride home.

I opened up another locker in the long line of metal doors and slammed it shut. Empty. They were all empty. *Why did gym have to be my last class of the day?*

Frustrated, I plopped down onto the cold bench and pulled my knees to my chest, hugging them closely. They didn't even leave my backpack, and, of course, that's where my phone was.

How could I have been so stupid? This year, I had Mr. Townsend for gym, and gym with Mr. Townsend meant running laps. Only laps. He thought running was the only kind of fitness anyone ever needed. Personally, I thought that that mentality had to be a werewolf thing because, well, running laps sucked. And yes, my gym teacher was a werewolf. Needless to say, by the time class ended, I was all sweaty and gross. I had planned to go shopping after school, just to kill some time before Marcy, my best friend, and practically sister, got home, so understandably, I had decided to grab a quick shower. Clearly, leaving my clothes unattended was a big mistake.

I glanced at my watch, 3:30. Another hour or so before the after-school clubs would finish. *Maybe I could make a dash for my locker then and grab my extra set of gym clothes?* The idea of running around school almost naked made my stomach roll.

For years, I had managed to avoid those ... those ... dogs. And now, I couldn't get away from them. I didn't even understand why Erika cared so much. Dominic hadn't spoken to me since that day. And honestly, I didn't even know why he had stopped to help me in the first place. Since he had become one of them, he had barely glanced my way.

I'm going to throttle that she-wolf!

The pack had always made their presence known in everyday Dog Mountain life. They prowled the streets, taking what they wanted when they wanted it. Well, maybe not really *taking*. Most of the residents of Dog Mountain willingly gave whatever it was that one of those stupid dogs wanted, but that wasn't the point. The point was that they never actually worked for anything; they just took. What happened to the days when werewolves had kept hidden?

The time ticked by slowly. I was starving, but then, I was always starving, and since I had just finished gym, I was extra-starving. My stomach rumbled, and I was starting to get a headache. I could feel it at my temples, radiating in circles through my head. *What a fan-freakin-tastic way to end the first week back at school.*

"Jade, you in here?"

Dominic. His deep voice rumbled through the door as he pushed it open a crack. My heart jumped in my throat, and I was pretty sure my whole body flushed. I felt it like a flash fever. Hot and sticky.

"Go away, Dominic," I yelped, scrambling from my seat. I whipped open one of the lockers and hid behind the metal door. "Don't come in here."

"Why not?" he asked, and I could hear the laughter in his voice. "It's not like I haven't seen you in your underwear before."

"Just stay out!" I hissed at him.

He didn't open the door any more than a crack. "I'm sorry, Jade. Erika ..." He paused, sighing long and loud, and then his hand slid through the small opening. "Look, I have your clothes. I'll just leave them here at the door, okay?"

I didn't say anything, and he didn't either. He just stood there, only his hand visible for a long moment. My stomach twisted in tender knots, and my heart beat loudly in my ears. The door inched open a bit further, and I couldn't stop the squeal that rushed from my lips. *Jeez, he's going to come in!* My brain was certain of it.

I frantically searched around for something, anything to hide my body. But there was nothing. Not even a towel. Those darn wolves probably would have stolen my bra and underwear, too, if they hadn't been in the stall with me.

But then, Dominic sighed again, and thankfully, he dropped my clothes onto the floor and pulled the door shut.

CHAPTER 2

AIDAN

I slinked behind an oak tree, pressing myself tightly against the rough bark, and held still as Dominic stomped out of the school. He walked by, without even a glance in my direction, and he was muttering something about *Jade being impossible.* Who Jade was, I didn't have a clue, and what he was doing here when he was supposed to be meeting me seriously had me annoyed. I may not have been the alpha for that long, but I was still the alpha — his alpha.

I had been tailing him all day, and so far, it had been a disappointment. The pack (or I guess it was *my* pack now) liked Dominic. I had been banking on the fact that it was only because he was a better option than Ray, the last alpha, if only slightly. But so far, following him around had only shown me that they actually liked him and what was worse, they trusted him. The problem was that I had a gut feeling that I couldn't trust him. Dominic was power-hungry. I could see it, feel it, and I was sure that he would be my biggest threat at the ceremony tonight. He had been Ray's beta, and now he was mine by default. Sure, I could choose someone else, and I wanted to, but as I said, the pack liked him. Stripping him of his title could lead to something I didn't want to face — yet.

I was beginning to feel a bit foolish, though, hiding behind a tree and stalking my beta. It didn't feel very alpha-ish. But then, I had never meant for this to happen. It wasn't that I didn't want to be the alpha. I did, and I was sure I'd be good at it, but that didn't change the fact that I hadn't meant to take out the last alpha.

I peeked around the tree trunk and scanned the parking lot for Dominic. He was leaning against his car, arms crossed, and, by the look of it, he was still muttering about something. This was the first time in the last twelve hours that I had seen his cool persona ruffled. And right then, as I watched him, I didn't know whether to be happy (or even more disappointed) that maybe I had been right about him.

He had been there when I had *disposed* of Ray last night, or I guess it was this morning, and he hadn't done much to stop it. Although it would have been against pack rules for him to step in, still, he didn't seem to care that much that Ray was gone. I figured that that was a good thing, seeing as the only reason I challenged the jerk in the first place was because I had found him beating his mate.

Just thinking about it made my stomach roll. Tammy had been covered in blood and barely breathing, huddled at Ray's feet when I had walked into the bar.

I had scented the pack at the border of this little hick town, and I had come close to just driving straight through. The last thing I wanted to deal with was a pack that I didn't know. And if I hadn't been so exhausted, I would have kept going. I'd been driving for thirteen hours straight, trying to put as much distance between my father and me as I could.

After checking into a motel, I searched for the pack

and found them easily enough at a little hole-in-the-wall bar in the center of town. My plan had been to let the alpha know I was in town and just passing through. This was purely out of respect for the pack, but when I saw him kicking the girl over and over, and not a single one of the pack members were doing a thing to stop him, I kind of lost it.

He was a big guy, dressed like a biker with a leather jacket and a green bandana wrapped around his head, and by the way the others were watching him, I knew right away that he was the alpha. They were all cowering back, clearly afraid to interfere. I shot them all disbelieving looks. They were all pack members; even the bartender had a distinctive wolf scent. Fury raged through me. I started toward the alpha and was about to pull him off the girl when Dominic stepped in front of me. "Leave it alone. She's the alpha female."

"The alpha female deserves more respect than this," I growled, staring him down. The alpha was still kicking her, oblivious to us, and for the first time in my life, I actually channeled my father.

I shifted, recalling everything the man had taught me about showing dominance. My legs were stiff and tall. My ears were erect and forward. My tail, vertical and curled. The hair on my back bristled, and I growled long and low. I stared at Dominic, advancing slowly. It didn't take long for him to drop his human gaze and shrink away from me, submitting. It was then that I knew he had to be the beta. The rest of the pack members followed him, moving back, hunching their shoulders, and making themselves look smaller. Not a single one of them shifted.

I let out a low warning growl, and the alpha stopped, motionless. The copper scent of blood was stronger in my wolf form, calling to me, reminding me of the thrill of the hunt. I took slow and sure steps toward her, baring my teeth, curling my lips, and claiming the prey as mine. If the alpha hadn't shifted, I don't know what I would have done. At that moment, all I saw was easy food.

He snarled at me, his fur bristled, and he crouched, ready to attack, guarding his food. The silver-white light of his alpha's imprint shone through his chocolate-brown fur as he gathered his scent, giving me a silent warning to back off. I growled again, and all at once, his scent blasted at me with a staggering force. The pungent, bitter scent overwhelmed me, reminding me of the days I'd spent locked away while my father tortured me — taught me — to ignore the call of an alpha with his own alpha scent. It was crippling, demanding me to give in. Submit.

He channeled his scent again, pushing it out at me in a steady stream. I tried to shake it off just as my father had shown me, and I pushed my own scent at him. He cocked his head to the side, confused for a moment, but without the imprint to enhance the power of my scent, his confusion was short-lived.

I kept my dominant posture, my lips curled even further, exposing my gums, and right then, he launched at me. For half a second, I almost submitted to him. I was exhausted and hungry, and I couldn't think straight, but then his teeth sank into my shoulder, and rage rushed through me again. Hotter and deadlier.

Swift clarity came back to me in a rush. An image of the girl curled on the floor, bleeding while Ray kicked her over and over surged through my brain.

I twisted, biting back. My teeth sank into his side, and then his legs, and in less than a second, he was pinned under me, his vulnerable neck exposed. The years of training under my father had paid off, making him an easy target, but he didn't submit. He snarled and kicked up, trying to throw me off him. He snapped out at my neck, his teeth grazing my fur.

I could feel the rest of the pack watching. Their tension and unease were palpable, and my inner-wolf responded to it. They had submitted, and he would, too. I pinned his neck down with my teeth, not biting, only holding him on the ground, but still, he fought, bucking and twitching under me. He snarled again, and a chorus of whimpers rang out behind me.

"End it," Dominic growled. "He will not submit."

And I did. My teeth found purchase in his neck, and I tasted his blood seeping into my mouth. And then, he stopped moving, stopped fighting, stopped breathing, and I let go.

I couldn't say how long I stood over the dead alpha, staring at him, waiting for him to take a breath before I had shifted back. I remember thinking that my father would have been proud if he knew that I had found my own pack and claimed the alpha rank. I had followed in his footsteps, just as he wanted. I could hear his words as if he were standing right beside me, *'You can run, but alpha is in your scent. You can't hide from it, Son.'* And I also remember thinking that I didn't know how I felt about it.

I didn't reach for my clothes piled behind me, marking where I had become a wolf. I was too stunned that I had won to realize that I stood in the middle of the bar, stark naked. I saw the beta pull the girl to her feet from the corner of my eye, and I noticed that she wouldn't lift her head. She kept her body curled, staying small and passive, and all I could think was, *How had that girl won the challenge?* How many females had she beaten to become the alpha's mate? And what had he done to her to break her so badly?

"The new alpha pair," Dominic said, once she was firmly on her feet and standing in front of me. He waved a hand at us as if he were introducing us to the world. The words shocked me. I hadn't considered everything before I challenged him, and the reality of my actions was slowly sinking in. Alphas do not lose their status if one of them passes on. What was his was now mine, and I was now hers. We were the new alpha pair.

"No," she whispered. "Please. I just want to go. Let me leave. I don't want the rank, and I don't want the pack." She looked up at me; her eyes were full of tears, pleading with me to let her walk away.

I slid my thumb across her cheek, wiping some of the blood away, and she cringed at my touch. "Are you sure?" I asked. I needed to know if she understood what she was doing. If she stepped down, there would no longer be a place for her in this pack. She would be ostracized, marked as weak, and, in time, killed or run out of town.

She didn't hesitate and said, "Yes, please take a new mate. Please. I'll leave town." Her voice was weak, and she dropped her gaze back to the ground. She quivered, shrinking closer to the floor with every passing second. I should have felt sorry for her. An alpha female should never show fear, not like this, and I couldn't even begin to imagine how broken she must have been. But right then, I had no sympathy for her. I only felt relief. I would not have to babysit a mate that I did not want, and clearly, she did not want me either.

"Go," I said. Just that. A simple command I had heard my father use countless times.

She let out a shaky pent-up breath and whispered, "Thank you," still refusing to meet my eyes, and she scurried from the bar without as much as a backward glance.

I had never seen a pack like this in all my nineteen years. Werewolves were supposed to be a protective bunch. It was ingrained in us. In our blood — our bones. But this pack ... whatever Ray (and I was certain it was because of Ray) had done had ruined them. Right now, though, my biggest worry was how close Dominic really had been to his old alpha. I needed to be sure he was with me. Tonight could change everything, and if he wasn't backing me ... I didn't even want to think of the chaos that could happen.

My phone began to vibrate against my hip, jerking me from my thoughts, and I fished it out of my pocket. Dominic. His name flashed on the screen. I tapped the flashing call button and brought the phone to my ear.

"I'm going to be late," Dominic barked into the speaker before I even had a chance to say hello.

"Anything wrong?" I asked, keeping my voice low and peeking at him again. He had folded one arm across his chest, and his body tensed as he leaned against the car.

He looked like he was considering what to tell me, and then, after a moment, he said, "No. I just need to deal with something." He relaxed slightly and sighed into the speaker, or at least I thought it was a sigh; it sounded like a crackly burst in my ear.

"With what?" I pressed, wishing I could get closer. I could barely pick up his scent from this far away, and I wasn't entirely sure if he was lusting after someone or completely frustrated. The scent was so diluted, mixing with the grass and leaves, and most of it was taken away on the breeze before it reached my senses.

"It's personal," he snapped with a rumbling growl.

I was about to tell him that nothing — absolutely nothing — was personal when his alpha was asking, but right then, the double doors banged open, and a girl stormed out of the school. She was of average height, maybe five-foot-six, slim with curvy hips and long brown hair, curled softly at the edges and around her shoulders. She was cute, and she looked furious, which in my opinion, made her look even cuter. She had a fiery spirit; anyone could have seen it just by looking at her. Her hands were clenched at her sides, and her cheeks were bright red. She squinted against the glare from the sun, and then her eyes landed on Dominic. If she had been furious before, she was murderous now.

For a second, she looked as if she were about to dart back into the school, but then Dominic turned to her, and she froze.

"I've got to go," Dominic growled into my ear, and the phone went dead.

CHAPTER 3

JADE

As soon as I walked out of the school, I spotted his silver VW. And then I saw him. Dominic was waiting for me. He was leaning against the driver's side door with one arm folded across his chest and his cell phone glued to his ear with the other. His short blond hair was sticking up as if he had been running his hands through it over and over. His jaw was set in a rigid line, and he really didn't look happy.

I probably should have guessed he'd be waiting for me, but in my defense, I was a tiny bit flustered. I figured I had an excuse, though, seeing as my clothes had been stolen, and my head was pounding as if it had its own heartbeat. I was about to turn around and run back into the school to find another exit when his hazel eyes met mine. He snapped his phone shut before I could make a move and strutted up to me. Yes, strutted. It wasn't a walk or a stroll; it was full of coolness, confidence, and more than a little conceit.

Dominic closed the distance between us faster than I would have liked, and when he was only inches away, he asked, "You okay?" although the tone of his voice insinuated that he really didn't care if I was or not, and he scanned me over, from head to toe — twice.

I wanted to yell at him because, really, I wasn't fine, far from fine. And it was his fault that Erika was picking on me. He could stop it. He could make them leave me alone. He was the beta, for Pete's sake. They had to listen to him. But he hadn't done anything about them, and clearly, he knew what they had been up to. He had just brought my clothes back.

I looked up at him with narrowed eyes, and I straightened my shoulders, masking myself with an air of confidence that I really didn't feel. "I'm fine," I said through clenched teeth, and with my chin held high, because I seriously didn't want him to know how much the *she-wolves* had upset me this time, I walked past him and into the parking lot. And the whole time, my werewolf survival mantra echoed through my brain, *Don't show fear. Stay strong. Be the dominant one.*

"Jade, just get in the car," he called after me.

I huffed and kept walking. "Leave me alone, Dominic."

"I don't think you should walk home alone." His footfalls echoed around me, and I almost started running — almost. It took a heck of a lot of restraint not to. Dealing with werewolves was kind of like being trapped in a horror movie; no matter how fast you ran, the evil villain would still catch you at a walk.

Suddenly, Dominic was in front of me, blocking my path. I gritted my teeth and glared at him. "I don't care what you think," I said, sidestepping him.

"Come on, Jade." He groaned and darted back in front of me. "Just get in the car. I said I was sorry. What more do you want?"

He towered a good six inches over my five-foot-six frame. I glared up at him; his broad shoulders blocked out the glare from the sun that was starting to make its slow descent, and he smiled sheepishly down at me as if his perfectly white smile could wipe out what had just happened. And dammit, but I missed that smile so much that I almost caved right there and then.

But I didn't. I rubbed my temples in small circles, wishing the headache away. I needed a clear head to deal with this. It helped a little. I forced my lips into a smile and said as sweetly as I could, "What I want is for you and your stupid pack to disappear." I batted my eyes at him in a way that I hoped was a little bit mocking, and then I stepped around him and started for the trail at the back of the parking lot.

I hadn't made it two steps when he grabbed my arm, not unkindly, but still with a firm grip, and started pulling me over to the car. "Just get in the car. The pack is stressed, and you're the last person that should be walking around alone right now."

"Let go of me, Dominic!" I squealed. My heart jumped into my throat, and my stomach twisted into a painful knot. I pulled back, trying to rip out of his vice-grip hold. I was pretty sure he was just trying to look out for me, but the thing was, he was creeping me out — just a little. I didn't like *this* Dominic. He was cold and intense, and he made my skin crawl.

Dominic stopped pulling me. He grabbed my other arm, spinning me in front of him and holding me tightly. He looked down at me and rolled his eyes. "I know you think I'm an ass, but I'm really just trying to help you here."

I laughed, but there was no humor in the sound. "It's your *so-called* help that got me into this mess." I yanked again, and he clamped his grip a bit tighter, pinching my skin. I could feel the bruises forming under his grasp, but he seemed oblivious to it. He looked ... distant ... hurt, gazing down at me but not seeing me. I almost felt bad for saying it. Almost.

After a long moment, Dominic blinked. "Jade ..." he growled. His eyes started to shimmer, golden yellow, around the edges, and I shuddered, completely involuntarily. Deep down, I knew he wouldn't hurt me. Out of all of them, Dominic was one of the best. Most of the time, he tried to keep the others under control. Well, he did when Ray wasn't watching. I knew it was Ray's fault that the pack was the way they were. They were being run by a drunken jerk that didn't care about anyone but himself.

Dominic opened his mouth, but he didn't get a chance to spit out whatever he was about to say. "The girl said, 'Let go.'"

Dominic didn't move, and he didn't let go. He glared down at me, still holding me tightly in front of him, as he growled, "Stay out of this, Aidan," sounding more animal than human.

Aidan? Who was Aidan? I looked over my shoulder, spotting the owner of the voice. He smiled and winked at me. "I don't think I will," the new guy — Aidan — said, folding his arms over his chest, making his broad shoulders look even larger. "Let her go."

I stared at him, and my jaw dropped. He was definitely new. He had to be because I knew I would have recognized that face if I had seen it before. He was smiling or smirking. It was hard to tell. It was one-sided, and his jaw twitched a little with tension. He was trying to look gentle, but there was a rough side to him that he couldn't quite mask. It shone through his chocolaty eyes, deadly and sweet all in one.

Dominic's grip tightened again, and a low growl rumbled from his chest. I winced, pulling my eyes away from Aidan's brown ones. "Dominic, you're hurting me," I said, just barely audible.

Dominic flinched as if my words were a physical slap, and the shimmer of golden yellow in his eyes vanished. For about half a second, he looked like he was actually sorry.

It didn't last.

"Whatever," Dominic snapped as he dropped his hands from my arms. He shot me an ice-cold look. "You want to walk home with Erika lurking about, then fine. Don't blame me when she finds you."

Dominic stepped around me then, glaring daggers at the new guy as he went to his car. The new guy didn't flinch. He stared back with the same intensity as if he were daring Dominic to come back. When Dominic opened the driver's side door, he growled something unintelligible and then jumped in, slamming the door shut, and his car rumbled to life.

What just happened? a voice in my head asked as I watched Dominic peel out of the parking lot. In all the years I'd known him, I'd never seen Dominic back away from anyone, even before he became a werewolf.

"You okay?" the new guy asked, pulling me back to the parking lot.

I glanced at him and offered what I was sure was a scary-looking smile. It felt forced and strained. "Um, yeah, thank you, um, Aidan, was it?" I asked. Confused didn't even begin to explain the turmoil swarming my brain.

"No problem," he said with a wink. His voice was deep but warm and held a bit of laughter in it, and I had to admit, the sound of his voice made tiny little butterflies flap in my belly. Or were the butterflies from relief? I wasn't entirely sure.

"You know Dominic?" I asked, squinting up at him and raising my hand to shield the glare from the sun. He was cute, in a rugged sort of way. His hair was shaggy, light brown, and uneven, and his strong jawline was rough looking with stubble. He looked about six-foot, and he was built, but not in a muscle builder kind of way — it was softer — but still showed his undeniable strength.

Aidan chuckled. It was deep and soft and the best sound ever, and he gave me a knowing kind of smile as he watched me take him in. I blushed. "Doesn't everyone in this town know him?" he asked.

"Yeah, they do, but you're clearly new." *Because if you weren't new, you would have pretended not to see Dominic dragging me to his car.* Aidan may have looked strong, but human muscles were more decoration than anything else against the werewolves.

"What's that supposed to mean?" he asked. A wide grin curled his lips. "I can't know people because I'm new?" Aidan chuckled again, and I couldn't help but smile at him. I just loved that sound. It vibrated through me and made my skin tingle.

"Okay, so that probably came out wrong." I dropped my gaze to the ground, trying to hide the burning blush that was rushing up my neck.

Then, a thought dawned on me; maybe he didn't know what Dominic was. Maybe the new guy wasn't stupid, just ignorant. And maybe that was why Dominic walked away. Dominic was giving him a chance to learn the pecking order, giving him a free pass this time. I looked up at him and blurted, "You should be careful. You don't know what you're getting into talking to Dominic like that."

He cocked his head to the side, searching my face. He frowned and sighed softly, and right then, I wished I could read his mind. The look he was giving me was so complex, full of sympathy and anger and something else that I couldn't place, except it did vaguely resemble guilt. He stared at me for a long time, long enough that I started to feel awkward, and it took everything I had not to start fidgeting. After what seemed like hours, he cracked a small smile. "Let's start again," he said, and he stuck his hand out to me. "I'm Aidan Collins."

"Jade Shaw," I said, accepting his hand and pumping it twice and effectively lifting the tension that had been brewing between us. "What are you doing here anyway?"

Aidan smirked. "Just finished registering for classes," he said in a way that made me feel like it should have been obvious.

"On a Friday when the school is closed." It was supposed to be a question, but it came out as a challenge. Maybe it was because new people never moved to Dog Mountain. It was a pack thing. There were never houses available for new residents unless they had the pack's endorsement, and with the way Dominic had acted, Aidan clearly didn't have it.

If Aidan caught my tone, he didn't let on. He just shrugged his shoulders as if to say *obviously*, and asked, "You need a ride somewhere?"

Yes. That's what I wanted to say. The way he was watching as if he wanted nothing more than to get to know me had my heart jumping like crazy. It was such a tentative look as if I were the only person around. But then I guess I was. We were standing in an empty parking lot, except the look in his brown eyes gave me the impression that it wouldn't have mattered if the lot was full. And it made me want to know him, too, even if it would be stupid to try. Aidan had just placed a huge target on his back, and he didn't even know it. Strangely enough, knowing that he was trouble, or more like knowing he had pissed off the beta, only made me want to know him more. But no matter how much I wanted to say yes, what came out was, "Actually, I don't live that far. I'll walk. But thanks."

"Sure," he said, sounding a little disappointed, or maybe that was just me hoping he was disappointed because, well, he was a cutie. He looked at me awkwardly for a second and raked his hand through his hair before sticking his thumbs in his back pockets. "I guess I'll see you around?" Was that a hint of hopefulness I heard in his voice?

"Yeah, um, sure," I said, stuttering slightly over my tongue. "See you." I turned from him, which was actually more of an effort than I had thought it would be, and started for the path. After a few steps, I glanced over my shoulder, and I was a bit shocked, and more than a little thrilled, that he was still standing there watching me. "Oh, and really, thanks," I called and gave a little wave, and then, before I lost my nerve and fully turned back to him, I headed for the trees.

CHAPTER 4

AIDAN

Jade disappeared into the trees. I wasn't sure if I wanted to follow her or pretend as if I had never met her. The one thing that I knew for sure about Dominic was that he didn't get angry or anything, really. He kept his emotions bottled up, hidden behind a mask. But that girl ... the way he had looked at me when I stepped in ... if I had to guess, I'd say he was jealous.

But then I really didn't have to guess. I could smell it on him, and I also caught a whiff of her hatred. It's funny how emotions could tamper with someone's scent. It made them an open book, really.

What was going on between them? Dominic hadn't taken her as his mate. Their scents were still distinctly separate. But there was something about the way that he had looked at her. It was as if she were his. It was full of safety — guarded protection. He may have been angry, but it had been clear that he would have never hurt her. Not really.

And I didn't know how I felt about that. When a wolf picked a mate, that was it. It was for life, and the thought of her being someone else's made my stomach clench. It was stupid. I didn't know anything about the girl other than that she was cute and she had pissed off more than one of my pack members, but when I spoke to her, I couldn't deny that I never wanted to stop hearing the sound of her voice. Even when she was clearly nervous, she had been confident about it. Her voice hadn't wavered. It was strong and sweet. Sure and stable. She knew exactly who she was, and she was so positive about it that I wanted nothing more than to know her, too. She was definitely ... intriguing.

Why had I told her I was registering for school? I should have come up with a better lie than that. I graduated last year. *Ugh!* I should have just left it alone. She was obviously on the verge of being spoken for, and besides that, I no longer had the luxury of choice. Alphas don't get to choose. A frustrated growl rumbled up my throat, and after another long look at the path that Jade had disappeared down, I turned and started for my car.

The cool breeze was refreshing as I made my way to the front of the school. Everything was still green, but soon it would change. The grass would die, the leaves would fall. Longer nights under the moon. For the first time in years, I was excited for the winter to come. I actually had a pack to run with. One that was not my father's.

Dog Mountain was small. Everything connected to the one street that ran through its center. There were a few shops, a handful of restaurants, a grocery store, and a hardware store. I was told that it was a busy place in the summer months, packed full of tourists coming to enjoy the hot springs that were tucked in the mountain, but it was hard to imagine it as I drove through the empty-looking town. A few people were walking on the street. Out of the ten people I saw, six of them were werewolves. At only 4:15, most shops were already closed for the day, with only the grocery store and restaurants still open.

I pulled into the driveway of the shabby-looking motel that I now called home and wasn't the least bit surprised to see Dominic's VW sitting in front of my room. He was leaning against his car, arms folded over his chest, and his legs crossed at the ankles.

I parked beside him, shut off the engine, and jumped out. "You were following me, weren't you?" he asked, not even bothering to look at me.

I walked past him, digging out the flimsy plastic key-card from my pocket, and unlocked the room door. I thought about ignoring the question, but seeing him leaning there, so calm and cool and with an obvious lack of respect, annoyed the hell out of me. "I was," I snapped. "Spread the word through the pack; Jade is off-limits." As soon as the words came out, I regretted them. I could almost feel the anger rolling off him instantly.

I pushed the door open and went straight for the curtains, pulling them closed. The room was an eyesore, and the sunlight dancing off the dust that coated the dark wooden surfaces of the desk and dresser only made it worse. I made a mental note to get cleaning supplies. I wasn't a clean freak by any means, but the dust was starting to drive me crazy.

"Dude, you can't claim her." Dominic was right on my heels, coming into my room and slamming the door with a jarring thud. "You lost that privilege when you became the alpha. You know how it works. You can't just pick a mate." There was a protective edge to his tone that cut through me like a jagged and dull knife.

Dominic pulled out the desk chair and spun it around before dropping down into it. I could feel the hostility rolling off him in waves, even if he did keep his tone even and the usual mask tightly in place.

"That's not what I meant," I said with a huff, except it kind of had been what I had meant, but I wasn't about to admit it. I knew the rules better than most of this pack. My dad had been drilling them into me since I was old enough to understand. "Make sure Erika knows to leave her alone. Same goes for everyone else, including you." I narrowed my eyes, and I could feel my eyebrows knit together as I glared at him. "This pack is going to learn to treat people with respect."

Dominic held my stare for a long moment, his hazel eyes shifting more yellow with every passing second. For a moment, I thought he was going to try to lecture me *again* on why an alpha wasn't free to pick a mate, but he didn't. Instead of arguing with me, he said in an acidic tone, "Yeah, sure, whatever you want."

The tension in the room was thick as we both glared at one another, neither of us willing to back down. Secretly, I kind of admired his gall. He had only known me for half a day, and in that time, he had watched me kill the alpha, and still, he stood up to me. This was the kind of beta I needed. One that wouldn't hesitate to tell me I was wrong. One that would stand up to me when I was making dumbass decisions. That's what my father's beta had done for him, and that's what I wanted, too. Except Dominic didn't stand up to me because he was trying to help, he did it because he had absolutely no respect for me.

"You will start showing me some respect," I said evenly, forging an authority into my voice that I didn't feel, but I was already getting sick of the way he challenged my every decision, and it had only been twelve hours now. It had to stop. "This is your last warning."

"You think you can run this pack without me?" He tensed in his chair, and his muscles shuddered under his skin as if he were on the verge of shifting.

I narrowed my eyes further and gritted my teeth. "Are you challenging me?" It came out as a growl.

Dominic considered it. He looked me up and down, insolently, and the first snap of a bone-breaking and grinding sounded loudly in my ears. Bristles of coarse hair littered his cheekbones, and his eyes glowed yellow as his shift to a wolf began.

Okay, so that wasn't what I had expected. My jaw hardened, and I widened my eyes, staring him down. My inner-wolf squirmed in my stomach, itching to come out, but I held it back, if only barely. Pins and needles rushed over my skin as my fur began to sprout. I stepped closer to him; a savage growl erupted from deep within my gut and rumbled through my lips.

Dominic's eyes widened, and for a split second, fear passed across them. It didn't last. "Nope," he said, shrugging his shoulders; any trace of the wolf vanished. "Just stating the obvious. Ray couldn't do it, and you won't be able to either." He spun the chair lazily in slow circles, and all the tension in him melted away, replaced by the cool conceit that I was getting used to seeing in him. "Once Bruce's pack finds out about you, they'll be here, ripping this town apart while you're weak, and I know them. I'm the one with the contact. I know how they work and where they'll hit." He chuckled and grinned. "You just focus on the games. Without a strong mate, you're as good as dead."

Again, I wanted to tell him to get out. How was I supposed to work with him? I didn't like him, didn't trust him. Everything about him screamed authority, and he wouldn't back down. He had made it clear more than once that he didn't want to be the alpha, but I wasn't buying it. No one would go to such extremes to show their dominance if they didn't want the position. There was just something about him that got my defenses up, and whatever it was, it only felt more intense with each passing minute.

He was still spinning the chair around in slow circles when I finally dropped my glare and padded over to the lumpy bed. I sprawled out, staring up at the off-white popcorn ceiling. I couldn't say how long we sat there, neither of us bothering to say anything, when I asked, "Why haven't you made a move for her?" I hadn't even really realized that I wanted to know his reason until the words were out of my mouth. I glanced over at him then, and he was smirking.

Dominic's smirk turned into a smile, and his shoulders began to shake as he tried to hold in a laugh. "Is that what you think?" He burst out into laughter and choked out, "Dude, I'm into men."

That hadn't been the answer I had expected, and I was sure that if I hadn't been able to smell the truth in his scent or hear the steady beat of his heart, I wouldn't have believed him. As I looked at him, though, even without those other things, I could see the truth written all over his face, and it confused the hell out of me. The kind of hatred I saw between him and Jade was the kind of hatred that stemmed from a lot of hurt feelings and a deep connection. *Maybe they were together before he realized?* I wondered.

"Why does she hate you so much?" I asked.

His smile vanished, and his laughter died abruptly. "She doesn't hate me." His tone was insolent, his jaw clenched. It was as if he dared me to say that Jade didn't like him.

"I'm not an idiot, Dominic," I growled and sat up, glaring at him.

He threw his hands up in surrender. "Seriously, she doesn't hate me exactly," he said with more than a bit of contempt. "Jade just hates the pack. She thinks we ruined her life. She'd be happy if there was no such thing as a werewolf." He was lying. I could hear it in his voice. It was defensive and wavered slightly. I was about to call him on it when he smirked and chuckled. "But don't worry about it too much. Soon enough, she'll hate you, too."

I lay back on the bed, forcing my tense muscles to relax. I didn't want to think about her, or anyone hating me just because I shifted into a wolf every once in a while. It was still hard to wrap my head around the town dynamics. Humans knowingly living with werewolves. It seemed wrong and utterly perfect all at the same time. I figured it would make life easier, not having to hide, and from what I'd heard about Bruce's pack, not hiding would make these people a whole lot safer. But still ... it was weird.

"We've got to get going," Dominic said. "You ready to defend your title and start the games?" There was laughter in his voice, and when I shifted on the bed to look at him, he was giving me an odd kind of look.

"I'm defending the title against you?" I asked, forging my voice to sound cool and uncaring as if he were a pesky flea and nothing to worry about, but in all honesty, out of all the males I had met so far, Dominic was the one I worried about.

He didn't answer. His eyes were dancing with amusement, and he chuckled as he rose from his chair and headed for the door. But then, I guess his laughter was enough to answer my question.

"I won't go easy on you," I said, sitting up. "I might not have meant to take over this pack, but I do intend on keeping it." Part of me wanted to launch at him right then and there and end this ... whatever this was that was brewing between us, but I couldn't. No. I wouldn't. I was going to do this by the rules. Every male had a right to challenge me once I overthrew the alpha. That was the point of this ceremony, and I needed to defend the title with honor and witnesses, not in a brawl in a grungy motel room. Tonight, I would either be taken down, or I would remain standing. I intended to remain standing.

Dominic stopped at the door and glanced over his shoulder at me. "Hurry up, man," he said with a smirk. "Let's get this over with."

CHAPTER 5

JADE

The walk home was quiet. Too quiet. I took the trail that cut through the woods. It ran from the school right past my house. It was probably just Dominic's insinuated threat that Erika was lurking about, but the whole way home, I was on edge. At every bend in the path, my heart literally stopped until I could see that nothing was hidden around it, and the hair on the back of my neck stood on end, sending prickling shivers down my spine. After the first two minutes or so, I was seriously kicking myself for not taking Aidan (or Dominic, for that matter) up on the ride home.

Me and my stupid pride! That's pretty much what it all boiled down to. I was too proud to ask one of those stupid dogs for help. And Aidan, well, I couldn't think of a good excuse for that. Stupidity was pretty much all I had there.

I wondered if Aidan knew about the werewolves. I was pretty certain that he didn't. If he did, he wouldn't have faced off with Dominic as he had. I thought about telling him, warning him to stay clear of the pack, but each time the words ran through my mind, all I saw was his smirk and laughing eyes. He'd probably think I was a lunatic.

"Jade, where have you been?" Marcy yelled from my porch step as I stepped out of the tree line. "I've been waiting for hours." She raced over to me, throwing her arms around me in a too-tight hug. "Don't scare me like that again."

Laughing, I pried her too tight arms off my waist. "Really, Mac? Hours?" To say she was a little dramatic would have been a complete understatement. Marcy was one of those all-or-nothing kinds of people, and she applied it to every aspect of her life. There was never a middle ground with her. And that was one of the things I loved about her the most.

She wrinkled her nose at me and tucked her long blond hair behind her ears. "Okay, maybe it was only ten minutes. But it felt like hours." She grabbed my hand and dragged me over to the porch swing. "Did you hear the news?" she asked as she plopped down, taking me with her. The swing creaked and cracked under our weight. She didn't even take a breath for me to answer before she huffed and muttered, "No, of course, you didn't. I shouldn't even know yet."

"What news?" I asked distractedly, noticing that the oversized driveway was empty, and the house was quiet. I glanced at my watch, 4:15. Where were my parents?

"If I tell you, you have to swear not to breathe a word," she said, giving me a stern look.

"Of course," I grumbled and rolled my eyes. Marcy had been going through this gossip phase. It started about a month ago, and each day since, there was another big piece of 'news' that I couldn't breathe a word about. It usually consisted of who was dating who, or what one of the *she-wolves* had worn; a bunch of useless information, really. But like I said before, she was an all-or-nothing kind of person, and gossiping was no different from anything else. At least her information was harmless to those she talked about. Marcy didn't have a malicious bone in her body. I leaned back on the swing, getting comfortable, and waited to be bombarded with whatever had sparked her interest today.

Marcy leaned into me; her vanilla spice lotion tickled my nose, and she whispered, "Ray is dead."

If Marcy had wanted my attention, she got it. "Holy sugar sticks!" I shrieked, and I swiveled on the swing, making the chains creak. My eyes felt as if they were bulging out of their sockets. "He's dead? You sure he's not just on a bender again?" It wasn't uncommon for the pack's alpha to disappear for a few days (or weeks) when he started drinking again. Clearly, Dominic wasn't kidding when he said the pack was stressed.

I felt sick. Guilt washed over me in nauseating waves of hot and cold. Had Dominic been reaching out to me because he needed a friend? Did I want to be that friend? *Yes. No. Yes. Maybe.*

Marcy held a finger to her lips and *shushed* me, and then she began wrapping a chunk of her hair around her finger, a nervous release she did often. That's when I noticed her puffy, bloodshot eyes and her wrinkly T-shirt. Marcy was a girly girl. She always looked perfect, and come to think of it, unless she was sleeping, I was pretty sure that I'd never seen her in a baggy T-shirt before. She tried to smile, but I could see through the act. Her lips were tight, forced into an exaggerated curve. If she had been wearing red lipstick, she would have resembled a demented clown.

She leaned into me again, dropping her voice even lower, as if she were worried someone would overhear her. "I overheard Dad talking about it at the station this afternoon, so I snuck into his office, and ..." she let her words fall short and visibly shuddered before whispering, "I saw the pictures from the investigation. Ray had bite marks all over him. You know what that means, right?" Her eyes were as wide as quarters, and that creepy smile twisted at the edges of her lips again.

I just sat there, staring at her speechless, and a small shiver rushed over my skin. *A new alpha,* a voice in my head, whispered, but I couldn't believe it. "Impossible," I said, more firmly than I felt. "We would have known already if someone had challenged Ray. The pack doesn't keep that stuff a secret. Are you sure the pictures were of him?"

Marcy pursed her lips and glared at me. "Of course, I'm sure. I do work there."

I rolled my eyes. I didn't think a co-op class was classified as actually working anywhere. Well, maybe it kind of was work, but really, she had only been doing it for a week now. There were two detectives in Dog Mountain, Marcy's dad being one of them, and he wanted her to follow in his footsteps. Or at least that's what he said, but truthfully, I thought it had more to do with her mom walking out on them last year than career training. He wanted to keep a closer eye on her, and what better way than to have her spend half of the day on the job with him.

A gust of cool wind blew over us, rustling the leaves in the towering oak tree that sat in the front yard, and I shivered again. Fall was coming. I could feel it in the air, crisp and fresh. It wouldn't be long now before the leaves changed. They were already starting; a slight hint of red and yellow-tinged the oak and maple trees surrounding my yard.

"I'm just saying," Marcy said with a shrug. "He was a werewolf. I highly doubt it was a *random drunk man falling into a ditch and being mauled to death by a wild animal* kind of thing." She arched a puffy brow at me then and asked, "What took you so long anyway?"

"Erika stole my clothes and left me pretty much naked in the gym locker room," I said absently, my mind reeling with the threat of a new alpha. The recruiting would start again, and then the power struggle, all wolves fighting each other for a higher standing in the pack. I had seen it happen twice in the last seven years, and each time had been worse than the last.

Marcy gasped and grabbed my arm. "You're kidding."

I let out a strangled kind of laugh. She was wiggling about on the swing, dying to hear the gossip. "Nope, and out of all the people who could have come by, it was Dominic that brought me my stuff back."

"Dominic? Really?" she squealed. "Please tell me you two have worked it out, and the two-year silent treatment is over."

With a long and drawn-out groan, I said, "Mac, seriously, he's a jerk." I cut her a look that I hoped showed how much I disapproved of the way she still idolized him. "You need to forget about him already. It's been two years."

Marcy, unlike me, had nothing against Dominic or the pack for that matter. It made no sense to me. It was their fault that her mother left, even if it wasn't intentional. Marcy's mom had never been okay with the whole werewolf thing (not that I blamed her), and last year she finally cracked — literally. She started doing drugs, drinking, and then a few months later, she just up and left without even saying goodbye. But, instead of blaming the pack, Marcy blamed her mom. I guessed there was something rational behind her blame, but seriously, shouldn't she hate the wolves just as much?

She smacked my knee playfully. "I miss him, and he's really not that bad. He hasn't changed as much as you think. If you'd just give him a chance ..." She looked at me, giving me one of those *I feel sorry for you* looks, and said, "I think he misses you, too."

Misses me. The idea of Dominic missing me made the hair on the back of my neck, and my arms stand on end and a small, but very noticeable, chill prickle over my skin. I tried to pretend that the shiver was from the brisk wind, but it wasn't. My stomach twisted and jumped; my body was alive with a craving — a longing — for him, one that I was beginning to think time would not dampen.

"Have you heard anything about a new alpha?" I asked, steering her back to the important stuff. My palms were starting to sweat, clammy and cold. My heart was aching. It was as if, with every frantic beat, a hand gripped onto it, squeezing it tight in my chest. The last thing I wanted to think about was the gaping hole that Dominic had left behind when he walked out on Marcy and me two years ago.

"Nope. Nothing," Marcy said. "The pack's not talking. Dad won't say a thing. I even tried to bribe him with that father-daughter day he's been begging me for after he caught me looking at the pictures, and still, nothing. He won't even tell me when it happened." She looked me square on and leaned in so close that our noses were almost touching. "They're trying to cover it up, Jade. Dominic came into the station, and Dad actually shoved me in a closet so I wouldn't be seen. He hid me from Dom. Our Dom," she paused for a second, and her skin turned a pasty white. "Dominic doesn't want a single breath spoken about Ray's death. Shit, I really shouldn't have told you."

No shit, I thought. Why the hell would they want to

cover it up? It made no sense. Alphas die. It happens
... sometimes. And Ray was a class A douche bag.
Why did Dominic care if people knew or not? He
didn't even like Ray, and he never tried to hide it, not
for a second.

Right then, I felt all kinds of guilty. It rushed over
me like a flash flood, cold and wet. I started to sweat,
my stomach turned, and for a second, I thought I was
going to be sick. Since when did I become such an
insensitive bitch?

"Jade," Marcy whispered and shook my hand as if
she were trying to get my attention, and she ripped me
from my thoughts. "Jade, please don't say anything.
Not even to Dominic. Please."

"Please," I said, waving her off. I stomped down the
turmoil that was swimming through my stomach and
smirked. "Tell Dominic? Not a chance. You know I
won't say a word."

The blare of a car horn made Marcy jump. We both
looked up to see Mom's blue minivan pulling up in the
driveway. She waved at us and turned off the engine.
"Hi, girls," Mom said as she opened the door. She
jumped out and then reached back into the car, pulling
out two big brown paper bags. When she turned back
to us, she smiled, but I thought it looked too big and
too nervous. Or maybe that was because I felt so
nervous that everything around me was suddenly
looking ... wrong.

"Hi, Mom," we said in unison, both jumping up
from the swing. Marcy gave me a pointed look as if to
say *Not a word*. I grimaced at her and then rushed over
to help Mom with the bags. Marcy was right on my
heels.

"Dad's busy tonight, so it's just us girls." Mom
grinned, letting us take the bags, which smelled
deliciously like fried chicken, and then she reached

back into the car and produced an armload of movies. "I brought home KFC and movies."

CHAPTER 6

AIDAN

Steam curled around me. I stood rigid on a platform of rock, looking down into a pool of black. The hot spring-fed the air with a misty fog, effectively reducing visibility for me as well as my challengers. Tonight was not just about strength. It was about the ability to fight with what you had around you. And I was ready, kind of, sort of, maybe.

The night air was cool but far from cold, and the canopy of trees blocked out any moonlight from above. I looked out over the crowd of twenty-nine werewolves standing just on the edge of the challenger's ring, defined by blazing torches which lit their faces. They all watched me with leery eyes. All but one. Dominic.

He stood in the center of the ring and nodded to me for the second time, a clear indication that it was time to start, and I gritted my teeth. Even when he was on the verge of trying to overthrow me, he still felt the need to act as my second and feed me cues. It was positively infuriating.

I moved to the side, stepped around the pool of water, and started down the carved rock staircase. "All of you who wish to challenge me, step forward," I said, my voice strong and firm and cold, not giving any indication to the fury that was brewing within me. For a moment, I'd thought that maybe, just maybe, Dominic and I would be a great team. Too bad the thought didn't last.

I continued downward, keeping my chin even and my shoulders back. Dominic held my eyes, and a smirk grew upon his face. I smirked back and raised an eyebrow. What was he playing at? Surely, he had to be a little bit nervous, but if he was, he wasn't showing it.

I reached the bottom of the stairs and stepped onto the damp grass. I paused for a second, scanning the crowd, and as I did, most of them cringed back or dropped their curious gazes to the ground. The only ones that stayed firm were the pack enforcers, but they were the least of my concern. Enforcers rarely challenged for alpha. For the most part, they were more than content with the power they already held over the pack, and I was sure that I wouldn't be going up against anyone from that team of five tonight.

I laughed a deep and belting sound that echoed through the clearing. I couldn't help it. My nerves were jumping like grasshoppers in my belly. All these people watching me. It kind of sucked. I could fight. I could be a leader, but public speaking was really not my thing.

"Is no one going to step forward?" I asked as I made my way into the center of the circle, feeling more confident with every step, and I took my place in front of Dominic. Part of me was hoping someone else would step forward. If I had to fight tonight, I seriously didn't want Dominic to be the only person I fought against. I wanted ... no, I needed a warm-up.

Dominic's grin widened, and he took a step closer to me. And that's when I noticed it. There was something in his scent. Something ... not right. Everything was too calm about him. No trace of adrenaline and no anger. Nothing.

He took another step. He was close enough that I could feel his hot breath puffing against my face and his hazel eyes shimmered with flecks of gold. He held my stare for a long moment, his muscles taut and his stance ready, and just when I thought he was going to attack, he asked, "I didn't fool you for a second, did I?"

"Nope," I lied, keeping my face hard as stone. I felt a sigh of relief inching up my throat, and I quickly swallowed it down. Relief washed over me in hot waves. From what I knew of Dominic, if he had wanted to fight, it would have been a fight to the death, and at that moment, I was shocked at how much I didn't actually want to kill the jerk.

He clasped me in a hug, smacking my back. "Now the fun starts," he whispered, except the tone he used made me think of anything but fun, and I stiffened slightly.

Dominic stepped back from me and looked out over the crowd once more, checking for anyone to step forward. When no one moved, he pulled the short wrought iron branding stick from his back pocket and walked over to one of the torches, holding it in the flame to heat. My jaw twitched. I could already feel the pain, and it hadn't even been done yet.

I turned to the crowd, a touch surprised at the silence. They were all watching me expectantly, waiting for me to speak. I swallowed hard and said, "You all have spoken by staying silent. Today marks a new day for this pack. New leadership and some much-needed change. Together, we will bring balance back into this pack."

It all felt too easy. All of it. What had Ray done to these people? The silence was deafening, and for a split second, I thought that someone might step up. Surely at least one of the males wanted to take the pack. They didn't even know me. I just couldn't believe that they would allow some new blood to walk in without fighting. But then I heard it. A soft clap. Just one. And that one was followed by another and another, and soon the clapping was louder than the silence.

I smiled, and warmth rushed through me. Acceptance. I hadn't let myself think that it could happen this quickly, but it was. Whether it was because they actually wanted me or because they were too scared to cross me, I didn't know, and right then, I didn't really care. This was mine. All of it. My life was changing and morphing before my eyes. In just a matter of hours, I had gone from a lone wolf, running from my father to an alpha. It was a rush. Adrenaline pumped through my veins, and my smile grew wider.

I stripped off my shirt, turned my back on the crowd, and closed the distance to Dominic. He held up the branding iron; the 'A' on the end glowed, burning like embers. This was the last step to claiming my new rank. The branding irons had been created long ago, back when werewolves ran wild and killed innocent people recklessly. They were infused with magic from the first pack and were distributed as new packs formed. When an alpha was branded with it, the magic bonded with their skin and bones. It gave them the power to use their scent, channel it, enhance it, and call upon it to control their wolves.

He mouthed, '*You ready,*' which turned out to be a pointless question because he didn't wait for my answer before he stabbed my right pectoral with the magic-infused, burning metal.

I locked eyes with him. My skin sizzled, and my jaw clenched, but somehow I managed to stay still and not make a sound. It hurt like hell. The metal burning and melting my skin. Leaving the alpha's imprint on my chest, but I didn't flinch. I wanted this too much. Craved it. Needed it. I could already feel the magic seeping into my bones as my flesh melted around the smoldering metal.

When he finally pulled it away, my skin stung as it quickly stitched back together, leaving a raised scar that looked as if it had been there for years. Dominic dropped the branding stick to the ground and snagged up a bottle of rye. He handed it to me, straight-faced, with awe shining in his eyes, and gave me a firm whack on the back before moving back into the center of the circle.

I quickly twisted the top and took a deep swig from the bottle. The rye burned down my throat and warmed my belly. My skin still stung, but the pain was tolerable. The soft buzz of the crowd drifted around me, and it grew louder and louder. I turned back to them just as Dominic raised a hand, silencing them.

The crowd inched forward, moving in closer to the edge of the circle, and I cringed on the inside as I watched the females shuffling in, snapping and growling at each other, even in their human forms.

Dominic stood still, waiting for them to settle, and as I watched him, I was certain that this was not the first time he had made this announcement. He waited patiently, playing his role of my beta perfectly. And right then, I got the feeling that Tammy may not have been the first alpha female Ray had had. Dominic seemed ... practiced. Sure of himself and what needed to be said.

"Ray's death has not and will not be leaked," Dominic said, belting out the words so loudly it was as if he had a microphone. "As you know, Tammy has left us, and with her gone, a new alpha female must rise up. So tonight not only marks the night of a new alpha male for our pack, but it also marks the start of the games for a new alpha female."

Hoots and hollers rang out through the night, and Dominic smiled, patiently waiting for them to die down before continuing, "Once the alpha pair has been established, we will let the news travel. You all need to be vigilant with your patrols. If any of you pick up the scent of Bruce's pack, we need to know immediately. He can't know that the females don't have a leader."

"You sound pretty cocky there, Dominic," someone shouted. "Last I checked, you lose your status when a new alpha male takes over."

Dominic laughed, a cruel sound. "You want to fight me for it, Joe?" Everything about him was relaxed as he spoke, his shoulders loose, his smile easy. He waited for a moment before another laugh fell out, and he said, "Yeah, that's what I thought." Then he turned to me and said, "You want to settle this, Aidan? Are you going to appoint a new beta?"

The pack erupted in a mess of noise. "Enough!" I yelled over the chaos. "Dominic will remain as my beta." I paused, waiting for any objections, but when none came, I said, "Let the games begin."

CHAPTER 7

JADE

I woke up feeling gross and greasy. The KFC had been delicious going down, but I wasn't used to eating that much grease at once, and it really wasn't sitting well at all.

Last night had been ... weird. Dad hadn't come home. Mom said he had a *boy's weekend,* and there was nothing to worry about, but the whole fact that she said there was nothing to worry about had me kind of worried. And it had been clear that I wasn't the only one. Mom had been hyperaware of every bump and thump. At one point, I had shifted on the couch, making the leather squeak beneath me, and she had jumped, tossing a full bowl of popcorn all over the floor.

Mom was never jumpy. She took everything in stride, and even when she was nervous, she always hid it well. It was a survival technique that I frequently used while dealing with the oddities of our town. But last night, she had been a nervous wreck.

Rolling over in bed, I looked out the big bay window. The sky looked like a dirty ball of wool had been unraveled, covered in clouds. I couldn't say how

43

long I had lain there watching the little rivers of rain slide down my window when my door squeaked open, and Mom peeked around it. "Honey, you need to get up."

"It's Saturday, Mom," I said with a groan and rolled over.

Mom pursed her lips, pushed the door wide open, and flicked the light switch on. The pot lights seemed overly bright against the dreary day outside. "You have company," she said evenly.

"Mac's not company," I groaned. "She's been a permanent fixture here for a year now." Since her mother took off last year, Marcy had pretty much moved into our house, and my mom had unofficially adopted her into our family. The only time she went home now was when her father forced her, or rather when he begged her. It wasn't that she didn't want to spend time with her dad, it was more that he was never home, always working, and Marcy wasn't really a solitary kind of person. She needed people, noise, and action.

I rolled up on my elbows and scrunched my forehead as my sleepy brain tried to process why I needed to get up. I guess I took too long because she marched into the room, shooting me one of that *stern mom* kind of looks.

"I'm not talking about Mac," she said with her hands on her hips, scowling down at me. "Get up. He's waiting for you."

"What?" I asked, squinting at her. "Who's 'he?'" I scrubbed my eyes, wiping the sleep from them, and yawned loudly.

Mom looked more put together today, not as jittery, that was for sure. She had her dark brown hair tied up in a loose bun, and she was dressed in a long, simple black knit dress. It hung on her slim figure loosely.

She arched a brow, and a small, devious-looking smile curled her lips. "Dominic's downstairs."

"You let him in the house?" I hissed and sat up with a start. I fought against my comforter, which was wrapped around my legs like a cocoon. "What's wrong with you?"

As soon as I said it, I heard his rumbling chuckle. *Darn those dogs and their impeccable hearing!* I glared at the door and gritted my teeth.

"Of course, I let him in. He's been your best friend since you were a baby," she said hastily and a bit too loudly as if she were trying to make sure he heard her reprimand me. "He stopped by to drop off your backpack, and he wants to talk to you." She walked over to my bed, flung the covers back, and glared down at me with her hands on her hips. "Now get up. I'm going out."

I gritted my teeth. *My backpack,* I thought, completely annoyed at myself for forgetting about it yesterday. I thought of a million reasons why I didn't want to talk to him or why I wasn't going to get out of bed, but each one sounded like a child throwing a tantrum. "Where are you going?" I asked instead. Heat settled in my cheeks, and my jaw was starting to ache from clenching it so tightly.

"Shopping," she said, not unkindly but with a definite edge, and then she grabbed hold of my feet and started to pull, dragging me off my bed. "Now get in the shower and make yourself presentable," she said.

Mom didn't leave my room until she watched me walk into the bathroom, and knowing her, she probably stood there until she heard the shower turn on. I couldn't believe she was still pushing her little dream on me. It was the only reason I could think of why she would leave the house with me in the shower and Dominic sitting just downstairs. Well, okay, maybe it wasn't the only reason. My parents knew he was gay, but still, they wanted nothing more than for me to date a werewolf, and pushing me toward Dominic would push me toward the straight ones. Twisted, right? They wanted their only daughter to hook up with an animal — literally.

I took my time in the shower and even longer blow-drying my hair. I was kind of hoping that if I stalled long enough, he'd just go away. I spent ten minutes staring into my closet before I finally decided on a pair of jeans and a powder blue T-shirt, and then, since I couldn't think of any other way to prolong the process further, I went to see what he wanted.

Dominic was lounging in my dad's recliner, and when I spotted him, I almost forgot how much I didn't want to see him. He looked ... good. Really good. His short blond hair was gelled, with the front flipped up. He was in jeans and a light blue polo shirt with the collar popped up, and he was smiling, something that he rarely did anymore, and darn it, but I missed that smile. It was a lot easier to hate him when he was all jerky and serious. But right then, at that moment, if only for a second, he was my best friend again.

I stood at the top of the stairs for a moment, watching him run a finger along the stacked bookcase beside him as if he were trying to pick something to read. He looked comfortable — at home — sitting in our country-style living room, amongst the blue and green-checkered curtains and the cherry wood floors. But then, I figured he should look comfortable since he was the one that had made and hung the curtains, and come to think of it, I was certain he had recommended cherry wood for the floors, too. I knew he had helped install them, at least.

As I padded down the stairs, trying to prepare myself for what I was sure would be a replay of yesterday, I stumbled, tripping over my own feet. I hadn't thought he'd even noticed me coming down the stairs, but the moment I slipped, Dominic jumped out of his chair, leaped over the coffee table, and caught me just before I did a face plant on the floor.

"That was graceful," he said, his voice oozing with sarcasm, and he helped me regain my balance. His lips twitched, and a cocky grin spread across his face.

"Wow, thanks," I said, snatching my arm from his hand. He chuckled, and his smile grew wider. I gave him my best *shut-up* look and said, "And you wonder why I don't like you. You do something slightly nice, and then you always ruin it by speaking."

Dominic crossed his arms over his chest; they bounced softly with his shoulders as he tried to hold in a laugh. His eyes shimmered with humor. "A simple thank you would have worked, too," he said. "You know, you're still so adorable when you're all mad, scrunchy-nosed, and flushed cheeked."

"Whatever," I snapped, putting every bit of snark I had into my tone. "Where's Mac?"

"She went home," he said, and then he gave me a serious look. "Jade, I want you to stay away from Aidan."

I laughed dryly and rolled my eyes before making my way into the kitchen. So that was what this little visit was about. The new guy. And by the look I was getting from Dominic, I'd guess it was also about a bruised ego. "And I care what you want because?"

Dominic followed me, stopping at the fridge to grab milk before moving to the cupboard and snagging two mugs. He scooped three heaping spoonfuls of sugar in one, added only milk to the other, and then filled them with steaming coffee. I watched him, stunned. The way he moved around the kitchen was as if he were supposed to be there as if he had never left. Once he had finished stirring in the sugar, he slid the mug over to me and grinned. "You still like it that way, right?"

I took the mug and drank a long, deep mouthful before looking back up at him. "What are you really doing here, Dominic?"

He stepped over to me and tucked a few strands of loose hair behind my ear, a gesture that used to be common, but now, it just felt wrong. "I saw the way you were looking at him. He's no good for you." There was more emotion in his voice than I was used to. It was gentle and pleading, strong and caring. It was as if we had stepped back two years, and he was still my Dom. My rock. My stabling force. My best friend. And I don't know why, but it pissed me off.

I almost pointed out that I didn't know anything about Aidan. I came close to telling Dominic that there was nothing to worry about because honestly, since finding out about Ray, I hadn't even given Aidan another thought, but I couldn't bring myself to do it. As far as I was concerned, it was none of his business who I looked at. "You don't have the right to play the concerned best friend card. Not anymore."

Hot guilt pulsed over me, and I almost took the words back. I felt like an insensitive jerk. Again, I wondered if he was trying to reach out because he needed someone to talk to about Ray's death. I almost asked him if he was okay, but just before I opened my mouth, Marcy's pointed look from yesterday flashed through my head and I bit my tongue. There was a reason Ray's death was a secret. I didn't understand why, and I really wasn't sure if I should let on that I knew about it — yet.

He narrowed his eyes, not harshly, but as if he were trying to get a better look at me and see something that may have been hidden under my words. "You're not being fair," he said after a long moment.

I glared at him. There really was nothing to say. He had abandoned me when I had needed him. Blew me off to climb the pack ranks. He had no right to try to tell me what was and wasn't good for me. Not anymore. If he wanted to talk about Ray, then fine, I'd be there for him, but I wasn't about to stand there and listen to him tell me what I could and couldn't do.

He must have seen what I was thinking, or maybe he still just knew me that well because he groaned. Dominic had a variety of groans. There was the long and drawn-out, annoyed groan. The short but loud *you've got to be kidding me* groan. But this one was one that I knew well. It was the *you are being so stubborn* groan. "Jade, you've got to forgive me already. It's been two years."

I clenched my teeth, trying to keep my jaw from dropping. If it wasn't for the look he was giving me, I probably would have laughed, but I could see that he was dead serious, and that made my head spin. "Exactly, it's been two years since the last time you made an effort. Two years since the first time you pretended not to know me, and two years since you left me to find my own way home because the pack was more important. You've never even pretended to be sorry."

Dominic crumbled at my words as if I had hauled off and punched him, and I almost felt bad — almost. He jammed his thumbs into the front pockets of his jeans and leaned against the counter, his shoulders hunched, and his gaze dropped to my stomach as if he couldn't look me in the face any longer. "I had to prove myself. They would have eaten me alive if I showed weakness, and you know it."

"Don't give me that crap," I snapped and banged my mug down on the counter. "Being a friend isn't being weak. You're just like the rest of them. You don't give a crap who you stomp on."

He groaned. It was the annoyed groan this time. "I'm trying to fix things. Stop being so stubborn."

"It's my natural defense, Dom," I said, giving him a dirty look, "the one I use against idiots, bullshit, and stupidity, and since you're here ..." I waved my arm around, in an exaggerated gesture in his direction.

He smiled a sad sort of smile, and it caught me off guard. My stomach dropped, and my eyes prickled. I quickly blinked the tears away. There was no way he was going to see me hurting. Mad was one thing, but seeing me in pain ... it wasn't happening.

"You haven't called me Dom in years." His voice was soft, just barely a whisper, and I may have been mistaken, but I was pretty sure his eyes looked a bit misty.

I couldn't even begin to count how many times I had wanted to have this conversation. How many times I had sat up all night waiting for him to call and *want to fix things*, but now that it was actually happening, it was the last thing I wanted to hear. "It's too late to fix things." I sighed, frustrated and angry and hurt, and I turned my back on him. "Just get out."

I didn't hear him move, and I jumped when the front door slammed. Seconds later, his engine rumbled, and then his tires squealed as he peeled out of the driveway. My body shook, my fingers trembled, and with him gone, it was even harder not to cry.

CHAPTER 8

AIDAN

I was a wolf, and she pretended not to see me.

Jade sat on the covered porch of a large log house, rocking back and forth on one of those dainty-looking, wire porch swings. She stared at what appeared to be a sketchbook in her lap. From where I sat, just past the tree line, in clear view of anyone who may have passed by, I watched as her blackened hand made sure and gentle strokes across the page. Every few seconds, her hand would pause, and her head would tilt in my direction as she stole a glance, but she never once made eye contact.

That was a mistake.

If I had been any other wolf, she would have looked submissive. And submission would not get her to where I was starting to think she should be. It would only put her at risk. But as I watched, it was clear that this was not actually submission. It was power. A cool and calm remoteness. She did not look as if she were giving in. Instead, it was as if she were too important, too high in the ranks, to pay me any attention. She was above me. And my inner-wolf craved her attention and acceptance.

It was an odd feeling, one that I was not used to. She should have been the one feeling this way, not me. It was maddening and confusing. She wasn't even one of us. And in all honesty, part of me didn't want her to be. The strength she emanated was intimidating. Crippling. What would it be like if she was part of the pack?

That morning, I had woken up, determined to avoid her. There was no point in knowing her. Not now. The games had started. The challenging females had made themselves known. Getting to know her now would only put her in danger. I had sparked her interest when we first met. Her scent had given her away, and she wouldn't give in easily; I was sure of it. And letting her know she had caught my attention would only make it harder. Jade didn't strike me as the backing down type, and that would be deadly, definitely, maybe. This was my life now, and for the most part, it was a life that I wanted. And she was just a girl.

But Jade ... she seemed to weasel her way back into my thoughts at the least expected moments. I wouldn't say I liked her, but she was undeniably intriguing. But then, that could have had something to do with Dominic hounding me last night to stay away from her, or maybe it was the way she had fought back yesterday. Whatever it was, she had caught my attention and refused to let go. And no matter how hard I tried to pretend that I had never met her, my brain wouldn't let me forget.

For a few minutes, I had successfully pushed her out of the forefront of my mind, or I had until Dominic had shown up late for our meeting this morning. Not just a little late, but thirty minutes late. At first, I had thought that his hard eyes and pasty-looking skin were directed at me, but then he had placed a hand on my shoulder and said, *'Sorry I'm late.'* Except, it hadn't been his words that had given him away. It had been the scent on his hand.

It was a scent that I knew or that I thought I knew. Almonds with a splash of fruit punch. It tickled at my memory, like a niggling reminder of something that stayed just out of reach.

And it was because of that scent that I had found myself as a wolf, sitting under an oak tree, outside Jade's house.

I hadn't known where I was going until I had arrived here. The rain had temporarily stopped, but it was bound to start again by the look of the blackened sky. My fur was drenched from running through the sodden woods, and I was starting to get cold, but I couldn't make myself leave.

What was it about her that made Dominic so uptight? I had to know. Each time her name had been mentioned last night, whether it was by one of the girls bragging about their little stunt or me, he had stiffened, each muscle visibly coiling beneath his skin.

I stalked closer, inch by inch. I didn't want to scare her away, but I had to get closer. Every animal instinct I had was insistently urging me to get her attention.

"Dominic, if that's you, you can screw off." She didn't look up as she spoke, and her hand continued to move deftly across the page, stroke by sure stroke.

Her commanding tone stopped me, pinning me in place. *Who was this girl?* I felt myself shrink, crouching lower and bowing my head. My brain was screaming at me to show my dominance, but my inner-wolf shrank anyway.

I whimpered. I tried to swallow it, choke it down, but I couldn't, and Jade's head snapped up. Her stare was piercing, penetrating, and I bowed my head further. *Who was this girl?*

I didn't move. I couldn't move. When she finally

dropped her eyes back to the page, my legs were trembling beneath me. I needed her approval. I didn't think as I bounded up the porch steps. I whimpered again and sat beside her, pressing my soaking wet body against her leg.

Jade stiffened, and a gasping sound hissed from her lips. I nosed her notebook, pushing it until it slid onto the swing beside her, and put my head on her lap. As I looked up into her big brown eyes for a moment, I thought she was going to push me away. She certainly looked as if she were considering it. But then, she smiled, a thin, tight-lipped smile, and placed a soft hand on my head. "I know, buddy," she said, stroking my fur. "I miss you, too."

JADE

It felt weird speaking to a wolf. I didn't know if he understood me, but I thought he probably did with the way he watched me. I buried my hand in his coarse fur, scratching his back, and he pressed into me further. He was soaking wet, and as he leaned against me, my jean-clad leg absorbed the moisture, and the fabric clung to my calf and knee.

I wanted to say more. I wanted to yell at him, laugh with him, and hug him. I wanted my Dominic back with every fiber in my body. This was the most attention he had given me in two years. I had tried so many times to talk to him, and he always pushed me away. This was my chance to get it all out, but instead of talking, I wrapped my arms around his neck and hugged him as he littered my face with sloppy kisses.

It seemed like only yesterday that he was bitten. The memory was still clear in my mind, cemented there, unwavering and unyielding. We were walking through the park, after watching a stupid horror movie. Dominic was a *Freddy Kruger* fanatic, me, not so much. There was just something about dying in a dream that made my skin crawl.

Late-night walks after scary movies were kind of a ritual of ours. It gave me time to unwind and reassure myself that it was only a movie. We were walking, arms linked, looking up at the star-speckled sky, when Dominic had stopped short and said, "You hear that?"

I smacked him playfully with my free hand and said dryly, "Not funny, Dom." He gave me an odd look, one that I really didn't understand, and then started walking again.

One of the things I had always loved about our friendship was that we had never needed to fill the silence with pointless conversation. We could spend hours just being together, doing our own thing without talking. And that night had been one of those nights. It was peaceful and perfect.

"Jade, there's something I need to tell you," Dominic said after we had walked for at least twenty minutes. That was when I had noticed how stiff his arm was in mine as if I were holding onto a steel pipe.

"Mmmhmm," I mumbled, hugging myself closer to his side, trying to keep myself out of the chilly fall wind. But instead of holding me closer, he only stiffened further.

I stopped short, looking up at him. A muscle in his neck twitched under his skin, throbbing like a heartbeat. His face was lined with crevasses, branching out from the corners of his eyes and lips like wild vines. "Ray wants me to join the pack," he blurted, all the words running together.

It took me a long minute to understand what he was saying, but sweat began to trickle down my back when I did. My stomach sank, and a chill rushed over my skin. For a moment, I thought I was going to be sick. I could taste the sour bile rising, burning up my esophagus. "You can't. They're a bunch of jerks, Dom. You can't." My voice screeched on the last word, loud and piercing.

"I know," he said. He hadn't needed to say more; I understood everything he wanted to convey in those two words. They would eat him alive. They were hard on him now, and we both knew they would be even worse if he was one of them. The pack had changed drastically since Ray became the alpha. They were vicious, even toward their own, and Dom ... well, Dom had a soft heart.

But Dominic never had a choice, not really.

The chilly night turned bitter. I remembered thinking that Erika must have been following us the whole time, waiting for the perfect moment to step out from the trees. I heard the crunch of gravel before I saw her. She stood in the center of the winding path with a purely evil smirk. The moonlight cast an unnerving silvery glow around her, making her black jeans shimmer in the light.

"Dominic, you have been summoned," Erika said. Her voice rang out, splitting through the silent night.

I moved in front of him without thinking, trying to block him from her sight. Thinking about it now, I realized that it would have never worked; he was half a foot taller than I was, but at the time, all I wanted to do was to hide my Dom. "No, you can't have him." My voice was strong, giving no indication of the twisted knots in my stomach.

Erika threw her head back and laughed. She locked her eyes with mine, and her skin rippled. Snaps and pops echoed through the cool night, and hair sprouted along her exposed flesh. Her face hazed over, distorting and shifting. Her legs snapped back, her arms extended and thinned. My stomach rolled as another deafeningly loud snap reverberated around me, and she dropped to all fours.

"Dom, run!" I yelled, glancing behind me, but he didn't move. I shoved him, trying to push him into action. It was as if he didn't even notice me; all he did was stare blankly at Erika.

A snarl ripped through the air, and I snapped my gaze back to where Erika had stood, just as a white wolf lunged at us.

Dominic hadn't screamed. He hadn't made a sound. It had been as if he had known all along what was about to happen. As if he had already given up. Before I could move, her teeth were embedded in his thigh.

That had been the night that I had lost one of my best friends. The night he had left me stranded. Erika held onto him until her muzzle was stained with red. She let go and chomped down three more times before sitting down on her haunches and staring up at him, his blood dripping from her muzzle. After an agonizingly long moment, she barked once and swung her head toward the trees.

Dominic hadn't looked at me. And he didn't look back while he trailed after Erika, head held high and shoulders stiff and straight. He left me there, tears streaming down my face, in the dark, alone.

I looked down at the big black wolf, his head still in my lap, and ran my hand along his fur, scratching lightly behind his ears. He huffed, a content kind of sound, and his sad-looking, golden eyes met mine. I smiled a little and muttered, "I'm sorry I kicked you out earlier."

CHAPTER 9

JADE

Monday came too soon. I wasn't ready to face Dominic. Not after confessing that I missed him, even if it was true. He always had a way of making me forget my anger, and as it turned out, even after two years, he could still worm his way into my heart. When he had whimpered, looking up at me with those sad dog eyes, I don't know, I had just ... caved. Part of me wanted to run to him and catch up on everything we had missed, but a bigger part of me wanted nothing to do with him. The pack had ruined him, and if I let him in, I was sure they would ruin me, too.

Dominic had followed me around as a wolf for the rest of the weekend. He had kept his distance, but I could feel him watching my every move. He had sat at the edge of the woods while Mac and I had lunch at Lucy's Diner on Sunday, and he was there, waiting when we had left the boutique. His presence had been comforting and nerve-racking and annoying all rolled into one. Why he felt the need to stalk me as a wolf, I had no clue, but that was exactly what he had done.

My alarm clock's insistent beeping started again, and I smacked the snooze button for the third time. For a split second, I thought about faking sick, but deep down, I knew that wasn't really an option. Sooner or later, I'd have to face him, and I figured it wasn't going to get any easier with time.

Marcy was waiting in the kitchen when I dragged myself downstairs. She was back to her old girly girl self, decked out in a cute, and way too short, pink dress that ruffled around her thighs. She was perched at the island with a jumbo-sized jar of strawberry jam and a plate of toast in front of her. She was giving me an odd look, as if she had something to tell me, but couldn't decide if she actually wanted to say it.

"You stayed here last night?" I asked, too groggy to try to figure out what the look was about. I padded over to the coffee pot and dropped my backpack to the floor. After our shopping trip yesterday, I had hidden in my room, tackling a stack of homework, and frankly, I couldn't remember hearing her leave.

Marcy, I assumed, had set out my travel mug and prefilled the mandatory three heaping spoonfuls of sugar. I snagged the coffee pot and filled it to the brim with steaming goodness before switching off the coffee maker and dumping the last little bit down the drain.

"Nope, came in about twenty minutes ago," she said. She opened the jam, slathered a thick layer onto her toast, and then took a bite. "Mom left while you were in the shower," she continued after she swallowed her mouthful. "She's back on mornings this week. Oh, and Dad's coming home today."

"Huh," I said as I made my way over to the fridge and rummaged through the crisper. Mom being gone already wasn't really a shock. Being an emergency nurse at the hospital meant that she often left the house before me. But Dad, on the other hand, well, I was dying to know where he had been all weekend.

I glanced over my shoulder at Marcy and didn't miss

the fidgety way she was sitting. She crossed and uncrossed her legs and slid the butter knife around; she just couldn't sit still. Her lips kept parting as if she were about to say something, but then instead of speaking, she shoved the last of her toast in her mouth.

"You ready to go?" she asked, around another mouthful of toast. She gave me an overly bright smile, popped up from her chair, and made her way over to the fridge, putting away the jam.

I snagged an apple from the crisper. "Yeah, I guess," I said and shut the fridge. I dragged myself over to my coffee and snapped the lid onto my travel mug. I shouldered my bag, and with a quick glance around, finding nothing that could delay leaving, I followed her out the door and locked it.

Not having a car sucked. It wasn't a bad day outside, but this whole walking to school thing was not for me. I really wasn't an exercise kind of girl, especially not in the morning.

The air was relatively warm for September, although by no means was it hot. I could already see the tiny goosebumps popping up on Marcy's bare arms as we walked against the breeze. The forest was a bit redder than it had been on Friday, and a few leaves had already fallen, scattering the gravel path with rich fall colors.

"I talked to Dominic," Marcy said casually, breaking the silence.

Hearing his name made a vein at my temple throb like a pulse, and I really didn't know if it was because I was nervous about seeing him or because he talked to Marcy about me. I cut her a look and said, "Don't want to hear about it, Mac."

She grabbed my wrist, pulling me to a stop. "He told me about this Aidan guy."

I groaned and shook her hand off. "He's

overreacting. I met the guy for like thirty seconds, and I haven't seen him since." I shrugged my shoulders and took a deep gulp of coffee as I started walking again. The gravel crunching under my shoes suddenly sounded too loud. "And besides that, Aidan was only trying to foil Dominic's kidnapping attempt."

Marcy laughed. Hard. So hard that she actually snorted. "Wow, seriously? And you say I'm dramatic," she said and shot me a rueful look. I opened my mouth to snap out a defense, but she threw her hands up and silenced me with a hard glare. Her laughter died instantly. "Don't even try it. Dom told me the whole story."

Two years had gone by without so much as a glance from my former best friend, and now this. I huffed noisily. And men said women were confusing. "Why does he even care? If I *was* into this guy, what does it matter to him?"

"Jade, he loves you," she said solemnly, giving me one of those looks that said that I should have already known it.

Ha! Loves me. What a joke. I didn't even bother to acknowledge that comment, and thankfully, Marcy didn't push it. If Dominic loved me so much, then where the hell had he been all this time? Ignoring me. That's where. Or playing cruel pranks on me and pretending he couldn't remember my name. Sure, the cruelness wasn't only directed at me, it was directed at all the *outsiders*, but still ... one weekend of playing nice didn't make up for all the nastiness.

We broke through the trees, stepping off the gravel path and into the parking lot, just as the warning bell rang out. The lot was full of empty cars, with only a few stragglers rushing into the school.

"We need your car back," Marcy said as we both began to sprint across the parking lot.

The hallways were packed with students rushing to their lockers or darting into homerooms. Marcy and I quickly parted, both mumbling, '*See you,*' before taking off to our lockers.

Dominic's locker was only a few down from mine, and I heard his laughter even before I rounded the corner and he came into view. He was leaning against the metal wall with Aidan, and they were laughing. Laughing!

I was stunned, gawking at them. Aidan was the first to notice me, and he smiled and winked at me. The way he looked at me was as if we shared a secret. And darn it, but those pesky butterflies started to wake up in my stomach. What was it about this guy that made my nerves all jumpy? He was cute, he had helped me out, but really, this was a bit ridiculous. I wasn't, and would not become, one of those boy crazy girls just because a boy winked at me, even if he did have a knee-melting smile.

Aidan hadn't shaved. That was the very first thing I noticed after getting over the shock of seeing him acting all buddy-buddy with Dominic. He was in dark blue jeans and a deep green hoodie that almost looked black. His hair was messy, not in a messy style, but just messy, flipping up at the sides. Everything about him, the way he held himself and dressed, said that he didn't care what people thought. And that alone made him, well, it made him seriously attractive. I loved confidence, and he emitted it like a tidal wave.

I snapped my mouth shut, realizing that my jaw had started to drop, and steeled myself, letting the thick doors within me slam shut, sealing off my emotions. It was something my father had taught me. '*Just imagine big doors, honey,*' he had said. '*And when you want to hide, just pull them closed.*'

It worked for about two seconds.

All the doors were sealed tight. I took a deep breath, gripped my travel mug a bit tighter, and I started down the hallway again toward my locker, focusing on my footfalls instead of staring at them. I could figure out why they were suddenly friends later.

I focused on walking, counting the tiles as I went. Anything for a distraction. I didn't get far. A pair of bright red heels came into my line of vision, and I looked up. Erika. The black leggings and a black, frilly empire cut shirt made her look extra-thin. Her pouty lips were painted to match her shoes, which, personally, I thought seemed like way too much effort for school, and her jet-black hair fell straight over her shoulders.

"I'm only going to tell you this once," Erika said, drumming her fingernails on her hips. "Stay away from them."

My eyebrows lifted so high it felt as if they were in the middle of my forehead. I didn't have to ask who she was talking about. It was clear by the way she stood in front of Dominic and Aidan as if she were trying to block them from my view. "And if I don't?" I asked with a strangled laugh. I don't know what made me say it, but it came out before I could stop it.

She made a *tsk* sound and wagged her finger from side to side. "It's really not up for debate, Jade. I know you've been sneaking around, trying to get Dom's attention. And I saw you checking out Aidan. They're mine. Both of them."

Erika held my stare, and she looked ... threatened as if I were standing in her way, and all she had to do was knock me over, and the prize would be hers. And that was confusing as all hell. Out of the corner of my eye, I noticed that Aidan was watching me intently with a half-smirk and curious eyes, and Dominic, well, Dominic looked as if he were about to burst out laughing. I couldn't say if it was at Erika or at me. His eyes were darting too quickly between us to really tell.

I smirked. "We'll see about that."

Her jaw dropped, and I stepped around her, feeling almost giddy from the dirty look she shot me, and I went straight for my locker. I know it was a horrible thing to think, but honestly, I was absolutely thrilled (and royally pissed off) that one of the *she-wolves* was considering me a threat, even if I really had no clue why.

AIDAN

Jade was livid when she stormed past me, and it was the cutest thing I had ever seen. It was also the most confusing thing I had ever seen. She shot me (or maybe — hopefully — it was to Dominic) an ice-cold glare. It was penetrating and commanding, and my inner-wolf clawed at my stomach, wanting to run after her and make her happy.

"I know what you're thinking," Dominic said.

My blood ran cold. He couldn't know that she was making me crazy. None of them could. If they knew ... "What's that?" I asked, glad that my voice sounded uncaring, and I glanced his way.

He laughed. "That she's adorable when she's mad."

"That she is," I agreed, watching as Jade disappeared around the corner and Erika scowled after her. My heart started to beat again, and the knot in my stomach loosened. He didn't have a clue. *Who was that girl?* The question echoed through my mind again, relentlessly. I just didn't get it. I could take down an alpha, command an entire pack of twenty-nine werewolves to submit, and grovel at my feet, but this ... this ... human girl could make me cringe with just one glance.

Erika turned to us with a big grin on her face and started over. I snapped my gaze to meet hers and said, "Don't you have somewhere to be?" It came out harsher than I had intended, but it worked, and without a word, she backed up a step and then took off down the hall.

"Stay away from her," Dominic said casually as if he were talking about the weather and not really trying to tell me what to do. I had heard the line more than I could count in the last forty-eight hours, and each time I heard it, it only made her all the more interesting.

"That's her call to make, not yours," I retorted, keeping my tone just as light. He still refused to enlighten me about his obsession with Jade, and spending the weekend following her around hadn't helped me figure it out either. The most I had gotten from that was confirmation that she missed him.

Dominic pushed off the locker and stretched his arms lazily over his head. He smiled a little. "She wouldn't even look at you if she knew who you were."

The second bell rang, signaling that we were late for homeroom, and we started down the hallway, neither of us in any rush to get to class. "Why are you so concerned about her?" I asked.

"I'm not," he said, cutting me a murderous sideways look.

I chuckled. "Not sure if I believe that this is your *I could care less* face."

Dominic stopped just outside our homeroom. The morning announcements began, and our principal's voice's distorted buzz droned through the old speakers. "She's lost enough to this pack," he said in a low whisper, just barely audible over the announcements. "She doesn't need to lose more than she already has." His voice, body language, scent, and everything about him said he was guilty. I just wished I knew why.

I pulled the classroom door open and gestured for him to go in. "You're really going to go through with this class stuff, aren't you?" he asked with a huff. "You know I don't need a babysitter."

I grinned. "Think of it as bonding time."

CHAPTER 10

JADE

Erika watched me. I felt her eyes burning a trail along my back in homeroom, then in English, and still in Math. Every move I made, she was there, watching. And it was starting to drive me batty. But she wasn't the only one that watched me. So did Dominic.

And I watched Aidan, if only to piss them off. Well, that and I couldn't bring myself to directly look at Dominic.

What was it about this guy that had them on edge? I really wanted to know. When Dominic wasn't staring at me, he was watching Aidan and Erika ... Well, Erika looked as if at any moment she was going to cock her leg and pee on him to mark her territory. Did female dogs do that? Well, if they did, I was sure she would do it soon. The whole thing was starting to make me feel a little sick.

Erika wasn't the only *she-wolf* acting like that, though. Linda, Becca, and Tiffany were all following Aidan around, giving dirty looks to any girl that looked his way. And they were snapping at each other just as much. They stared each other down and shoved each other around. It was the strangest thing I had ever seen. Weren't girls usually more tactful than this? What happened to the snide comments and mean girl manipulation?

Aidan took it all in stride. It was as if he didn't even notice. He talked to everyone. He was friendly. He smiled. Everyone seemed to like him, especially the pack, and darn it, but I did, too. And it made my stomach sink. No matter how hard I tried, I couldn't come up with anything that would get the pack away from him. It was clear that they were recruiting him, and the more I thought about it, the more the sinking feeling in my stomach grew.

But the weirdest thing was that no one was talking about Ray. The police still hadn't said anything. His death hadn't been in the paper, and as far as I knew, the pack hadn't had any kind of service. The only thing I managed to find out was that Ray's wife had vanished. Their house was empty. It was almost as if neither of them had ever existed.

I still hadn't talked to Dominic, but then, he hadn't made an effort to talk to me either, and I was beginning to think it was better that way. All I was getting from him was a bunch of what I thought were supposed to be meaningful glances, except I didn't know what the meanings were. I figured he was trying to make a point, but the joke was on him because whatever the point was, I wasn't getting it. I was pretty much ready to chalk up the weekend to a weak moment. It was probably better to just forget it. And if he had stopped watching me, I would have done just that.

I sat in class, watching the clock slowly tick the minutes away. Lunch couldn't come soon enough. I needed a break, not that I had been doing much in class. I couldn't focus on anything other than the burn of Dominic's eyes and the sneer on Erika's face.

When the bell finally rang, I forced myself to stay

in my seat until they left. For about half a second, Dominic looked as if he was going to approach me, but before he could, Aidan slung a loose arm over his shoulder and led him out the door.

The cafeteria was already packed by the time I got there. I glanced at the overly long line of students waiting to be served and spotted Marcy at the front. She waved what I thought was a boxed salad at me, and then she pointed to a table and mouthed, *'I got it.'*

Ben and Ann were chowing down on French fries and gravy when I plopped down at my usual table. The fraternal twins were dressed the same, as always, in blue jeans and black hoodies. I've always thought that they secretly wished they were identical. They sure tried hard enough to look the same. Ben had even dyed his blond hair brown to match Ann's, and Ann always wore blue contacts, the same shade as Ben's natural eye color.

"Hey, Jade," Ann said and smiled. "I'm surprised you're sitting with us." She didn't mean it to be unkind; I could see that from the soft smile she was giving me, but the statement got my back up anyway.

"What? Why?" I asked. My voice sounded harsher than I had intended.

Ben cut Ann a narrowed eye glare and said, "We heard that you and Dom made up." He smirked at me and then dropped another fry in his mouth.

I snorted. "Hardly." I leaned forward, resting my elbows on the table and my chin in my hands. *Rumors.* How did kicking Dom out of my house translate into us making up? It took everything in me not to turn around and look at him. I could hear his laughter, and it made my heart twitch. It wasn't quite a squeeze or a twist, but it was enough of a twitch that I noticed it.

Thankfully, Marcy slid into the chair beside me and pushed a salad (or what was considered a salad by high school cafeteria standards: a bowl of lettuce and a single cherry tomato) in front of me. I was about to ask her when she was leaving for the police station, desperately wanting to change the subject, when she said, "And another one gets taken."

"Another what?" Ben asked, looking at Marcy with an utterly blank face, and Ann let out a loud groan.

Marcy rolled her eyes and then nodded in Aidan's direction. "The new guy seems pretty close with Dominic."

There goes trying to change the subject. "He doesn't look like he was taken," I said dryly. "He looks willing." And that made my head spin. I could have sworn they hated each other, or at least that Dominic really didn't like Aidan. Why else would he tell me to stay away?

Ben sighed, and he dropped the fry he had been about to shove in his mouth back into the container. "I didn't think it was possible, but Dominic is getting hotter."

"I know, right?" Ann said with a grin and elbowed her brother playfully. She didn't even try to hide the long and very appraising look she gave Dominic, and as she stared, the grin melted away. "Jade," she said, still watching him closely, critically, "have you noticed the way the pack is hovering around Dom?" Frown lines began to litter her forehead, and she scrunched her nose. "It's like he's ... more important somehow."

My breath caught in my throat, and my heart stopped. I swiveled in my chair, not bothering to try to hide it. Dominic sat at the head of the lunchroom table, which was ridiculous because really, it was just a plastic fold-up table, but he made it look ... regal. Aidan sat on his right, Erika on his left, and along the edges, six other pack members watched him, engrossed in whatever he was saying.

Dominic was smiling. His eyes were bright. He looked ... happy ... content ... proud. My heart started to pound again, and my stomach rolled. Dominic never looked happy. Not anymore. He always had the same mask. Hard and cold and cruel. Not happy. Never. And the way the others were watching him, listening to him ...

I locked eyes with Marcy and whispered, "No." I didn't mean it as a whisper, but the rock-hard lump that had suddenly formed in my throat wouldn't let my voice rise any louder.

Her eyes were wide, and the color rushed from her face. "He ..." she started, but she must not have believed what she was about to say because she promptly snapped her mouth shut.

I pushed my chair out, the legs scraping across the linoleum floor with a screech, and I stared at Dominic for a long minute. Clippings of the last few days flitted through my mind as if I were looking at newspaper articles. *The pack is stressed. He's no good for you. I'm trying to help you.* All his subtle little hints and warnings rang out through my head, and heat burned in my cheeks. Suddenly, I felt sick and utterly stupid. I wasn't part of the pack. He wouldn't have been able to warn me of anything without seeking permission unless ... The thoughts were swarming so loudly in my brain that I couldn't understand any of them.

And then I was standing over him, and I heard my voice, cold as ice, say, "Dominic, we need to talk."

Dominic didn't even look up. "Kind of busy," he said dismissively.

I gritted my teeth, and I really don't know what came over me, but I grabbed hold of his ear and pulled. "We need to talk now."

That got his attention, as well as the attention of all the werewolves at the table. They all glared at me. Even

Aidan was giving me a death stare. Dominic jumped up from his chair and smacked my hand away from his ear. He took hold of my bicep firmly and said, "I'll be right back, guys," before he dragged me from the cafeteria.

As soon as we were through the doors, he dropped his hold and asked, "What do you want?" His tone was sharp, and his shoulders, rigid.

"It's you, isn't it?" I asked. I guessed the look on my face wasn't sweet because he backed up a step and the pink flush in his cheeks turned white. I poked him in the chest, and he flinched back another step. "You took out Ray."

Dominic trembled slightly under my stare, and he sucked in a noisy breath. His shoulders sagged a little as if he were trying to shrink further away from me. He dropped his eyes to the floor, and then he gave his head a forceful shake, pulled in another loud, sucking breath, and hesitantly met my gaze. "You threw me out of your house. Blew me off, and now you think you can just ... just ..." He grunted and threw his hands up in the air, completely frustrated.

"Stop it," I snapped, and he flinched again. "Just cut the crap, Dom. You followed me around all weekend; you can damn well answer my question!"

Dominic cocked his head slightly and searched my face. His brow furrowed in confusion, and any hostility that had marred his body softened. "What are you talking about?" he asked.

"Come on, Dom, I know that the black wolf that trailed me all weekend was you," I shouted. I didn't mean to shout. It just sort of happened, and a burning blush rushed up to my neck. I took a deep breath and smiled awkwardly. "Look, it doesn't matter. You've made your point, okay. I'll stay away from Aidan, but don't be like Ray. Don't start the recruiting. You're better than that."

"Jade, I'm a brown wolf, and I'm *not*," he punched out the word, letting it hang in the air for a moment as if he wanted to make sure I grasped it before he continued, "the new alpha. And it would be really smart for you to forget that you know anything about Ray."

AIDAN

Crap! It seemed like that was the only word my brain could formulate as I listened to Jade and Dominic. It was also the first time in my life that I hated having enhanced hearing. It would have been nice to pretend that they were just having a friendly conversation.

Erika leaned into me. "You were following her?" she snarled in my ear and then leaned back. Her lips curled into a sneer, and she laughed darkly. "Did you hear that, ladies? It looks like we have another contestant."

Crap! Crap! Crap! The banter stopped instantly, and four sets of glowing yellow eyes landed on me, expectantly. Waiting. I slouched a little, trying to look relaxed, and shrugged my shoulders, brushing it off as no big deal. I held their eyes for a long minute before I said, "She's nothing."

"I don't know about that," Erika said and laughed again, but there was no humor in it. "She seems smitten, and by the sound of your wild heartbeat, I'd say you are, too."

CHAPTER 11

JADE

"Dom, what do you mean it wasn't you?" I asked. My voice was barely a whisper, and the metal-lined hallway suddenly seemed ... small ... tight ... airless. I had hugged that wolf, and I had let it smother my face with wet kisses. I felt ... violated. At least I knew why Dominic hadn't tried to talk to me yet, although knowing it didn't really make me feel any better.

"I'm not a black wolf," he said again, a little helplessly this time. He took a step toward me, and when I took a step back, he put up his hands in surrender. "Jade, you're not looking so hot. Are you okay?"

I focused on breathing. In and out. In and out. I wasn't entirely sure why I was so upset, but my throat was burning, and I fought hard to swallow the tears that were threatening to break loose. My heart was breaking — again — just like it had two years ago. And I realized, unexpectedly, that part of me, even though I had been fighting it, had really hoped that I was going to get my Dominic back. That he'd heard my confessions. That he wanted to start over and *fix things* like he'd said. And I was pretty sure that the fact that he hadn't heard me say all those things was distressing me more than knowing some other wolf was stalking me.

I shook my head. "Nope," I said calmly, and before he had a chance to make me even more *not okay,* I turned from him and started down the hallway.

"Jade, wait!" Dominic called. His footsteps were extremely loud in the vacant hallway as he jogged to catch up to me.

I spun back around and put up a hand to stop him. "I can't do this right now, Dom. Just tell Mac I'm not feeling well. Please." My voice sounded as hollow as I felt, and it really didn't sound like my own. I tried to close the doors. I wanted to hide my feelings, but I couldn't. I couldn't focus. I could barely breathe. Each small breath I managed to suck in hurt, burning down my throat like a lit fuse and into my lungs.

But Dominic didn't seem to have the same problem. His face hardened as he closed himself off from me, and it made my stomach drop. I could see the doors slamming shut as he proceeded to lock me out and cut me off, and I hated him for it. He nodded. "Take the sidewalks."

I offered a weak smile and a little wave, but he didn't respond. He just looked at me with those cold, uncaring eyes and waited for me to leave. And that's exactly what I did. I left. Just like he had left me two years ago. Without a backward glance, I weaved through the empty hallways and out the school's front door.

My key was stuck in the lock. It wouldn't turn, and I couldn't get it out. It was frustrating as all hell, and without thinking, I kicked the door. Hard. It hurt. I yelped, and my big toe throbbed.

But it was worth it. I yanked on the key again, and it came out just as the door flew open.

Dad smiled at me. It was the kind of smile that only a dad could give. A bit excited, a touch worried, and a lot happy. It was one of those smiles that encompassed every emotion he had, and it was exactly what I needed.

"Hey, Dad," I said, and without warning, I launched myself at him for one of his epic bear hugs. "Welcome back."

He caught me just as I knew he would, squeezing me tightly and spinning me over the threshold. But the hug didn't last nearly long enough. He put me down and held me at arm's length, giving me one of those concerned fatherly looks. "Hi, honey. What are you doing home?"

I wiggled out of his soft grip and slid by him, kicking the door shut with my heel. "Wasn't feeling good," I lied and padded into the living room. I dropped down on the couch, focusing all my effort on looking sick.

He didn't buy it for a second. "You never get sick," he said bluntly, following me into the room. He sat down beside me and asked, "What's going on?"

Dad looked tired but relaxed. His silver-dusted black hair was flat on one side as if he had been sleeping on it, and he had pillow creases indented on his cheek. He had on his favorite navy blue jogging pants and a gray T-shirt, and by the tightness of his lips, I guessed he was fighting against a yawn.

"Sorry I woke you up," I said. "How was your trip?"

"Jade," he said with a no-nonsense tone, "what are you doing home?"

I bit my bottom lip and wiggled on the couch as I considered lying again. But then I looked into his bright blue eyes, and I saw the concern painted on his face, and the floodgates burst open. Everything rushed out in a mess of words. I told him about Erika and the locker room. I blurted about the black wolf. About Dominic. About Ray. About how no one was supposed to know he was dead. I told him about Mom being all jumpy. I talked about losing Dominic and about how much I missed him. It was as if I were stuck in a tornado, gushing everything out in a spinning gust of wind, unable to stop.

But just like a tornado, I touched down and ran my course, and when there was nothing left, I flopped back on the couch, feeling drained and a little deflated.

Dad considered my story for a long and way too silent moment before he asked, "Does Dominic know about the black wolf?"

"What does that matter?" I asked a little breathlessly. He had to focus on the black wolf out of everything that I had blurted out. I wanted to be upset, or angry, or anything, really, but I couldn't. It all seemed like too much energy. And all I felt was empty. Not in a bad way. It was more of a contented kind of empty as if I had expelled all the badness, and all that was left was ... exhaustion.

"He has always watched out for you, honey," he said softly, and he reached out, brushing some hair from my forehead. "Even if it didn't feel like he was there, he was. He always will be. You know that."

Did I? Not really. But I nodded and smiled anyway. "I'm going to lie down," I said, hauling myself up from the couch.

"Wait," he said, taking hold of my wrist and pulling me back down. He wrapped me in a hug, leaning his chin on the top of my head. "I know you think we are pushing you, your Mom and I, to join them, and I don't want you to think I'm trying to give Dominic an

excuse. He hurt you. He knows that. You know that."
Dad sighed, and his shoulders slumped a little against
me. "But you can't judge them all from his stupidity. I
just want you to be safe, honey. I know you can't see
it, but the pack is safe. They always have been, and
having the wolves as friends isn't as bad of a thing as
you think it is."

I knew he was trying to be comforting, or give me
some kind of life lesson full of wisdom, but it really
wasn't helping. There was nothing safe about the pack.
It didn't matter which way he tried to spin it;
werewolves were not safe.

I pushed out of his arms, giving him what I hoped
was an agreeing look. "I'm going to take a nap," I said,
and I left him sitting there with concern marring his
face, and I headed to my room.

It wasn't until I got to my room that I realized he
hadn't told me about his weekend, but at that point, I
was just too drained to care.

♥

I screamed. There was something on me, smothering
me. I couldn't breathe. I tried to push it off, flailing my
arms around, pulling at the comforter. I couldn't move.
It was dark. Too dark. I was drowning. Suffocating.
Another scream ripped from my lips, but it was
muffled and distorted with barely any sound to it.

"Chill out, Jade." Marcy's voice belted out,
wrapping around me like a soothing blanket. She
grabbed hold of the comforter and pulled it down. I
sucked in a ragged breath, and it burned through my
empty lungs. She was laughing and grinning, and she
was sitting on top of my stomach.

I pushed her off me, giving her a dirty look. "What the hell?"

Marcy giggled. She flopped onto her stomach and made herself comfortable on my bed, resting her chin in her hands. "What happened to you today?"

I grabbed my powder blue comforter, pulled it back up to my chin, and wiggled under the covers, trying to find the sweet spot again and hoping that she'd just go away. I closed my eyes and kept wiggling, but I just couldn't get comfortable.

Marcy cleared her throat dramatically loud. I opened my eyes and gave her another dirty look, but she just grinned.

"Nothing happened," I said. "I just wasn't feeling well."

"Liar," she said, pursing her lips. "You never get sick."

I groaned and rolled onto my side. "Whatever."

My curtains were open, revealing the star-speckled night sky. The silver moon was almost full, and there didn't appear to be a single cloud. I must have slept for hours, but yet, I was still exhausted, and I was sure if Marcy would just leave, I would have no problem falling back to sleep.

Marcy had another plan. She smacked at my legs. "Get up. We're going out."

"Just let me sleep, Mac," I said, snuggling a bit deeper under the blankets.

"Not happening." She laughed evilly and crawled over me, so we were nose to nose. She was grinning mischievously, and her eyes danced with laughter and what looked a lot like secrets. "We're going to get ice cream, and you are going to spill everything. Especially the part about why Erika was asking about you. Whatever you said to Dom, she's fuming about it."

Her smile widened, and she giggled a little. "And I have awesomesauce news of the boy variety."

CHAPTER 12

AIDAN

That night, Dominic was the moody one. Not that I was overly moody per se, it was just that Dominic was never really anything, except when Jade was involved. Again, I found myself wondering what that girl had done to make my pack so uneasy around her. It wasn't just Dominic and Erika; it was most of them. They all watched her with leery eyes, and she seemed oblivious to it. The girl was too busy being overly sure of herself, and I couldn't help but think it was a complete act. No one could be that tough, not when they knew what they were up against.

Dominic hadn't spoken a word to me since lunch. After Jade left, he had talked to her friend and then stormed off. I still couldn't believe that Jade tried to drag him out of the cafeteria by his ear, and if I hadn't been the reason for her anger, I'd probably be laughing about it now.

We were sitting in my motel room watching the night descend upon us; well, I was sitting. Dominic was pacing. I had figured he would have come around by now, but he hadn't. Every once in a while, he would stop his relentless pacing to slam something around, but still not a word.

The first challenge was scheduled for tonight. I was sure Dominic wouldn't be here otherwise. Erika wasn't wasting any time. She was determined and strong and competent, and I absolutely hated it. She was a bitch and not really someone I wanted to spend the rest of my life with. But then, none of the challenging females really sparked my interest. They were all just so ... bitchy and conceited and fake.

But Erika, she had to be the worst of them. Actually scheduling a challenge ... it just wasn't normal. Females were usually more creative, not relying solely on strength to beat their opponents. They picked their times carefully and rarely broadcasted when the attack would happen. It gave them the edge of surprise. As long as there was one witness to testify to the outcome, the winner would move forward.

Erika, though, wanted an audience. Most likely, she was trying to intimidate the others, letting them see what she could do. And I didn't like it. She was too full of herself, and conceit wasn't really a great leadership quality.

A frustrated growl penetrated my eardrums, and Dominic slammed a coffee mug onto the dresser, shattering it.

"Stop slamming things around and just spit it out already," I said, sprawled out on my lumpy bed, staring up at the popcorn ceiling. I couldn't take much more of his brooding. The stress of tonight was eating at me, and he was only making it worse. And at the rate he was going, I wouldn't have a single mug left in this crap hole of a room.

"I asked you to stay away from her," he said through clenched teeth.

"And I told you that wasn't your call to make." I

tried to hide the amusement from my voice, but it leaked out completely unintentionally. Seriously, he sure acted like a crazy jealous person for a guy who didn't even like women.

He stiffened, every muscle in his body tensed, and he glared at me. "She's not going to join the pack."

I offered up a smile. "I never said I wanted her to."

The smile worked ... a little. Dominic sat down in the desk chair and leaned forward, resting his elbows on his knees. "Then what are you doing with her?"

Now that was the question, wasn't it? What was I doing with her? I didn't even know. I hadn't meant to go to her. I hadn't even realized it was her scent that I was following, but once I was there ... I just didn't want to leave. No, that wasn't entirely true. I wanted to go, but my inner-wolf had wanted something different. She was born to be an alpha. She had the strength. She had compassion. She could make me tremble with a single look. Jade had it all, or she would if she was one of us. *And I'd have her.*

The sudden and completely unexpected realization made my stomach squirm in a nervous, happy kind of way. I could almost picture her standing beside me, not a step behind. From the way the other females treated me, I knew they would always be hiding in my shadows. But Jade ...

I shook off the thought, or rather my inner wolf's elated dream. Instead of telling Dominic all of that, I said, "You know, I hate to point it out because this whole thing is actually quite entertaining to watch, but haven't you considered what could happen if you keep telling me to stay away from her? It's like she was just a girl, and now she's forbidden fruit. You are making her so much more intriguing." He shot me a foul look, and I chuckled. "Oh, and not to state the obvious, but I didn't even speak to her."

"We only have one black wolf in the pack," Dominic snapped, but then he chuckled, and a mischievous grin began to pull at his lips. "You think I'm worried about her safety, but really, I'm not. Jade can take care of herself. It's you I'm looking out for here. She'd tear you apart if she knew who you were."

I laughed and rolled my eyes. "A bit dramatic, don't you think? She's just a girl," I said, except I kind of believed that it wasn't all that dramatic.

Right then, my phone rang, a loud shrill, and the sound felt like doom. Okay, maybe not doom exactly, but definitely one step closer to it. And by the way Dominic was watching it vibrate across the nightstand, I figured he was thinking close to the same thing.

"You going to answer it?" he asked, without lifting his gaze from the phone.

I reached over and snagged it up, tapping the flashing call button, and then held it to my ear. "What's the verdict?"

"You've got to come down here," Joe said in a rush, panting as if he had been running and was completely out of breath. "Erika's lost it."

My jaw clenched, and I gripped the phone a bit tighter. "Against the rules, man. I can't interfere." This was the part I hated the most about the games. Alpha males were not allowed to attend the challenges. It was supposed to stop distractions and provide each female with a fair playing ground.

"Aidan, she's going to kill Becca," Joe said. "Get down here."

My gut twisted. *Dammit!* I had hoped it wouldn't come to this. I took a deep breath and said, "I can't. They knew the risks. If Becca won't submit ..."

"Becca already submitted," Joe snapped, cutting me off. "She submitted five minutes ago."

"Where?" I asked, jumping off the bed and snagging

my keys. I mouthed, '*Let's go,*' to Dominic, and threw the door open. According to pack law, fighting to the death was fine if neither of them would give up. But killing after submission was punishable by death.

"The park, and hurry up," Joe said, clearly flustered. I could hear shouting in the background, tinted with panic. "She's already bit a few of us that have tried to step in."

"I'll be there soon," I said and hung up.

When I jumped in and started it up, Dominic was already in the car. I threw it in reverse, and the tires squealed. My muscles were so tight they burned.

"What going on?" Dominic asked as I shifted gears and spun onto the road.

"Erika's trying to kill Becca. Where the hell is the park?"

It was a tense and silent drive to the park. I was actually a bit stunned that Dominic didn't have anything to say. He always seemed to have something on the tip of his tongue. He listened as I told him the little bits Joe had said, which took less than a minute, and then he sat there staring out the window with a locked jaw.

It took four and a half minutes to drive across town and reach the park. I figured that was one of the pluses to living in a small nowhere town, but it still felt like a long drive. As soon as I parked, Dominic was out of the car and running toward the crowd gathered in the center of what looked like a soccer field. The sky was clear, and the extra-bright moon cast the ground in dull silvery light. I took a deep breath and emerged from my car, letting the door slam, and I started over.

The field was set back in an alcove. On three sides, tall pines hid most of the view from the rest of the park. If the parking lot hadn't been directly in front of it, I wouldn't have even noticed it. Raised bleachers outlined the playing area, and a walkway skirted the open end.

As I approached, Dominic was already pushing everyone back, opening up the circle of onlookers. With a quick scan, I was relieved to see that they were all part of the pack, and for half a second, my focus settled on the head of the enforcers. Jared stood just outside the crowd, watching. He smirked at me, and my blood boiled. "You couldn't have dealt with this?" I snarled.

"Not my job to keep the peace, alpha," he said with laughter in his voice. "I only deal with those who have broken pack law, and that hasn't happened here yet."

I gritted my teeth, focusing back on the crowd. I had never liked the enforcers in my father's pack, and the ones here were no different. Always waiting on the sidelines to deliver punishment, but never stepping in.

And then my eyes landed on Erika.

She was in wolf form, her white coat speckled with blood. She was snarling, circling around a gray wolf that lay motionless on the ground. The wolf was still breathing; I could just see the slight rise and fall of its stomach. Erika stalked toward her, growling, low, and menacing.

"Enough!" I shouted, closing the last few steps to tower over her.

Erika swung her head, fixing her eyes on me. She let out another growl, baring her teeth. A rush of raw adrenaline coursed through my veins, and my skin prickled. I pulled off my shirt and pants and tossed them aside as my bones started to break, reshaping and changing. It was a rush, hot and cold. Spine-tingling and thrilling. A hot chill slithered over me, and my body shifted, forming into a black wolf.

I growled and snapped out at her. My fur bristled along my spine, and I curled my lips, exposing the full length of my canines. Erika backed up a step, her eyes darting between Becca and me. Blood dripped from her muzzle, and she snarled again, savagely.

I held her eyes and stalked toward her, a low growl rumbling from my throat. I gathered my scent, letting it trickle through my imprint and into the air. It was as if she just realized who I was because a flash of panic suddenly flitted across her eyes. For a second, she looked as if she were going to bolt, but then she dropped to her stomach, shimmied across the ground until she was at my feet, and began to lick my chin.

I snapped at her to stop, and she whimpered, rolling onto her back, exposing her vulnerable neck and belly to me. I looked down at her for a moment, disgusted, and then I turned from her and let my body reform to human.

As soon as I stood up, Dominic handed me my jeans, and I tugged them on. The crowd was silent, still as marble, watching to see what I would do. I dug my keys out of my pocket and tossed them to Dominic. He snatched them out of the air. "Get Becca out of here."

"What about her?" he asked, nodding toward Erika, who was still on her back, whimpering softly.

I looked back at Erika and gritted my teeth. I could have her locked up, but it wouldn't hold. Technically, she hadn't done anything wrong yet. Becca was hurt, but she was breathing. The enforcers would let her walk no matter what I said. If I hadn't stepped in ... I gave my head a shake, banishing the thought. If I hadn't stepped in, I would have lost both of them.

"Let her go," I said, more than a little reluctantly. I heard Jared chuckle, and I didn't doubt for a second that he'd been hoping I'd slip up and make a stupid call. The enforcers were the only ones who had the authority to deal with reckless or unfair alphas, and they were the only ones who wouldn't be punished for standing up to me. "She hasn't broken any laws."

I glared at Jared for a moment, and his dark, laughing eyes held mine. He smirked at me and gave me a nod that looked like approval. I knew what he was doing. Testing me. He was trying to decide if I would abuse my rank and whether I needed to be under constant watch. I figured I passed the test, though, because he turned his back on me and walked away.

I scooped up my shirt, and as I tugged it over my head, I heard someone say, "Shit, Jade. We need to go."

CHAPTER 13

JADE

Marcy was worked up. So worked up that I had absolutely no clue what she was saying as she spoke. She was speaking in half sentences, starting the thought in her head, only giving me bits and pieces, and then jumping from one topic to the next so quickly that I was completely lost. The gist was that I had pissed off the pack ... again, which really wasn't a new thing. I tended to piss them off a lot. Not that I meant to. It just kind of happened. I've always liked to believe that it was because Erika couldn't deal with the fact that Dominic and I had a past, although I couldn't swear on that, because really, it wasn't just Erika that I seemed to piss off.

Marcy was dragging me through the park, hell-bent on getting freakin' ice cream. The wind was cold. The sky was black. And all I wanted to do was lie in bed and pretend as if nothing was wrong. I wanted to forget about the black wolf that wasn't Dominic. I wanted to pretend I had never met Aidan, and I seriously didn't want to think about Ray's death and why no one was talking about it. But no, of course, I couldn't do that. Marcy needed ice cream.

Baskin Robbins was just on the other side of the soccer field. We stuck to the path, rounding the field, and from this distance, it looked as if the shop lights were dancing through the night as the silhouettes of customers moved past the window.

"Shit," Marcy said. Her arm weaved through mine, and she jerked me to a stop. "Jade, we need to go." She started tugging on my arm, pulling me back the way we had come.

"I thought you wanted ice cream," I said, cutting her a sideways glance. Even in the dark, she looked guilty.

"Marcy!" someone shouted, and I swiveled, looking into the secluded field. Someone was walking toward us, but I couldn't tell who it was. Behind him, a small group of people, maybe ten, were gathered.

"Shit. Shit. Shit." Marcy looked up at me with wide eyes and chewed on her bottom lip for a second, thinking. "If he asks, you begged me to go out, okay?" she whispered, her eyes pleading.

"What?" I asked, completely lost, and I glanced back at the group. Had they been there the whole time? I didn't know, and not knowing made me crazy nervous. I should have noticed them. I should have been alert, not worrying about some boy that I had hardly talked to. If Aidan wanted to be part of the pack, that was his problem, not mine.

"Trevor," she said urgently. "He told me to stay home tonight. Please, Jade. Just please say this was your idea."

I wanted to shake her by her shoulders — literally. "What does Trevor have to do with anything?" I asked, not bothering to try to hide how pissed off I was.

"He's my awesomesauce news," she mumbled, averting her eyes from mine. She started kicking at the ground, digging a little hole in the grass with the toe of her shoe.

Clearly, she needed more than just a shake. Awesomesauce news and Trevor seriously didn't mix. Trevor was not awesome anything, werewolf or not. He was a complete douche bag. And I was about to tell her as much until I caught movement out of the corner of my eye. Trevor was moving in on us, closing the distance quickly, so I bit my tongue and started pulling her down the path. I didn't move fast enough.

"Mac, what the hell are you doing here?" Trevor shouted, snagging her arm and tearing her away from me. He spun her around to face him. "I told you to stay home."

Trevor stood stiff, looking down at her. He wasn't much taller than I was, but his bulky frame seriously increased his intimidation factor. His hoodie was snug, hugging his thick arms and chest, and his white baseball cap shielded most of his face. His jaw was locked, and his grip on her arm looked painfully tight.

Marcy shot me a desperate look before focusing on him. "Um, Jade wanted ice cream. It's a girl thing. We eat ice cream when we're upset." As she rushed out the explanation, her voice squeaked unnaturally high, and Trevor shifted his glare to me.

His scrutiny made the hairs on my neck prickle, and like a wave, they slowly rose as a shiver traveled up my back and neck. I took a step toward him, trying to hide how nervous I was, and clenched my fists. "Take your hand off of her, Trevor, before you lose it," I said, glad my voice was strong and didn't jump the way my stomach was.

"You're not helping, Jade," Marcy hissed at me and moved closer to him, wrapping her arms around his neck. "I'm sorry. She was upset about the whole Dom thing. I couldn't say no."

Trevor stood stiff, not moving closer but not moving away from her either, and he kept his gaze focused on me. "You should have called me," he said through gritted teeth. "I told you I didn't want you walking around alone. Is it really going to be like this again, Mac? Not even a day, and you're already trying to push the limits."

"I didn't want to bother you," Marcy said sweetly. She brought her hands up to his cheeks, pulling his gaze back to her, and she batted her long lashes at him. "You said you had pack stuff to deal with tonight, and it's not like *Baskin Robbins* is far." She glanced over her shoulder at me and laid the sweetness on thick. "Look at her, honey. She's a mess. Ice cream is totally mandatory right now."

Trevor cupped her face with both hands, thankfully not looking back at me. I was sure that he would have known she was lying if he had. "You make me crazy, you know that, right?" He bent a little, planting an incredibly hot kiss on her, so hot, in fact, that I blushed and had to turn away.

I glanced back at the field as I waited for them to stop, and relief washed over me. The group had pretty much dispersed, with only two of them left watching us.

The relief died fast.

The two left were heading over, and as they neared us, I realized who they were. Dominic and Aidan. Dominic gave me a completely fake smile and cleared his throat. "Sorry to interrupt, guys, but did she just tell you that Jade wanted ice cream?"

Marcy made a throaty whimpering kind of sound, and Trevor chuckled. "Yeah," Trevor said, his voice muffled by Marcy's lips.

My body temperature dropped and a painfully tight knot twisted in my stomach. *He wouldn't,* I thought. Dominic grinned at me and winked, and sweat beaded up on my upper lip. "Shut up, Dom," I hissed, and his grin widened.

"Jade's allergic to dairy," he said. "Trev, your girl is lying to you."

I felt my jaw drop. Aidan moved a bit closer, and Dominic laughed. I was stunned. Absolutely stunned. Did he really hate me that much? Really?

"You lied to me?" Trevor asked, pushing Marcy back and holding her at arm's length. His eyes raked over her as if he wasn't really sure if he should believe Dominic or not.

"Wwwhat?" she stammered, her eyes growing wide and panicked. She cut Dominic a disbelieving and completely betrayed look and said, "No, of course not. Why would I lie about ice cream?" It probably would have been believable if her voice hadn't trembled so much.

Knots twisted in my stomach. I couldn't think. We had been so close. So close to just walking away.

Trevor growled. It came from the back of his throat, and his eyes flashed yellow. Marcy started to squirm, trying to shake him off. I shot Dominic the coldest look I could muster, and he chuckled and mouthed, '*Do your thing.*'

It took me a second to process it, but once I did, I almost laughed. If I hadn't wanted to kill Dominic at that very moment, I probably would have roared with laughter. He was setting us up. Except, we had been seconds away from walking away, and Marcy had been handling it just fine without Dominic's seriously unneeded help. I wanted to march over to him and smack that grin off his face, but instead, I groaned and stomped up to Marcy. "Have you lost your mind?" I snapped, grabbing her arm and tugging her out of Trevor's hold. "Mac, he's already broke your heart once. What the hell is wrong with you?"

Marcy didn't miss a beat. Confusing Trevor had always been the easiest way to get his temper down to a bearable level. And Trevor, well, he wasn't exactly the smartest werewolf of the bunch. She jutted out her bottom lip in a pout. "You're supposed to be happy for me."

Dominic chuckled, swiftly moving between Trevor and Marcy, cutting off Trevor's attempt to grab her again. I tugged her a bit further away before throwing my hands up in the air. "He cheated on you."

Dominic's chuckle turned into a full-bellied laugh, and I shot him a murderous glare. Why he felt the need to set up a distraction was lost on me. He could have just ended it, pulled rank on Trevor, and made him walk away, or even better, let us handle it.

"It was a misunderstanding," Marcy said, pacing around me until both Dominic and I were effectively blocking Trevor from her.

I followed her movement, crossing my arms over my chest and rolling my eyes. "Oh, I've got to hear this," I said dryly. "A misunderstanding? How exactly did you misunderstand seeing his tongue down Erika's throat?"

"Okay, so maybe it wasn't entirely a misunderstanding. But he promised he won't do it again." She went up on tiptoes and glanced over my shoulder, smiling sweetly. "Right, honey?"

"And you believed him?" I said before Trevor had a chance to answer.

"I'm happy, Jade," she said and stomped her foot. "Can't you just let me be happy?"

Dominic was roaring with laughter, and it took everything I had not to burst out, too. Trevor looked so lost, his gaze shifting back and forth between us as if he were watching a game of tennis. Another minute or so of this, and we'd be able to walk away; I was sure of it.

"Babe," Aidan said, stepping in front of me, "give her a break." He slung an arm around my waist, pulling me against him, and nuzzled my neck. "Trust me," he whispered in my ear, his lips brushing against my earlobe. My breath caught in my throat, and I tried to push him away. He looked down at me with that knee-melting smile of his and whispered again, "Trust me."

AIDAN

Jade gave me a dirty look. Not just a little dirty, but mud puddle dirty. I tried to pretend that it was directed at someone, anyone else, but it wasn't.

I should let go, I thought. *I should let go and just walk away.* But watching her manipulate one of my wolves without a shred of violence ... It was amazing. She was amazing. And all I could think about as I watched her was touching her. Being closer to her. I needed her.

I held her tightly against my body, and she tried to push me away, but it was a halfhearted attempt. I could feel her frantic heartbeat pounding against my chest, and her breath was coming fast and short. I pulled her a bit closer, and she melted against me. Too bad she still glared up at me with hatred. It was frustrating as all hell, and all I could think of was wiping that look off her face.

I smirked at her and bent forward, brushing my lips against hers lightly, teasingly, and she responded instantly, wrapping her arms around my neck.

A primal need surged through me, crippling me. And before I could stop it, the teasing kiss changed ... morphed ... into something close to savage. Jade bit my bottom lip, sucking it between hers. She moaned and dug her hands into my hair, pulling me closer, crushing me against her.

This crush is going to be the death of me.

That's all it was. A crush. Simple attraction. Something to forget. I knew that. I just wished my gut (and my heated lips) would accept it, too. She had been doing just fine without my interference, but if I was being honest with myself, I had only interfered for a chance to get closer to her.

"Aidan!" Dominic growled.

I didn't want to stop. I really didn't want to let her go, but at the sound of his voice, Jade jerked away from me. I held on tight, keeping my arms firmly around her waist, and after a second, she relaxed against me again. She looked up at me through hooded eyes. They were the sexiest eyes I had ever seen. They had this bedroom quality, deep brown, with full, thick lashes. I brushed my lips against hers, just a featherlike sweep, and let my hand travel slowly down her silky smooth arm, entwining my fingers with hers.

"You have my keys, Dom," I said, keeping my eyes locked with hers. "I'll see you back at the motel." Then, I stepped back from her, giving her hand a little tug, and started walking. I knew this was stupid, but I couldn't let go, not yet, so I said, "Trevor, the girls want ice cream. You coming?"

Trevor looked as if he had no clue what was going on, and I bit back a laugh. Dominic had said he knew what he was doing, but this was not what I had expected. He shook his head as if trying to clear it and then grinned. "Yeah, sure, come on, Mac." He held his hand out to her, and she rushed over, grinning.

We had only made it a few steps when Jade stopped abruptly and spun back around. "Dom, wait," she called. There was desperation in her voice, which lit my nerves on fire. She tried to pull her hand away, but I didn't — wouldn't — let go. Not only did I not want to, but Becca was already in the backseat healing, and the last thing I needed was to try to explain to Jade why there was a naked and very bloody girl in my car.

Dominic didn't turn back. He reached for the car door and swung it open. "Not now, Jade," he said and climbed in, shutting the door quickly.

She stood still, watching him pull out of the parking lot as if she thought he'd stop. He didn't. The car disappeared down the road, yet she still watched, even after any shred of taillights was gone.

"You okay?" I asked as I took a quick glance over my shoulder. Trevor and Marcy had already disappeared into the shop.

"What the hell are you doing?" Jade asked, keeping her voice low. She tugged on my hand and started walking. Her hand was stiff in mine, and she made a point not to look at me, but she didn't let go.

"Hanging out with friends." That wasn't really a lie, was it? The pack was sort of my friends. I wanted to tell her who I was so bad it hurt, but I just couldn't do it. What if Dominic was right? What if she hated me just because I was one of them? I didn't think I could live with that.

"They're not your friends, Aidan," she snapped. "Are you blind or just stupid?"

"Stupid," I said, looking down at our hands laced together. "Definitely stupid." But everyone needed to be stupid once in a while, right? What fun would life be if I always played by the rules?

CHAPTER 14

JADE

My mocha was cold. Not just cool, but freezing, and I sipped it slowly, trying to make it last. The coffee shop was busy. The chatter of students buzzed in the air. Each one of the cracked up red, faux-leather booths was occupied, and for once, not a single pack member was invading the space. I fiddled with the saltshaker, twirling it around, watching the tiny grains shift through the glass. Marcy was talking about, well, I really didn't know, because I honestly wasn't listening.

Once she started gushing about Trevor, I zoned out, and well, I was too busy forcing myself not to look at Aidan again to really hear what she was saying. I was really beginning to feel like a crazy stalker. Aidan had been sitting in the booth a few down from us, reading for close to an hour now, and he still hadn't glanced my way. It was maddening. Never in my life had I been ignored as much as he ignored me. It had been almost two weeks since we kissed in the park. And since then, he had been more than a little distant. He was always polite when I forced him into a conversation, but that was it. A distracted politeness, as if he always had somewhere else to be that was more important.

And that attitude made me want him more. He'd only been living in Dog Mountain for a short time, but Aidan had quickly climbed to the top of the social ladder at school. The pack loved him, and with the pack's endorsement, so did the rest of the students. I figured being popular in a small town wasn't all that hard. It wasn't as if there were a ton of competition. Except, I knew that being popular in my small town was a challenge. But Aidan hadn't needed to even work at it. Even after standing up to Dominic, he had managed to penetrate the popularity ranks. And he had done it with a cool detachment as if he didn't care one way or another.

This was the first time I had seen Aidan without Dominic or one of the other werewolves flanking him in the last two weeks. It was also the first time I had seen something other than aloofness on his chiseled face. His hair was spiky with gel, and his brown eyes were wide as he flipped the pages of his textbook as if it were the most absorbing thing he had ever read. He was gentle with the pages, letting his fingertips caress them delicately. I got the impression that he was one of those people who could read a book ten times without making it look like it had been opened. I didn't know whether I liked that about him or if it was another thing that drove me crazy about him.

"I like him, Mac," I said, still twirling the saltshaker in my hands. "Like really like him." It seemed like such a stupid thing to admit. I hardly knew him. How could I possibly know if I liked him or not? But my stomach didn't seem to agree. Every time I saw Aidan, birds took flight in my belly.

Marcy cocked her head to the side, looking at me as if I were nuts. She arched a brow. "Who?"

I tilted my head and jutted my chin in Aidan's direction.

She glanced over her shoulder and then turned back to me, wrinkling her nose. "Really? But he's ..."

"Perfect," I said, cutting her off and shooting her a dirty look.

"Dominic is perfect. Trevor is perfect. He's...," she paused, and her eyebrows moved together as she tried to find the right words. She snatched the saltshaker out of my hand, smacking it down on the table. "Cold."

I laughed. I didn't mean to. It just came out. "He is not, and Dominic doesn't count in this."

"Yeah, he kind of is," she said, and her frown grew. "He's barely spoken to you since the park."

"It's an act," I said defensively and with a lot more conviction than I felt.

Marcy considered this, and as she did, a sly smirk spread on her lips. "Then go get him."

"I can't." I sighed, looking down at the table. What was it about him that made me lose my nerve? Anyone else, and I wouldn't hesitate, but Aidan, he seemed so out of reach. Above me. As if he were above us all.

"Why the hell not? Who says you have to wait for him to make a move. We're not in the Middle Ages, Jade."

I sighed. "He hasn't even noticed I'm here."

"Wow, really? When did that ever stop you before? You want him, then get your skinny butt over there and make your presence known." I gave her a look, and she grinned her epic idea grin. She leaned in across the table and dropped her voice to a whisper. "Remember back in eighth grade, before Dominic came out, and you wanted his attention?" she asked.

"Um, not sure ..."

She cut me off. "Yes, it's perfect."

AIDAN

Keeping a straight face was a challenge. Jade and Marcy sat a few booths over from me, but I could hear them as if they were right next to me. Jade looked, well, hot. But then, she always did. It wasn't just her perfect figure with all of those peaks and curves, or her glossy hair, or her full lips that made her hot. It was her confidence. Even when she doubted herself, she was still confident about it. It was far from conceit, though, nothing like Erika and the others. Jade was a girl who knew exactly who she was, and she let the world know it, too. It made her even more appealing, really.

Staying away from her these past few weeks had been brutal. But I didn't really have a choice. Erika had taken down another one of the challenging females, and with only four of them left, it wouldn't be long before I was tied down to one of them. There was absolutely no future for Jade and me, and the sooner I accepted that, the easier it would be for her. So far, Erika hadn't caught wind of our little moment in the park, and she had forgotten the absurd idea that Jade was a threat. And I wanted to keep it that way.

From the corner of my eye, I watched a storm of emotions pass across Jade's face before she settled on the confidence that always burned in her eyes. She slid from the booth, stood up, and ran her hands down her thighs, smoothing out her jeans.

"Okay, I'm going to do it," she said, looking at Marcy as if she wanted Marcy to stop her.

Marcy grinned and leaned back in the booth. "Good luck."

Jade's shoulders rose and fell three times before she spun on her heels and walked up to me, or marched was more like it. Everything about her said determined. I had expected her to say *hi* or slide into the booth across from me, but she didn't. She dropped down beside me, and before I could even get a word out, she grabbed the collar of my shirt, balling it in her fist, and yanked me toward her.

Her lips were on mine before I could even think. They were soft, warm, and tasted like mocha. They felt even better pressed against my mouth than I remembered. She worked her lips over mine with the same passion that she had for everything else she did. Urgent and hot. My lips parted as did hers, and as soon as they did, she flicked her tongue against mine, and suddenly, my hands were wrapped in her silky hair and

...

"Sorry, I'm late." Dominic. At the sound of his voice, we broke apart, both of us breathing more than a little heavily. She looked at me; her eyes were full of heated excitement. She licked her lips as a smile pulled at the corners of her mouth. "Jade?" Dominic asked in disbelief. "Out of all the pack members in this town, you go after him again!"

Jade made a sound. It came from the back of her throat, a mix between a gasp and a growl. The heat that had been in her eyes iced over, and she leaped out of the booth.

"You're one of them," she spat.

I narrowed my eyes at her, searching her over. My brain was foggy, and my eyes kept landing back on her swollen lips. It took a few long seconds for me to figure out what she was talking about.

"I'm not just one of them," I said just as nastily, and every muscle in my body tensed as I slid out of the booth and glared down at her. I had never had someone look at me with so much hatred, so much disrespect. "I'm the alpha."

All the color drained from her face, and I instantly regretted telling her. For half a second, she looked as if she were going to pass out. She wobbled a little, and Dominic placed a hand on the small of her back, keeping her steady. He was smirking at me, a cocky smirk, and all I wanted to do was punch him.

Jade rocked on her feet for another second, and then, scarlet streaked up her neck, settling in her cheeks. She spat on the floor and wiped her mouth so hard with her sleeve that her lips were burning red when she stopped. "I feel sick," she whispered.

JADE

I needed air. Aidan was the alpha. I kissed the alpha. And I wanted to kiss him again. So much so that it hurt. He was staring down at me with cold eyes, and his jaw was twitching as he clenched and unclenched his teeth. Dominic was saying something to him, but I couldn't hear it. My ears were ringing too loudly, and my heart was pounding even louder.

I swallowed hard, but it didn't help to move the bristly lump lodged in my throat. *I kissed the alpha.* The birds flapped in my stomach, begging me to move closer to him and do it again.

Suddenly, a montage of images invaded my brain. I saw Dominic. His smile. The way he held me in the picture that sat beside my bed as if I were the only thing that mattered. The proud big brother. The best friend. Then I saw him as the beta. The cold eyes. The hatred. The aggression. His back faced me as he walked out of my life. And my irrational mind blamed Aidan for it all.

I felt my face twist into a sneer, and for a moment, I saw the pain in Aidan's eyes. It didn't last long, and in a blink, he had his cold mask back in place.

Aidan didn't see it coming, but then I hadn't either.

I took a step toward him and slapped him with everything I had. A burning sting rushed through my hand. Dominic chuckled, and I spun on him. Whatever it was that he saw in me made him take a quick step back, and without even a small glance over my shoulder, I left the coffee shop.

CHAPTER 15

Jade was like a flash thunderstorm, calm one second, and the next, a burst of ferociousness. It was amazing and troubling and more than a little confusing. And she could really hit. My cheek burned, and I was pretty sure there was a nice red handprint there. I really hadn't seen that one coming, not after the seriously hot kiss she had just planted on me. I could still taste her mocha on my tongue, and dammit, but I wanted more.

The door slammed behind her, and the glass shuddered from the impact. "You okay?" Dominic asked, although his tone clearly said that he really didn't care one way or the other. He was smirking and looking as if it were an effort not to burst out in laughter.

"Fine," I said, scanning the coffee shop. Everyone was silent, waiting, watching, and the reality of what I had just done sank in fast. I dropped down into the booth, noticing the weary eyes and the stiff postures of everyone around me. Ray's death, and my position, had been kept quiet for a reason, and because of that ... that ... girl, it was all going to go up in flames. "Shit," I blurted, resting my head in my hands. "Did I really just announce that?"

The silence was ruthlessly loud. The pounding hearts and breathing of all the people around me were like bad music blaring in my ears. Too loud to think. I wanted to run after Jade. Force her to listen. Make her see me again for me. But I had a pretty good feeling that that would be a useless effort, and Jade hating me seriously wasn't the important thing. Not now. But Bruce's pack getting wind of a new alpha, one without a mate, was.

"I'll make the call," Dominic said abruptly and pulled his phone from his pocket. Any humor that had been on his face vanished. His back stiffened, his jaw hardened, and he paced to the back of the shop, his phone already to his ear as he began barking out orders.

Shit! The pack wasn't ready for this. I didn't know enough about the cougars yet. How they worked. How many there were. The last count Dominic had been able to get hold of was eighteen, but that was only a count of the males. From what I understood, the female numbers were and always had been an unknown factor.

I knew Bruce was vicious, and he was always looking for more females to lure into his clutches. I still couldn't figure that one out. From what Dominic had told me, Bruce only recruited females, and so far, his contact wouldn't reveal the why. I also knew that they had been coming closer to town these last few days. Their scents were scattered along the edges of our woods.

How could I have been so stupid! This little game with Jade ... this stupid crush, was putting us all in jeopardy. Not just the pack but also the town. But still, even knowing that all I wanted to do was run after her.

For about half a second, hot regret washed over me. If I had just kept driving. If I hadn't stopped in this stupid hick town, I wouldn't have to deal with any of this. I wouldn't have to worry about a pack of werecougars. I wouldn't have to deal with twenty-nine werewolves that acted as if they were the only things that mattered. I wouldn't be an alpha with a beta that fought me at every turn. And I wouldn't have met Jade.

I sighed. Not meeting Jade ... My fists balled in my hair, and my jaw tensed. That girl was ruining everything. But then, I figured it was my fault. I had been letting her and the pack walk all over me. Maybe I had been too nice, too forgiving. Maybe Ray had had the right idea all along. Evoke fear in the pack and the town. I wanted to call my dad. I needed advice, but I couldn't bring myself to dial the number. He would only tell me what I already knew. I was being too soft with them all.

I didn't hear the door open or her footsteps, but I felt her slide into the booth, pressing up against me. Erika. I glanced at her. Nervous whispers and the synchronized clattering of mugs against tables suddenly invaded my brain. I glanced up to find the booths around me were now empty as people filed out the front door or moved to the opposite side of the coffee shop, giving me a wide birth.

I inched away from her, pressing closer to the wall. She wore her typical skintight black tank. It was cut so low that her breasts were barely covered, and she also sported black jeans and a leather jacket that fit like a glove. Her bright blue eyes and even brighter red lipstick were the only color on her.

Her nostrils flared, and her eyes sparkled. She studied me long and hard, taking in deep breaths, and when her lips started to curve, my stomach sank.

"Leave it alone, Erika," I warned, putting every bit

of authority that I had into my tone. "She's not part of this."

She smiled, not a nice smile, and it sent a chill over my skin. "Too bad what you say doesn't really matter, not when it comes to this. She's left her stench all over you."

CHAPTER 16

JADE

I could still feel Aidan pressed against me. The warmth of his body. The softness of his lips. The sweet taste of his tongue against mine. The butterflies in my stomach turned into a flapping nest of birds just from the thought of him. But then they stopped. How could someone so ... so ... perfect be such a monster?

It was strange how my perception of Aidan could change drastically with a single word. I thought I had known who he was. Not that I really knew him, but I had this idea of who he was supposed to be, except that idea crumbled as soon as I heard *alpha*. In a split second, everything had clicked into place with surprising clarity. The pack loved him not because he was a nice guy but because they had to. And it made me wonder how much of what I thought I knew about him was a lie.

The last few rays of the sun had long since flickered out on the horizon, and the sun-warmed ground that I sat on had grown cold. The wind was fierce, cutting through my jeans and sending goosebumps rushing over my skin. Leaves flew around me, falling from the trees, and were yanked from the ground as another gust of bitter wind rushed through the park. I should have gone home. Marcy would be worried, and so would Mom and Dad. But I didn't want to leave. Not yet.

To be honest, I was a bit surprised that no one had come looking for me yet, but I figured Dominic had a hand in that. He was really the only person that Marcy or my parents would have listened to if they thought I was missing. I guessed I should thank him for that. For giving me time to breathe.

I traced the engraved stone, running my fingers along the grooves. The moon cast light in silver strips on the stone, cutting through the trees. I had always loved this place. The wall of faces. The monument stood in the center of the park. It was supposed to be a tribute to the alphas, their faces engraved there as they took over the pack. For me, though, it wasn't a tribute. It was a reminder that they were not invincible.

Leaves crunched under shoes in the distance. I listened as they approached, not bothering to look behind me. I probably should have, but I couldn't make myself care. The crunching stopped at what sounded like only a few feet from my back, and her voice cut through the air, making the already bitter night turn arctic. "You should have stayed away from Aidan."

"Go away, Erika," I said, letting my finger trail along the grooves of another face.

She laughed darkly. "I don't think so."

I straightened a little as tension flowed freely, thick and suffocating, between us, but I still didn't bother to turn around. Erika was one of those girls that thrived on others' fear, and I wasn't going to let her think that her presence bothered me, not even for a second.

A string of snaps and pops echoed through the park. I leaped up from the ground, but not out of fear. I was furious. Why couldn't she just leave me alone? I spun toward her and gasped. She was a white wolf, larger than I remembered her to be. Her eyes were wide, staring at me, and she bared her teeth, snarling.

I snarled back. I felt it in my belly, vibrating up my throat. All of my anger bubbled up, and it burst out into a growl. I stalked toward her. It was probably stupid. A voice in my head was screaming at me to run, but I couldn't. I wasn't going to let her think I was scared, and in all honesty, at that moment, I was too angry, too hurt, to feel the fear that should have been jolting through me.

Erika snapped out at me and let out a rumbling growl. But I kept moving in on her, my eyes locked with hers. "You're not going to win," I taunted. My voice sounded wrong — savage — and my lips twisted into a sneer as I snarled at her again. I sounded feral like an animal. It was wrong. So wrong. But at the same time, it felt ... right. Strong and fervent. Eager to end her reign of terror once and for all.

I towered over her wolf form. She pulled her lips back further, the pink of her gums exposed. For a second, I froze, and white-hot anger surged through me as I stared into those yellow eyes. I blinked, only a quick flutter of my lashes, and when I opened my eyes, she lunged forward.

Raw adrenaline pumped fiercely through my veins. I jumped out of the way, hitting the ground hard. Grass and dirt bit into my side as I skidded along the ground. I rolled out of the skid, jumping back up to my feet.

Erika stalked toward me again, snarling savagely, and right then, my stomach rolled. *What the hell am I doing?* She circled to my right, and I swiveled, matching her movements. I swallowed the dread that had begun to trickle over my skin and scanned around me, looking for something, anything, I could use.

My eyes fell on a branch, and another frustrated

growl ripped through me. The branch looked thick, sturdy, and perfect, and it lay on the ground just behind the snarling white wolf.

The fur along Erika's back bristled, standing on end along her spine, and her ears straightened as she pushed them forward. With stiff, straight legs, she sidestepped, continuing to circle, and I kept moving, matching her pace. The branch was getting closer with each cautious step. Her eerie, glowing eyes never strayed from me. They were intense and cold and calculating.

Suddenly, Erika stopped and leaped into the air, moving faster than my eyes could follow. And then she was on me. I barely felt her teeth sink into my ankle. My blood was pumping fast, and my breath coming short as a new burst of energy coursed through me. I did the only thing I could think of. I kicked out at her, throwing her off balance enough that she let go, and before she could sink her teeth into me again, I lunged at her, grabbing her muzzle with both hands, and held it closed.

Erika bucked and swung her head from side to side, but I held tight. Now that I was actually touching her, all the fear I should have felt in the first place was pressing at me from all sides. She growled and yanked, and I held on certain that if I let go, I'd be dead. My arms were throbbing and shaking, and my hands were slick with drool. I didn't know how much longer I would be able to hold on. With every shake of her head, my hands slipped, and I had to scramble to keep hold.

A low, rumbling, and more than a little frustrated growl ripped from me. "Stop it!" I yelled in a voice that did not sound like my own. It sounded too cold and too forceful, full of command that I had never known I had in me. And then, Erika just … stopped.

She looked up at me, her eyes widened, and her entire body trembled. She bowed her head, breaking eye contact. Her ears flopped down, and she whimpered, lowering herself to the ground at my feet as I let her muzzle slip from my hands.

AIDAN

"Did she ...?" Dominic started, his voice trailing off.

We tracked Erika since she rushed out of the diner, watching and waiting. She had been right. I had no say in the alpha female games. I couldn't stop Erika from challenging Jade, but Jade was just a human, and I figured that that fact alone could overrule the *no alpha males allowed at a challenge* rule. If Erika had tried to pull the crap she had with Becca, Jade wouldn't have stood a chance. Or at least that's what I had been trying to tell myself to justify my proximity to the challenge. Clearly, I had been wrong.

"She did," I said as Erika bowed her head and sank to the ground. The copper scent of blood filled the air. I felt sick, and a cold sweat broke out over my back. I should have stopped this. I could have stepped in. And if I had, Jade wouldn't be ... *She'll hate you even more when it sinks in*, a voice echoed through my head, triumphantly, as if my conscious was actually happy that my life was crumbling all around me.

Dominic looked at me, stunned. "Aidan, you're not going to ..." he started, but his voice trailed off again as he looked back at the girls. Erika lay silent, her tongue darting out as she licked at Jade's ankle.

I nodded. "I am." I wanted to smile; I could feel it in my belly, but I didn't. The scent of blood was growing, wrapping around me, and I watched as Erika's tongue darted out again, coating Jade's bleeding ankle with her saliva. My conscious was yelling at me, telling me this was nothing to be happy about, but I couldn't stop it. I was happy and sick and stunned.

"She doesn't know what she did."

"Doesn't matter. You know the rules. She probably won't win anyway. She'll give up." Even to my own ears, my voice sounded cold, uncaring, and it was ... odd. My heart was thumping; my nerves were alive, rushing and sparking over my skin. But my voice ... my voice was like my conscious. Cold and disappointed.

"But she's not one of us," Dominic said, a pleading note to his voice. "And she doesn't know how to give up."

"Dominic, go help Jade," I said, cutting him a look. "She's bleeding."

CHAPTER 17

JADE

She bit me. She bit me. She bit me.

My ankle was bleeding. Erika's tongue tickled my skin as she lapped up the scarlet trail that leaked from my flesh, catching it before it reached the ground.

She bit me. She bit me. She bit me.

I couldn't move away. I wanted her to stop. My stomach rolled, and bile rushed up to my throat.

She bit me. She bit me. She bit me.

Erika whimpered, and her tongue flicked out again, sending a hot rolling chill up my leg and over my skin. She was salivating. Her drool was warm and cool all at once. She nosed my leg, trying to get my attention.

She bit me. She bit me. She bit me.

"Erika!" The voice was loud. Commanding. Furious.

Erika whined and pressed her head against me, cowering at my feet. She looked up at me. Fear shone in her eyes, and she whined again.

"Erika, get away from her," the voice demanded, but she didn't move. I didn't know how she could resist the urge to obey. That voice. It made my insides shiver, not in a good way.

She held my eyes and tilted her head to the side. She barked once, just a little yip, and then bowed her head again.

"Shit," the voice said. A hand touched my shoulder. It was gentle and warm and familiar. "She's waiting for your command," it said softly in my ear.

"She bit me," I said. I felt empty. Hollow. Vacant. "She bit me."

A growl rumbled through the air. I shuddered. So did Erika. I felt her trembling against my leg. I bent beside her. I don't know why. I didn't want to, but I couldn't stop it. "It's okay," I whispered and patted her lightly, letting my fingers trail down her back.

The growl came again. Louder. Stronger. And the white wolf cringed into me. She licked my chin and flattened her ears.

"Jade, stand up. Don't let her hide behind you. You can't protect her from her alpha. It's not your place."

"She bit me," I said again, hating myself for saying it. I looked up, and Dominic smiled a sad, sad smile.

"I know, honey," he said. "But you need to step away from her. Tell her to go with Aidan."

I furrowed my brow and looked around. What was he talking about? There was no one else here. I opened my mouth, ready to demand an answer when suddenly, I was face to face with *the* black wolf.

I jumped a little and rocked on my feet. Erika whimpered, and Dominic snapped, "Don't show fear. It'll ruin what you've already done." I started to look up. The realization of what had really happened hit me hard and fast. "No, don't look away from him, Jade. Stand up slowly, keep your eyes open and fixed on him."

The black wolf snarled and bared his teeth, and I fought the urge to close my eyes. This was Aidan. Aidan was the black wolf. I thought I would be sick, and I swallowed hard, pushing the rising bile back down my throat. I stood up on shaky legs and held still. I wanted to run. I fought against the scream, trying to push up from my stomach.

We locked eyes for an agonizing and terrifyingly long moment, the black wolf and me, and then he shifted his focus, growling at Dominic. And Dominic ... Dominic dropped his eyes and shrunk, rolling his shoulders over and making himself as small as he could without dropping to the ground.

Erika crawled toward Aidan, her belly dragging along the ground, and licked his chin until he snapped at her to stop. With one last piercing glare at me, he left, with Erika trailing behind him, her tail between her legs.

"Why did you make me do that?" I asked, my voice cracking over the words. The last bit of Erika's white form disappeared into the trees.

"Because Erika is treating you like an alpha, and if you bowed to him, you would lose that respect," Dominic said as if it was matter-of-fact.

"But you bowed to him," I countered. I wish I hadn't said it. I didn't want to talk. I didn't want Dominic's help. Cold sweat was dripping down my forehead, and the bitter, sour bile was fighting its way back up my throat.

"Yes, but I'm his beta," Dominic said. He sounded so distant. So far away. "I'm lower than him."

The world around me was spinning and shifting. The night seemed darker, blacker, and bitterer. My stomach rolled, and my head spun. I looked at Dominic and whispered, "She bit me."

♥

I woke up to a wonderfully familiar smell. It was musky with a hint of apple, and I pulled in a long, deep breath, savoring it. His hand brushed lightly across my forehead, pushing away my hair, and I cuddled up closer to him, burying my head in his chest.

"How are you feeling?" he asked. His voice was whisper soft, and he pulled me closer still, wrapping his strong arms around me.

"Tired and thirsty. Really, really thirsty." His sweater muffled my voice, but he still heard me and laughed.

"Thirsty?" he asked and chuckled again. "I think that's the first time I've heard that one."

I kept my eyes closed. I didn't want to look at him. I didn't want to see the pity or the understanding that I was sure would be on his face. The sun was beating through the window. Its warmth touched my exposed skin, and it felt so … real. All of it felt real. I wondered how long I had slept. Was it a few hours? A few days? Was I already in transition? I wanted to be angry, but I couldn't bring myself to drudge up the feeling. What point was there? It was done. I was, or soon would be, one of them. Anger seemed like such a waste of effort.

We lay there silently for a long while. Dominic rubbed soft and soothing circles onto my back, and although I couldn't say it, I was glad he was there. Who would have thought that this would be what brought us back together? I surely hadn't, but in a way, I was glad for it. His arms around me made everything a bit brighter. Fuller. Easier to handle. I could still feel Erika's wet tongue on my ankle, tainting my blood.

"What's going to happen, Dom?" I asked. I squeezed my eyes tighter, wishing I could just go back to sleep and pretend none of this had happened.

"Well, um ..." he started and squeezed me a bit tighter before continuing, "the first thing that's going to happen is that you are going to have a shower, and then you'll get dressed, and then you need to talk to Aidan."

I bolted up, pushing him off me, and a surge of white-hot rage rushed over me. "What!" I shouted and then took a long breath, trying to rein in my voice. I narrowed my eyes at Dominic. He was still lying back on my bed, cool and calm, smirking at me. "I'm not going to talk to him. I never want to see that jerk again." Okay, so maybe anger wasn't all that hard to feel after all.

That wiped the smirk from his lips. "Jade," he said, with a commanding force that made me sit a bit straighter. "There's no place in this town for a lone wolf, and with what you did to Erika ..." he trailed off and took a long, deep breath. "If you don't join the pack, you'll run the risk of creating your own, and trust me, you don't want that. Not here."

AIDAN

Dominic's voice was loud. It drifted down the stairs as if it were seeking me out, making sure I didn't miss a beat of his conversation with Jade. I wished I had missed it all. The venom in her voice when she said she never wanted to see me again had my inner-wolf doing backflips in my stomach, just itching to run to her and beg her to accept me.

She was meant to be an alpha. Not just an alpha, but *my* alpha mate. I could feel it with every fiber, every vessel, every nerve ending in my body. I wasn't sure how Dominic managed to speak to her the way he was. His voice held so much command. It didn't waver in the slightest. I assumed it was because of their past, whatever that was, but still, the rest of the pack had been treating her with hostile caution, and he acted as if she were just a girl. And right then, I wished I had done exactly that right from the start.

As it was, it took everything I had in me not to run up those steps and punish him for speaking to her that way. It was as if my inner-wolf had already claimed her and accepted her as my equal.

Mr. Shaw didn't seem to notice my turmoil. He just stared at me, long and hard. It was distracting and annoying, and I could feel my blood pressure rising with every passing second.

He seemed like an okay guy. And I figured he had a right to be a little pissed about his daughter, but the longer he stared at me, the more I felt as if he wasn't really that angry. It was as if he were sizing me up, taking in every little detail and trying to decide my worth. He reminded me of my first girlfriend's father, which made me overly nervous.

Mrs. Shaw had been a lot easier to deal with. I'd met her briefly this morning, and it had only taken a few short minutes to convince her that Jade would be fine. She didn't even bother checking in on her daughter before running out the door to work, entrusting her fully to my care. And she had actually seemed happy about the fact that Jade had been bitten.

We had been sitting in the living room for about an hour waiting for Jade to wake up when he finally cracked an odd kind of smile and said, "So my daughter is part of the competition."

"Yes, sir," I said, a bit stunned. I looked him over again and furrowed my brow. The inner workings of a pack's rank were not something that a human should know. He was staring at me, waiting for more, and he was giving me a no-bullshit kind of look, one that had me certain he knew exactly what was going on. Most likely more *Ray* damage, I figured, and I continued with caution, "She broke Erika last night. And she didn't back down from me after the challenge."

That shocked him. I saw a quick flash of it in his eyes, but he covered it up quickly. "I don't doubt that. Jade has spent a long time hating your pack. She wouldn't back down." He stretched his long legs in front of him and crossed them at the ankles. "Has she accepted the rank?"

I held his eyes, unblinking and unflinching. "There are still three other females fighting for it. Nothing to accept yet. And as far as I know, Jade doesn't have a clue what she's signed up for. She might step down when she does."

He laughed, a full-bellied laugh. "Jade doesn't give up," he said and laughed again. He sounded so much like Dominic, it was a bit ... weird, and it added a whole shitload of questions to the rising pile in the back of my mind that centered on Jade. Again, I found myself wondering, *Who was this girl? And how deep of a connection did she have with my beta?*

Mr. Shaw's laughter died down, and he gave me a somber look. "Be honest with me, kid," he said, sounding a little deflated, "does she have a chance, or should I be packing her up and taking her away?"

It was a fair question, and I had to really think about it before answering. "If she left now, she'd have Erika following her. It was a struggle to get her to leave Jade's side last night." I paused, collecting my scattered thoughts, and scrubbed at my face before looking back at him. "I think she has what it takes, sir."

Mr. Shaw considered my answer. He folded his arms over his chest, and one eyebrow rose. "And how do you feel about my baby girl?" There was no-nonsense in his tone as he asked the question, and I got the feeling that there was only one right answer. Too bad I didn't really know what the right answer was.

"Doesn't matter," I said with a shrug. "Alpha pairs are about strength and dominance and leadership. How I feel, or who I want, doesn't make a difference in who will win."

"You don't know who I am, do you, son?" he snapped, and I got the sinking feeling that sticking with the truth of the situation wasn't the right answer.

I shook my head from side to side. "No, sir. Should I?"

"He works for you, dumbass," Dominic said as he padded down the stairs. "Who do you think I called yesterday when you were stupid enough to tell the whole town who you are?"

Every muscle in my body coiled like a spring. "You," I said, snapping my gaze back to Mr. Shaw. My nostrils flared as I sucked in breath after breath, but all I got were wolves and humans. No trace of cougar. Nothing but human was coming from this man. "You can't be."

Mr. Shaw chuckled. "Nice little trick, isn't it?"

CHAPTER 18

The doorbell rang again in three short and shrill bursts. I could hear Dominic laughing and the deep rumbles of Dad's voice, but yet, the doorbell was still ringing. I secured my towel around me, tucking it tightly, and whipped the bathroom door open. "Answer the door," I yelled, and with a glance down the hall, just to make sure no one was there, I slipped out of the bathroom and headed for my room.

I didn't get far.

Someone cleared their throat and started shuffling up the steps behind me. I spun around, figuring it was just Dominic. I was about to give him an earful about the door, but the words clogged in my throat. "Aidan," I said, and I hated how my voice squeaked on his name. I sounded like an awkward teenager, and I was sure I looked it, too.

He wasn't smirking. His jaw was locked tight, but he didn't look unhappy, annoyed, maybe. He reached the top of the stairs and just stood there, staring down at me. And right then, I didn't find him intriguing. It was a weird feeling as if something that should be there was just ... gone. I figured that it was because I knew who he

129

was now. The mystery was gone, and at that moment, all I saw was barely concealed power and authority, and it made me shiver. My stomach constricted, twisting tight as a corkscrew, and I chewed on my bottom lip nervously.

Aidan took a step forward, and I almost did the same. Almost. His fitted gray T-shirt hugged his muscled chest and sculpted arms, and as I looked at him, I suddenly felt alive, as if someone had flicked my power switch on. All I could think about was touching him. An urging need ran through me. It was primal, deep-seated, and more than a little bestial. It was nothing like the butterflies or birds that I usually felt when he was near. This was so much more that it consumed me like fire consuming a fluttering piece of paper. My skin burned, and my heart pounded. I wanted to know what that power felt like under my fingertips. His eyes raked over me, and he licked his lips, and Jesus, but my knees started to tremble. He had that look in his eyes, the one he had had when we first met as if he saw nothing but me. It was so intense as if I were the only thing in the world that was worth looking at.

And that's when my senses came back to me. I flushed. It burned over my skin like a fever, and I reached up, pulling my towel around me tighter. I blinked, and I took a step back. He took another step toward me. Everything about his tense posture urged me to move away, but I couldn't. Dominic slid his hand to the small of my back, pressed his lips to my ear, and whispered, "He's testing you, Jade. Don't back down."

I jumped then. I hadn't even seen him approach us. I had heard him downstairs, and I knew he must have walked right by both Aidan and me. "You didn't tell me he was here," I hissed back. My heart was racing, and my knees still shaking.

"Well, I am," Aidan said, "and we need to have a chat." He shifted his hard gaze to Dominic and said, "You've got to stop helping her. She needs to win this one on her own."

"I don't think I want her to win," Dominic said, his voice full of defiance. His hand pressed a bit harder on the small of my back, and I slapped it away before he forced me to move closer to Aidan.

Aidan laughed, a shocked and strangled kind of sound. "Not your call, Dominic."

"What the hell are you two talking about?" I snapped, but they ignored me. I looked between the two of them. Aidan stood a bit straighter, and so did Dominic, rolling his shoulders back and puffing out his chest. Aidan's chocolaty eyes brightened, and a golden ring shimmered around the edges. He growled. Yes, growled. It was deep and low and rumbling, and it made me shiver again. The power behind that sound was intoxicating. Alluring. And something deep within me responded to it. I wanted it. I wanted that power more than I wanted to breathe.

The face-off didn't last long. Dominic slunk back a step and dropped his gaze, but the tension lingered. Silence fell over us, thick and awkward, and with every passing second, I became hotly aware that I was standing in the hallway wearing only a towel. Aidan was staring at me as if I were some hot fudge sundae that he really wanted to lick.

"Aidan, let my daughter get dressed," Dad hollered up the stairs, breaking the seriously uncomfortable tension.

Aidan smirked then and winked at me. "Sure thing, Jeff," he yelled back in a way that was far too friendly. He turned from me then and started down the stairs. Dominic followed him, his eyes on the ground and shoulders still hunched.

"Stop right there," I said. Aidan glanced over his shoulder and smirked. "How do you know my dad?"

He chuckled. "Again, I ask you, can I not know people just because I'm new?"

AIDAN

I think walking away from Jade was the single hardest thing I had ever done. I had expected her to be dressed, not almost naked. That little white towel had left little to the imagination, hanging just below her bottom, and cinched tightly over her chest. Each silky curve of her body begged me to get closer and see if her skin was as soft as it looked. All I could think about was seeing what was underneath that thin cloth. I had never wanted something so badly. Never.

And that scared the hell out of me.

Wanting wasn't in the cards for me. Not until she won. Not until she was mine. And my gut was telling me that once she knew the score, she'd happily step down. I had seen it in her eyes. The loathing. The hatred. I was certain that's what the look had been. The girl who had been haunting my every move had been unattainable before, and she had just moved even further out of my reach.

Dominic followed me down the stairs, not saying a word, and her father stood at the bottom, eyeing me suspiciously. I waited for the soft click of her door and looked the man straight in the eyes, and said, "We're not going to tell her. She won't stand a chance if she knows." And then I spun on Dominic. "If you go against me again, I will strip you of your title and kick you out of this pack. I'm not playing your games anymore."

Anger flared in his eyes for about half a second, but

it quickly vanished when he noticed I was serious. Clearly, playing nice hadn't worked yet, and I was done. Done with all of it. If this pack was going to continue to push me, I would push back. Especially now. With Jade's transformation, I couldn't risk her inner-wolf losing respect for me. I wouldn't risk it. If that happened, if I couldn't maintain a position as her equal, even as a hated equal, I'd risk losing the entire pack. And I wasn't ready to lose yet. Not when it meant another male would take her.

"I'm sorry," he whispered, dropping his eyes to the ground.

Jeff turned gray, all the blood rushing from his face, and he sucked in a loud gasping breath. "You can't keep this from her."

"She won't fight for me," I said calmly, even though saying it out loud sent rage coursing through me. "I'm pretty sure your daughter hates me, Jeff, and you know what will happen if she doesn't fight. It's not just my pack I'm worried about. Now that the news of a new alpha is out, your pack will be hovering, and she needs to be focused."

"Are you kidding me?" Erika's voice screeched through me, like rusty brakes on a car. "She'll fight for you. She wants you."

"What are you doing here?" I asked, well, okay, I demanded, and Erika flinched.

"Jade didn't show up at school," she said. Her voice was whiny, and she sounded as if she were going to cry. She lifted a stack of books and stepped closer to me as if she thought I hadn't noticed them. "I brought her homework."

I just stared at her and gritted my teeth. My own scent wafted around me — pungent and commanding. I pulled on my alpha wolf, pushing it forward, channeling it into my human form. The vibe was unmistakable. I might as well have ripped off my shirt, beat my chest, and yelled, '*I am alpha.*'

"Aidan, we get it," Dominic said with a slight tremor to his voice. "You're the alpha. Could you tone it down a little?"

I didn't have a chance to respond. "Erika?" Jade snapped. I swiveled and looked up the stairs, and for a second, I started to smile, but it died fast. Her scent was just as strong as mine was, and it came close to overpowering me. "Seriously, you have a lot of nerve," she spat. "Get the hell out of my house!"

"Um ... I'm just ... homework," she said, jutting a stack of books out. Her arms were shaking, the books sliding around in her hands. "Please don't hate me," she whispered. "I won't be a problem. I promise. Just ... I can't live with my alpha hating me. Don't make me go." She started inching toward the stairs, keeping her eyes averted from Jade, and it made my blood boil.

"Erika, she is *not* an alpha," I said more harshly than I had intended, but with Jade so close ... projecting so much authority, I just couldn't pull it back. "She's not even part of *my* pack."

Erika stopped at the base of the stairs but didn't turn back to me. She curled her shoulders over and dropped her head as if she hoped that I wouldn't notice her. "Jade and I have some business to deal with. She'll see you tomorrow," I said as gently as I could, which still turned out to be sharper than I wanted, and Erika shuddered, but she still didn't move. I turned to Dominic. "Take her home. Don't come back here tonight."

"No," Jade growled from deep within her belly. She fixed an icy stare on me and held it for a long minute. When I didn't flinch, she said, "We have no business. Erika, come up here. You can help me with my homework."

Erika started up the steps, and Jade smiled at her encouragingly before she glanced at her father. "Dad, if Mac comes home, send her up, okay?" And then she shifted her gaze to Dominic and said, "Oh and Dom, I'm starving." Her tone was sharp, commanding, and impossible. I loved it and loathed it. She smirked at me, clearly pleased with herself, and started to turn her back on me. She hadn't even made her first shift, and she was already falling into the ranks with ease as if she had been there all along.

Dominic's laugh pulled me out of my stupor. "Sure thing, boss," he said. "One Lucy's Griller coming up."

Everyone was moving, jumping at her orders. My whole body went rigid. "Stop!" I shouted. I couldn't make my muscles relax. My jaw flexed, and it took everything in me to just stand still. Dominic froze, and Erika blanched. "Get out."

"Aidan," Jeff said. His voice was calm, but I heard the warning in it, and he squeezed my shoulder with a firm, pinching grip.

I didn't let him finish. I didn't want to hear it. This wasn't going to help, I knew that, but I couldn't stop it. She was being impossible, even if she didn't know it. I turned to Jeff and looked him straight on. "I said get out."

CHAPTER 19

JADE

Okay, maybe I took it a bit too far. But in all fairness, Aidan was pissing me off. Who the hell did he think he was coming into my house and commanding my guests as if they were nothing more than slaves? It was wrong on so many levels. But what was worse was that something inside me growled when I caught his scent. It was intoxicating, and in seconds, my own scent ramped up and matched his. I didn't know what was happening to me, but I loved it almost as much as I loved the idea of being alone with him. It was all completely animal, and it excited and scared me all at once.

My dad gave him a crazy disappointed look but didn't argue. But then, of course, he wouldn't. He was the pack's number one fan. "Mom and I will be at Joe's tonight if you need us, pumpkin," he called, and then to my horror (and absolute pleasure), he left, pushing Erika and Dominic out the door.

"You need to leave," I said, but my voice betrayed me. It shook, and all of the command I had had just moments ago was gone.

"Has Dominic told you what to expect?" Aidan

asked, completely ignoring me. His tone was as sharp as his body language. Commanding and demanding answers. Every part of me screamed to give him anything and everything he wanted. I wished he hadn't ignored me. Really, I wished he would just go because all I could think about was jumping down the stairs and ripping off that shirt of his. I wanted to kiss every inch of his body, taste it, lick it, and oddly, I really wanted to rub against it. It was driving me crazy. He was driving me crazy. I had never wanted something so much before. It hurt in a wonderful kind of way.

"I already know," I said and let my eyes trail down his lean body again. "Grew up here, remember? I'll shift in three days unless my blood rejects it, and in that case, I'll die." His muscles looked deliciously strong, and as I descended the stairs, moving closer to him, I could feel the heat radiating from his sun-kissed skin.

"You won't die," he said. He started to smile. I saw a hint of it touching his full lips, but it vanished quickly. "I can already smell the wolf coming from your skin. You'll shift."

"Huh," I said. He was watching me closely as my foot fell on the last step. I wanted to run at him, but I fought against it. What had Dominic said? Don't back down? I tried to imitate Dominic, keeping my head high and shoulders back. I pictured his strut and his confidence, and I channeled it. Honed it in and projected it.

Aidan noticed. His face lost a little color, and he sucked in a loud breath. "I'm not going to tolerate you stepping over me. If you want to be part of my pack, you better learn your place."

"Who says I want to be part of your pack?" I purred. *Purred!* I almost laughed at myself. I really wasn't the purring type. Blunt and direct was more my style. But this guy ... I licked my lips. Completely involuntary, I swear, and my eyes raked over him again.

He arched a brow and smirked ... a little. "Your hatred towards me is a bit much, don't you think?"

Hatred? Clearly, he was misreading me. He squirmed a little, and his face went a bit whiter. And I grinned. I couldn't help it. I had never had a guy squirm from my stare before, and I had to admit, it was a bit exhilarating. "Actually, no, I don't," I said, playing along. "You lied to me."

He sighed, a frustrated kind of sound. "You never asked, Jade. You just assumed I was human. I never lied."

We were only a few feet apart now, just a couple more steps, and I'd be able to run my hand over his chest. I shrugged lazily and took another step. "Lying by omission. It's the same thing, genius."

He chuckled. The sound was like velvet. Soft and strong, and it made my knees go weak. He noticed that, too, and chuckled again. "I can't omit anything that I wasn't asked about."

I was about to tell him that he was an ass-hat. What a stupid cop-out. And by the look he was giving me, he knew exactly how stupid he sounded, but I didn't get a chance because Marcy came barging through the front door.

"Jade, I'm so sorry. Dom made me leave this morning." She slammed the door behind her, turned around, and ran smack into Aidan's chest. "Oh," she squealed, surprised. She took a step back, realized who it was, and then she gave him the dirtiest look I had ever seen. She put her hands on her hips and narrowed her eyes further. "What are you doing here?"

Aidan gave her a quick once over and said, not cruelly, but with a definitely uncaring tone, "Trying to decide if I want her in my pack or not."

Marcy gasped and hopped another step back. "You can't ban her."

He smiled and then laughed uneasily. "Yeah, I can. It's not an automatic entry. She wasn't recruited. She picked a fight and got bitten."

"I didn't pick a fight," I said, folding my arms over my chest. My bottom lip jutted out, and I hated myself for it. Really? Was I really going to pout about this? Technically, I had picked a fight. I could have walked away. But still, hearing him say it, seeing that look on his face, it was as if he thought I was nothing more than trouble.

"Aidan, dude, you're being a douche bag," Marcy blurted. Aidan's eyes flared, and her hands flew up in surrender. "Settle down, boy. I'm all about team werewolf, but she hasn't even shifted yet. Can't this, you know, wait? Maybe you could come back tomorrow or something?"

Aidan didn't even think about it before he shook his head and said, "Nope, someone's got to stay with her."

"I'm not going anywhere," Marcy said, standing a little straighter, and she fixed her glare back in place. She was aiming for fierce, I was sure of it, but right then, she looked more like a little kitten testing out her claws.

"I mean a pack member, Mac," he said with a groan. "Someone needs to monitor her just in case ..."

"You said ..." I started, but Aidan promptly cut me off.

"Things can always go wrong, Jade."

"Trevor," Marcy blurted. "Can he stay with us?"

Aidan gritted his teeth, and it almost looked as if he were trying to find a reason to say no, but after a moment of consideration, he fished his phone out of his pocket. He scrolled through his address book, tapped on the screen, and then brought the phone to his ear. "Trevor, come to Jade's. I need you to stay here with the girls." There was a long silence, and Aidan stiffened. One by one, deep lines began appearing on his forehead. "When?" he asked. Another pause. "How many?" He must not have liked the answer because a growl slipped out, and he turned his back on us. "Just get here," he snapped, and then he shoved his phone back into his pocket.

"What's wrong?" I asked, although my voice didn't sound like I cared even to my own ears. His back was stiff, the muscles under his skin coiled and bulged, and the urge to touch him again was unbearable. I took a step, moving toward him, and he spun around.

Aidan's eyes were golden. Not a speck of the delicious brown left. Strands of coarse hair littered his cheeks, and his skin looked as if it were crawling. Seeing him on the verge of shifting awoke something in me. Something ... deliriously physical. My muscles began to ache in an amazing kind of way, and prickles ran over my skin. It was as if my body wanted to shift with him. Anything to be closer to him.

"Jade, you will not let anyone other than Trevor and Marcy through those doors. Am I clear?" His voice was a deep growl, and his eyes held me with such intensity that I couldn't move.

"Crystal," I whispered.

I couldn't say how long we stood there watching each other. It could have been seconds, minutes, or hours, but it didn't matter. Right then, I could have stayed there forever, lost in his shimmering eyes.

"Trevor's here," he grumbled, shattering the perfect moment into millions of sharp-edged shards.

There was a loud bang on the door, and Aidan turned away from me, grabbed the handle, and pulled it open.

Trevor looked ... rattled, and there was a jagged rip across the front of his blue sweater. There was also a gash along his right cheekbone that looked like it was starting to heal. It was still bright pink, and there was dried, crusty blood along the edges.

"What happened?" Marcy shrieked and rushed over to him. She started fussing over his sweater and his cheek, making a bunch of anxious gasping sounds.

Trevor grabbed her hands, holding her still, and exchanged a long look with Aidan that I couldn't even begin to understand. And then Aidan glanced at me and said, "By the way. You'll need to learn how to control that."

"Control what?" I asked and hated the pout I heard in my voice. He stepped out the door, keeping his back to me, and I hated that, too. He was leaving, which was a good thing, maybe, kind of. Well, it should have been, but darn it, I didn't want him to go.

He glanced over his shoulder and winked. "Your lust. Your scent is screaming sex." And then he walked out the door, shutting it quickly behind him.

CHAPTER 20

AIDAN

It was easier leaving than I had thought it would be. My inner-wolf wanted Jade so badly that it took everything in me not to shift. With Jade's enthralling scent and Trevor's news, I really hadn't thought I would have been able to walk out that door and leave her alone, but I did it. As soon as I shut the door behind me, I let out a pent-up breath that I hadn't even realized I'd been holding, and I dug my phone out of my pocket. I fired off a text to Dominic telling him to meet me at my motel room and bring Jeff. I had some questions for both of them, and it was time that they started talking.

I got into my car, started it up, and pulled out of the driveway before I could change my mind. She was handling it all better than I had expected. She didn't need me. And knowing that she didn't need me made it so much harder to deal with. I wanted her to need me.

But what I really needed was a shower. Preferably a cold one.

Jade's scent had held a distinctly alpha quality to it, and she was responding to me exactly how I had hoped she would. I was an unclaimed alpha, and her inner-wolf had picked up on it immediately, even if she didn't know that it had happened. Female wolves' hormones tended to go a touch haywire when there was an unclaimed alpha nearby, and since she had liked me beforehand, well, it was all a little more ... intense.

Thankfully, when I arrived back at the motel, the parking lot was empty. I darted into my room, and knowing I probably only had a few minutes before Dominic would get there, I stripped off my clothes and jumped into the shower, turning the taps as cold as I could stand.

The shower helped ... a little. I had just turned off the ice water when I heard a thudding knock at my door. I got dressed in a rush and yanked the door open, and just as I did, Jeff's fist slammed into my jaw.

I stumbled back a step, and a sharp pain shot through my face. What was it about the Shaws that made them want to hit me? Yesterday, Jade. Today, her father.

Dominic was on him in a flash, grabbing his arms and holding them behind his back. Jeff didn't struggle. He stood just outside my door, glaring at me.

"Okay, yeah, I probably deserved that," I said, rubbing my aching jaw. The skin was already hot under my hand. "But I warn you, Jeff, don't do it again. I'm not Ray, and I will not humor you." I turned from them, padded over to the lone desk chair in my room, and took a seat before I said, "Let him go, Dom."

"Yeah, you did deserve it," Jeff said, shaking his hand out. "Don't you ever try to kick me out of my own house again."

Dominic slid by Jeff and sat on the desk beside me. He wouldn't look at me, but I wasn't really surprised about that. I was surprised that he was taking his place beside me. I really hadn't expected it. After ripping him away from Jade and threatening to boot him out of the pack, I had figured he would have stayed clear of me, at least for a while.

Jeff looked stunned, too. His jaw dropped slightly, and his eyes widened. Clearly, Dominic had said something to him when they had left. Jeff looked as if he were about to say something, but he held it back. After a second, he crossed the room, letting the door slam behind him, and he took a seat on the edge of the bed.

"Where's Jade?" Dominic asked. He tried to sound casual, but it was a useless effort. His voice was like gravel, and his scent was a mix of hot fury and concern, and it held a tangy edge of jealousy.

"At home," I said with a chuckle, as the dirty look she gave me flashed across my mind. "She kind of kicked me out. But I have some good news. She doesn't entirely hate me, although I think she wishes she did."

"I never thought she did," Dominic said through clenched teeth. "You sparked her interest the first second she laid eyes on you."

"How could you leave her alone?" Jeff asked. His complexion paled quickly, and it looked as if it were a struggle for him not to jump up and run out the door. "What if one of them attacks before she's ready? What if ..."

I raised my hand, and he sucked in a breath, holding in whatever he was about to say. "She's not alone. Mac and Trevor are there. And she did beat Erika as a human. I'm sure the other three won't be a problem for her."

Dominic shifted on the desk and finally looked at me. "What if she rejects the change?" He held my eyes, and I saw his fear. It was shining through his mask, although by his tense posture, I was pretty sure he was trying to hide it.

"She won't," I said, keeping my tone light. "Actually, I wouldn't be surprised if she has her first shift today. She smells more wolf than human."

"Aidan, please let me go stay with her," Dominic said. He reached out, placing a hand on my shoulder. "She hates Trevor, and she needs someone to help her through this."

I shrugged his hand off and stretched my legs out in front of me, crossing them at the ankles. "Bad news, too, though," I said, ignoring his plea. "It's time for you to come clean. Because honestly, if I catch another whiff of jealousy on you, I'll rip you apart." I said it all with a smile, but there was no mistaking how serious I was.

Jeff sat still. So still, in fact, that I was pretty sure he was even holding his breath. His hands were clasped in his lap, and his graying hair looked like it could use a good brushing. When I had first seen him, he was kind of intimidating, big, and burly. The father of the girl I liked. Right now, he looked small and scared. It was ... weird and a little perfect. All I had needed was to show my authority, and I could make this man tremble before me.

Dominic sighed and hopped off the desk. He padded over to the big window and pulled open the curtain, letting the sunshine glitter through the glass. He was nervous. I could smell it, and his heartbeat picked up, thrumming a little quicker against his ribs.

"There's nothing to come clean about," he said and glanced around the room. He snagged the garbage can and made his way back over to the desk, picking up the scattered protein bar wrappers and empty coffee cups.

I watched him pick up all the garbage and then begin to straighten the textbooks on the coffee table. The tension was growing; his nerves were making his hands tremble slightly. "I know something's up with you two, Dom, and I want to know what it is."

He turned to me and gave me a blank look. "Shouldn't we be dealing with your exposure? The pack needs to prepare. If we aren't ready, she's the easiest target."

"She's not an easy target," I said, not backing down. "She doesn't even need to move to pin someone in place. I know you felt it. You jumped pretty quickly when she said she was hungry."

I let my scent roll off me, filling the room, and folded my arms over my chest. He was giving me an insolent look, one that clearly told me that he did not, and would not, agree with me, and I was done putting up with it. I hadn't wanted to use my alpha scent like this. I hadn't wanted to turn into my father, but I couldn't fight him and deal with everything else.

Dominic held my stare for a moment before his body visibly started to shake. He laughed a strangled sound and put his hands up, backing up a step. "I swear nothing is going on between us," he said with a desperate note in his voice. "We grew up together. We were best friends. She kissed me once. I told her I was gay. Without the whole sex issue between us, we got closer. I got bit. I ditched her. She hated the pack and me for it. That's it."

I felt the change in my eyes, the soft sting as they began to glow, and he shuddered back another step. "If that were all true, you wouldn't be so jealous," I said, watching him drop to his knees before me.

Guilt washed over me hard and fast. Dominic's face twisted with agony, and a quick flash of how this felt slammed into me. I remembered the pain burning over my skin when my father had let his alpha wolf out. I remembered the scent clawing through my body, making my inner-wolf convulse. I remembered the power behind it, and that memory was what made me pull it back.

Dominic gasped in a breath. "I love her like a sister," he said, panting and crumbling to the floor as I pulled back the last of the invasive scent. He took a few breaths and pulled himself up, propping his back against the wall. "I don't want her hurt. She hates hard, she loves even harder, and if she doesn't win, she'll be crushed when she realizes that means she won't get you." He laughed, but there was no humor in the sound. He gave me a look, and if I didn't know better, I would have thought he actually cared about me. "And you'll have to walk away from her. How many times do I have to tell you I'm looking out for you! Not her. If she lost right now, could you walk away? I'm not blind, Aidan. You're attracted to her, and that's dangerous. If you help her, give her any kind of advantage, she'll be killed, and you won't be able to stop it. The pack won't stand for it, the enforcers will step in, and I don't trust you enough not to help her. You've already interfered with her once."

The cocky strength was back in his voice, and the color was quickly returning to his cheeks. As I listened to him, I felt as if he had swung a baseball bat into my gut. "That's different," I scoffed, but I knew it wasn't. "You were dragging her to a car."

Dominic got to his feet, still a little shaky, and paced toward me. "Yeah, I was. But if she had have been my mate, she'd have been put on trial for crossing me. And you would have had to hand down the sentence."

I scrubbed at my face. "You're going to tell her, aren't you?"

"Nope. You were right. She won't fight for you. Not because she doesn't want you but because she's stubborn. She's pissed at you, and with Jade, that can last a while." He sighed long and loud and ran his hands roughly through his hair. "She'll lose everything while she chews on her hatred."

I didn't say anything because I was pretty sure he was right. Sooner or later, Jade would gain control of her inner wolf, and when she did, I was pretty sure she'd turn her back on me. Dominic let out a gusty huff and took his place beside me, sitting on the desk.

"I want to be free to help her with the change," he said with determination. "I want to be able to help her win, and I can't do that without your consent. Before you shoot me down, just think for a second about how close you are to having two packs in this town. Erika will follow her anywhere, and I'm sure others will, too."

"Dominic, she needs to know what's happening," Jeff pleaded. It was the first time he'd spoken in a while, and honestly, I had kind of forgotten he was even there.

"Shut up, Jeff," Dominic snapped. "This has nothing to do with you. She's our problem now, and if you still want us to protect your wife, you'll stay the hell out of our way."

Where the hell did that come from? Dominic could be cold. I knew that. I'd seen it, but this ... this was more than a little cold. Jeff inched back a little before he could catch himself. Just hours ago, I would have sworn they were close. Really close. They were so much alike, the way they spoke, the way they held themselves. It was as if they were related. But just like everything else that confused the hell out of me, it pointed back to Jade. *Jade.* That girl was going to be the death of me. I was sure of it.

I glanced over to Dominic and said, "I'll think about it. That's all I can give you right now. But I promise I'll consider your request." He offered a small smile, and then I shifted my gaze to Jeff. "You know, I've been thinking," I said. "You're the only person in this town that would have the ability to leak the information of a new alpha. Even with my slip up yesterday. You're the only one that could have gotten it to them."

Jeff sat up a bit taller and glared fiercely at me. "My alliance has always been with this pack."

I narrowed my eyes. "Three of the cougars attacked one of my wolves on the outside of town today."

"Shit. Who?" Dominic asked.

"Trevor. He's fine. The cougars aren't, though." I hunched over in my chair, leaning my elbows on my knees and leveling my glare on Jeff. "There's something that just doesn't add up here. Why didn't you change your daughter, and why are you so intent on her being part of my pack?"

For a moment, I didn't think Jeff was going to answer me, and white-hot rage simmered in my veins. He must have noticed the change in me because, in one breath, he blurted, "Our pack would have used her. She's young. They don't take mates the way you guys do. Women are a community possession. I couldn't let that happen to my baby. As far as they know, Jade and my wife died three years ago when their bodies rejected the change. Dominic, please talk some sense into him. Jade needs to know what she's gotten herself into." A small tear snaked down his cheek and dripped off his chin, soaking into his sweater.

"Nothing has changed," Dominic said icily. "We aren't friends. I have always tolerated you for Jade's sake only. I can see through you, Jeff. You only want her to know because you want her to hate Aidan more than she is going to hate you when she finds out what you are and what you've done."

Jeff bolted up from the bed. Red rushed to his

cheeks, and he balled his fists. "I haven't done anything!"

Dominic slid off the desk and stretched lazily before closing the distance between them. "I watched you do it," he snarled and then hauled off and punched Jeff. Jeff grunted, and he dropped back onto the bed, out cold.

CHAPTER 21

JADE

I'm a werewolf.

I laughed. I'd been laughing since I heard Aidan drive away. Marcy was sitting on the couch looking at me as if I were a nut case, and well, I probably was. This wasn't really something to laugh about, but the irony of me becoming a werewolf, well, it was just funny in a sick kind of way.

Once Aidan left, Marcy had promptly showed Trevor to the bathroom so he could get cleaned up, and then she had made her way back to me. The cut was supposedly from screwing around with some of the guys, but I wasn't sure if I believed him. When he'd said it, his heart rate had picked up, and the scent that pulsed from him smelled like a lie. It was tangy and salty, and it just didn't feel ... true. But whether he was lying or not didn't really matter.

I sat in Dad's recliner, feet up, arms sprawled over the armrests, staring at a lot of nothing. My stomach was starting to ache, but the laughter just kept coming. I figured it was a form of shock, although it really didn't feel anything like shock.

"Jade, what the hell did he mean about you smelling

like sex?" Marcy blurted out. She was clasping and unclasping her hands nervously as she watched me.

My laughter died fast, and my cheeks burned. "Um ... well ... dammit, Mac, if you hadn't shown up ..." I let my words fall short, and heat flushed over my skin. I didn't want to admit what he'd done to me, just by being in the room, or how much I wanted to run after him right then.

"You want him?" she asked, and her eyebrows shot up. "After the coffee shop, you still want him?"

I sighed and something pressed against my stomach as if it was trying to chew its way out. "More than ever, and I hate it. He makes my body burn and tingle."

"Maybe it's part of the change," she offered. I thought she was trying to be helpful, but she wasn't. There was so much disgust in her voice that I felt sick for even considering him.

"It's not part of the change, but it is normal," Trevor said, walking into the living room. He glanced at me, just a quick look before he dropped his gaze to the ground and made his way over to sit with Marcy. He had scrubbed the dried blood off his face and had replaced his torn sweater with one of my dad's zip-up hoodies.

"What the hell is that supposed to mean?" Marcy shouted.

"Mac, I've had a bad day," Trevor snapped. "Don't push me." He went to put his arm around her, and she smacked it away.

"You've had a bad day?" she said, jumping up from the couch and glaring down at him. "My best friend is turning into a werewolf. She's lusting after some jackass alpha. My boyfriend thinks he has a right to treat me like dirt. You think you had a bad day? Stop being so goddamn selfish, Trevor, and answer my damn question."

I bit back another laugh. I wanted to jump up and clap. It wasn't often that Marcy got mad, but it was an awesome sight when she did. And for her to finally tell off Trevor, well, I had never thought it would happen. Her petite frame was all puffed out, and she balled her fists. She looked as if she was ready to haul off and punch him.

"When there is an unclaimed male alpha, female wolves get a bit crazy," Trevor said, looking up at her with barely concealed rage. He held her stare for a moment before he shifted it to me. "Jade, your inner-wolf is reacting to him. It's natural."

"Clearly, I'm missing something," Marcy said with a noisy huff. She dropped down beside Trevor again, and this time when he tried to pull her into his arms, she let him, but then that was Marcy. She didn't know how to stay mad, and Trevor knew it. I was a bit disappointed.

"Why did Erika come after me, and why did she call me her alpha?" I asked once they were settled. Marcy cuddled into his side and rested her cheek on his chest as if she hadn't just blown up at him.

"She did?" Trevor asked as if his brain couldn't understand what I was saying.

"Yeah, and Aidan kind of freaked out about it. He said I wasn't an alpha, and I needed to learn my place."

Trevor chuckled. "He's threatened."

"You've got to be kidding me," I said with a groan. Aidan, threatened? I didn't believe it. Not for a second.

Trevor shook his head and chuckled again. "You don't get it. You make him nervous. You make all of us nervous. Even before you were bitten, you've always projected power. You've always been dominant. It's why you've never been recruited. Ray didn't want someone who would stand up to him. And everyone knew if you were changed, you'd make your way into the alpha pair."

"The alpha pair?" Marcy questioned before I could and shifted her head to look up at him.

"Packs have alpha pairs, or they're supposed to," Trevor said as he brushed some hair out of her eyes. "Two alphas. One male and one female. We've never really had that." He shrugged a little as he looked back at me. "There's always been an alpha pair, but the females have constantly cowered behind the males."

"Hold up," Marcy said and sat up a little. "Are you trying to say that Jade's the alpha?"

"Not yet, but I think she could be."

Marcy looked at me with wide eyes, and she made a gurgling sound from the back of her throat as she choked on whatever she was about to say. She started to cough, a wet and painful sound and Trevor rubbed circles into her back.

I sat up slowly, pushing on the footrest of the recliner until it clicked, locking into place. I was pretty sure that this was where I was supposed to crack. I sure felt like I was going to crack. *Me ... an alpha.* The idea was almost laughable ... almost, and if it weren't for the rush of energy that shot through me at the thought, I probably would have actually laughed. And what the hell was an alpha pair? I had an idea of what that might entail, and I was suddenly a bit ashamed, enough that my skin began to tingle at the thought of being paired with Aidan.

I stood up abruptly. I needed air. It was too hot. I was starting to sweat. It beaded up on my forehead and ran down my back. I spun on my heels without a word and darted for the door.

Trevor got there before I did. "Where are you going?" he asked. He folded his arms over his chest and leaned against the door.

"Out," I snapped and tried to shove him out of the way. It was like trying to move a thousand-pound boulder; he didn't move an inch.

"I can't let you do that, Jade," he said with more than a little caution. He eyed me hesitantly.

"You're going to stop me?" I growled, and I was stunned at the viciousness that coated my voice.

Trevor unfolded his arms and grabbed my shoulders firmly, pushing me back a step. "Jade, don't make me call Aidan back here. He has more important things to deal with than your change."

That hurt. Really hurt. Even if I didn't want to admit it, part of me wanted to be the most important thing on Aidan's mind. I deflated like a popped balloon.

♥

I didn't go out. Not because I thought Trevor would actually stop me if I pushed the issue (or at least that's what I had been telling myself) but because I knew if I had left the house, I would have run to *him*, and I really didn't want to do that. I sent Dominic a slew of text messages, begging him to come over, but he still hadn't replied.

Marcy had given up trying to talk to me hours ago. She was curled up on my bed, snoring softly, and Trevor lay beside her. He pretended to sleep, but I knew he wasn't. I could feel him watching me through slitted eyelids.

I sat on the window seat in my room, watching the stars slowly fade into the gray-blue sky of predawn. My bones ached but in a good way. I could feel the change coming, and it scared me. It had only been about forty hours since I had been bitten. The change shouldn't have been happening this quickly. But it was.

I had expected it all to be unbearably painful. It had always sounded painful. Bones snapping and reshaping. But each time a bone began to crack, a rush of steamy adrenaline pumped through me. It was like a high, and I was actually starting to crave it. So far, only a few bones here and there had tried to reshape, but as soon as they snapped, they quickly mended back in place.

My stomach was a tender ball of knots, and every few minutes, a burst of heat rushed over my skin as coarse hair sprung out and receded again. My nails were the only thing that stayed constant. They had morphed into claws about an hour ago and had yet to change back.

"We should go outside," Trevor whispered, sitting up and sliding off the bed, careful not to wake Marcy. "I've been timing it. It's only about seventy seconds between each break now."

"I'm not ready," I said, looking back out the window. During the last twenty minutes, an increasing number of wolves had been gathering along the edge of the woods in my backyard. At first, it was just one, a rusty brown one that sat at the edge of the tree line watching my window. But as the minutes ticked by, more gathered.

"You are ready, Jade," he said, although I didn't believe him. I rolled my eyes dramatically, and he laughed a little awkwardly. I knew Trevor didn't like me, and I couldn't stand him most of the time, but it was kind of *nice* having him here. He shuffled in place for a second and then grinned at me. "You're going to make an awesome werewolf. You just need to let it out," he said as he fished his cell phone out of his pocket.

"What are you doing?" I jumped up from the ledge

and rushed over to him as he tapped the screen. Panic gripped my throat, and my heart jumped in my chest.

"Calling Aidan. He ..."

"No, please don't call him," I said, a little desperately, cutting him off. "Trevor, please."

He cut me an apologetic look and raised his hands helplessly. "He told me to call him when you started to shift, Jade. I don't have a choice. I can't ignore a direct order from him. He'll throw me out of the pack."

Right then, I caught a scent. It was a scent that I knew, one that I would have recognized anywhere, and one that made sparks race over my skin and birds take flight in my stomach. I looked back out the window, and my breath caught in my throat. "He's already here," I whispered, locking eyes with the black wolf.

CHAPTER 22

JADE

He howled to me. The sound wrapped around me, and warmth pooled in my stomach. My heart fluttered for a second and then drummed fast in my chest. I was transfixed, unable to look away from his midnight black coat. Behind him stood at least fifteen other wolves, all a mix of browns, grays, and whites, and they joined in his song.

The black wolf looked up through my window. His golden eyes searched my face, and then he tilted his head back and let out another skin-tingling howl.

"It's time, Jade," Dominic said, and he placed a hand on my shoulder. I jumped. I hadn't heard him come in, but darn it, I was glad he was here. "You need to pick."

"Pick what?" I asked, and my voice shook. I looked up at him, and my eyes burned with the threat of impending tears. Everything was falling into place and falling apart at the same time. I was becoming what I hated most, but by becoming that, I was also getting back what I wanted most: Dominic.

He smiled a crooked smile and took my hand, pulling me up from my seat. "He's giving you a choice to pick the pack. Aidan brought them for you."

"I ... I don't understand," I stammered and snuck another quick look at the black wolf.

Dominic reached out and tucked some loose hair behind my ears. "Every wolf has a choice. Pack or solo. It's simple. You can walk away from us, or you can join us."

I glanced back out the window. My skin was crawling, and my face was starting to feel ... wrong. Different. I could feel the coarse hair poking out along my arms and the pressure on my bones. The wolves continued to sing below me, and the sound of them called to me. It was as if they were calling to me and only me. Asking me to join them. Waiting for me to sing with them. And every fiber in my body wanted exactly that. To be a part of them. I wanted to throw up and laugh, scream, and cry.

"Um, Jade ..." Marcy's voice was shrill, and as I looked over at her, she scurried back on the bed. "You have a muzzle."

AIDAN

Maybe I was wrong about Jade. Maybe she wasn't ready. But the truth was, whether she was ready or not, I couldn't wait any longer. She was vulnerable until she shifted, and I couldn't worry about her not being able to defend herself.

I had rounded up as many pack members as I could, hoping that with this many wolves present, her inner-wolf would respond to them. But having them here meant leaving very few watching the perimeter of Dog Mountain.

I tilted my head back and let another long howl out. I waited, listening to my pack calling her for what felt like forever. I was about ready to give up, but then I heard it. The click of a door. The soft drop of clothes onto the ground. A gasp. A moan. A grunt. The pat of paws on cement.

And then I was flying through the air and crashing onto the ground.

She stood over me. Her fur was black as pitch, and her eyes, a brilliant gold. She grinned, a toothy grin, and hopped a little, ready to play.

The pack was silent, and the tension was thick. Her scent was powerful, sharp. I rolled back up to my paws and shook the grass from my coat. My scent ramped up a notch, and a chorus of whimpers filled the air. But Jade ... she didn't back down. I straightened, and I let a warning growl rumble from my chest. My lips curled up, and my eyes widened.

She cocked her head to the side as if she didn't understand, and I growled again. I needed her to fall in line. She had to choose to follow me. She had to choose the pack. I wished I could speak to her. I wished she would grasp it. But she nudged me again, nipping playfully at my side.

JADE

I thought Aidan was trying to tell me something, but I couldn't focus on it. His scent was wonderful. Powerful. Perfect. And all I wanted to do was run and play and rub against him. I had so much energy. Too much energy. It was soaring through me, and I couldn't stand still.

He seemed ... annoyed, and I wished he would stop growling at me. The tension that rolled off the other wolves was suffocating, and he was only making it worse. Each time he growled, they would whimper and shrink further away from us.

And I didn't want them to go.

I nosed his side, and he snapped at me. He growled again, louder, longer, and my insides shivered at the sound.

I stood a bit straighter and pushed my ears forward. I growled and snapped back at him. *I want to play.* Why wasn't he getting it? It was so frustrating.

Aidan shivered. I could see it move along his fur. It was amazing. Tantalizing heat surged through me. He growled again, and I growled back.

Aidan took a step closer to me, his canines bared, and he snarled. His scent changed then. It became stronger, and something in me trembled. He barked and followed it with another growl that made my knees shake. A voice in my head screamed at me to stay standing, but my knees started to buckle, and with each second, it was harder to hold his stare. I felt my head dropping inch by slow inch.

Something tore into my skin. I yelped and tried to jump away. My flesh ripped. It felt as if a bunch of little and very sharp knives was stabbing into my hip over and over. The silence was painfully loud. All the growling and howling stopped. The knives bit into my flesh again, and a snarl exploded from me.

The copper scent of blood drifted up to my snout. I pivoted on my hind legs, my right side burned, and I came face to face with a dirty-gray wolf. Her lips were curled back, and blood — my blood — covered her teeth and dripped from her muzzle.

Sounds of a scuffle rang out from behind me, but I didn't take my eyes off the wolf in front of me. She crouched down, snarling and snapping at me. I tried to mimic her movements, but my back end hurt so badly. I could feel the warm trickle of blood running down my leg and matting my fur.

She lunged at me, tackling me to the ground. I

landed on my back with a breathtaking thud, and her teeth came at me, aiming for my neck. I kicked out, my back paws planted in her stomach, and I kicked her off me before her teeth could sink into my neck, and I pushed back up on all fours.

I could barely put weight on my injured leg. I didn't understand what was happening. Dominic had said they had come to welcome me. Why wasn't he helping me? And where was Aidan? The gray wolf was circling around me, and she looked as if she was ready to jump on me again.

What's happening? a voice in my head shrieked. *Why were they letting her do this to me?*

I snarled at her, and for a split second, she froze, and her eyes widened. But then she growled and came at me again.

I stood my ground for two reasons. One: Dominic told me not to back down from them. And two: I couldn't run even if I wanted to. I stretched my body, standing as straight and as firmly on the ground as I could, preparing for the impact. I growled a menacing and slightly freaked-out sound.

The gray wolf was barreling toward me with her canines exposed, and my heart was jumping around like a rabbit in my chest. Her teeth sank into my right shoulder, and she wrestled me to the ground.

Dirt and grass burned against my side as we slid and rolled over each other. I bit out blindly, desperately, and I instantly tasted the salty sweat in her fur and the iron taste of her blood. The blood seeped into my mouth, and I latched on tighter. I growled and yanked and flung her onto her back.

She made a whimpering sound, and I sprung up and towered over her. Rage and fear and something that I really didn't want to understand fed through my veins. I felt my lips curl, the cool air brushed against my gums, and the world seemed to stand still, vanishing away and leaving only the gray wolf cowering at my feet.

It scared the hell out of me, but at that moment, I wanted to kill her. I wanted to rip her apart and roll in her blood. It was as if the animal that I had turned into was taking over, and all I could think about was the taste of her blood. I felt a growl rumble around me. Her shoulder was gushing blood, a large chunk of skin was gone from where I had bitten her, and her meaty muscles were exposed. It would have been so easy to kill her. I could see it all. My teeth in her neck, tearing out her throat. The taste of her blood. The rush of victory.

The growl came again, followed by a soft whimper, and then a cold nose pressed against me. I swiveled, baring my teeth and snapping out. A rusty brown wolf dropped to its belly and then rolled onto its back and licked my chin. Standing right behind that wolf was the midnight black alpha.

I snarled at him furiously, and he snarled back. For half a second, I thought about lunging at him. I was so mad, so hurt ... but instead, I shook off the thought, turned, and limped away from him and the pack.

CHAPTER 23

AIDAN

"What the hell did you do to her?" Marcy screamed. She ran at me, her fist balled, and she punched me over and over in the chest. And I let her. She was crying. Her shoulders convulsed as gasping sobs fell from her, and she continued to punch me.

Trevor rushed over, ready to pull her off, but I shook my head. I hardly felt her weak hits, and I figured she probably had a right to be mad. So I just stood there until she was done. Playing the tough alpha seriously wasn't easy. It's not as if Marcy knew I had no choice but to let Jade fight it out. I hadn't expected the attack to happen, not on her first shift, but the females had a right to fight her, and I couldn't do much to stop it.

It took a full sixty-four seconds for her tears to win out, and Marcy crumpled against my chest, crying uncontrollably. "Mac, I didn't do anything to her," I said softly.

"You should have stopped the wolf!" she shrieked and pulled away, glaring up at me. "I told Jade you were cold. I told her to stay away from you. I was right. You're just like all the alphas before you." She pulled her arm back and swung at me, open-handed. I caught her wrist tightly in my grip.

"Marcy," I snapped, my patience wearing thin. "Don't think you can talk to me like this just because you are dating a member of my pack." She struggled, trying to jerk her hand away, but I held onto her wrist firmly and looked at Trevor. "Take her. I don't want to see her again."

"Aidan, Jade wants her here," Trevor said, refusing to look at me. He stepped up to us and wrapped his arm around Marcy's stomach, pulling her away.

Fury spiked through me, and I hated it. I hated giving orders and using my alpha status to get what I wanted. I loathed demanding things from the pack and forcing them to submit. I hated my father for doing it, and I hated myself just as much. But this pack was just too screwed up. They didn't listen when I asked nicely. And now Jade, the wolf I intended to make sure won the challenges and became my mate, aided their disobedience. *That damn girl is going to be the death of me.*

"I don't really care what Jade wants," I said, seething. I let my scent roll off me, and Trevor started to tremble under the weight of it.

"I'll take her to her room," he said with a desperate note in his voice. "You won't even know she's here." He still wouldn't look at me as he started to drag Marcy away and up the stairs. She shouted at me through a garbled mess of tears that I couldn't even begin to decipher.

When he reached the top, he looked back in my direction, his eyes fixed on the floor at my feet. "Aidan, please stop." His voice was like gravel grating under tires. "She's just as much my alpha as you are. Don't make me pick one of you." He turned on shaky legs, with Marcy still crying in his arms, and disappeared down the hallway.

I gritted my teeth for a long moment. I'd never seen anything like this. Never. How in the hell was Jade able to dig into Trevor so quickly? She wasn't branded. She didn't have the extra power that came with the alpha's imprint. Her scent was strong, but without accepting the position, it was still bearable. I cursed myself for letting Trevor stay with her, waiting for her to shift. His loyalty was shifting, just as Erika's had, and I didn't have a clue what to do about it.

I stood at the bottom of the stairs, counting them, up and down, attempting to relax my nerves. It wasn't working. My fists clenched and unclenched, seemingly on their own, and each second that passed, my skin grew hotter, and my blood boiled further. "Dominic!" I shouted.

Dominic was out of Jade's bedroom and standing in front of me in a flash. Surprising relief washed over me at his quick response; at least it did until he said, "Just go, Aidan."

I laughed. It sounded cruel even to my own ears. "I'm going to see her, Dom." I took the first step, and he grabbed my bicep, yanking me back from the stairs and pulling me into the kitchen. He stopped in front of the stove and turned on the fan before glancing at me. When he did, I figured I looked just as pissed off as I felt because he skittered back a few steps.

"She doesn't understand what's happening," he whispered. "She thinks we allowed the attack."

I shot him a cold glare and, through gritted teeth, said, "You should have told her to submit once she walked out of the house. You were supposed to guide her. You're the one who asked to help her." I was already regretting letting him. I thought he got it. I thought he'd tell her what to do; clearly, I was wrong.

"I did tell her. Dammit, Aidan! You're such a jackass! You can smell it. She's an alpha. It's in her scent. Her inner-wolf will only submit to you if yours submits to her." Dominic's voice rose with each word until he was flat out yelling in my face.

I wanted to punch him. Just haul off and punch him. Somehow, I really don't know how I held the urge back. "She has to prove herself for that, and so far, she hasn't."

"She took down another challenger," Dominic said as if that was proof enough.

I shrugged. "There's still two more."

He looked at me then, as if I was an idiot and an even bigger fool, and said a little helplessly, "She just wanted to play."

JADE

I could hear him. Aidan was whispering. I couldn't make out the conversation, but the sound of his deep voice made me shiver. I shouldn't have been able to hear the notes of his voice. He was downstairs, and my bedroom door was sealed tightly. But his voice wasn't the only thing that found me. His scent, musky and powerful, wrapped around me.

I sat on my bed, watching the last of the scars on my hip fade away to nothing. By the time I finished showering and scrubbing my body clean of blood, my wounds had closed. It had only been thirty minutes. Thirty freakin' minutes since that wolf attacked me, and the marks were already gone. I didn't know whether I wanted to pass out, hyperventilate, or jump around. My senses were hyperaware of everything around me, and it was terrifying and exciting and a little sickening. I had never had so much energy before, and I didn't know what to do with it all.

Aidan's voice rose and fell as he argued with Dominic. He was beyond mad. I could hear it in his growled murmurs and smell its heat in the air. It was almost like the scent of hot pavement as the first drops of rain fell, except stronger. Each time it got louder, my body shuddered with a mix of pleasure and spine-tingling fear. My inner-wolf was doing backflips in my stomach. One second my skin was burning with desire for him, and the next, my inner-wolf was cringing and begging me to lie down at his feet.

I wanted my dad. I wanted to talk to him. I needed to hear the reassurance in his voice. He always knew the right thing to say, and since Dominic wasn't explaining anything that made sense, I thought maybe, just maybe, Dad would know what was happening to me. He'd been involved with the pack for as long as I could remember and knew a lot about how they worked. I dialed his number for the last five minutes, and each time I called, it went straight to voicemail.

The front door slammed, and footsteps pounded up the stairs. I pulled my blankets up around me, listening to the scuffling as Aidan and his amazing scent made his way down the hallway. It was weird knowing instinctively who was walking on the other side of the walls, but I did. I could feel his presence in my bones. With each step closer to my room, my heartbeat quickened. My bedroom door squeaked open, and he stepped into my room, closing it behind him.

He was wearing black jeans that sat low on his hips and a snug black T-shirt that showed off the ripples of his abs. He had toned up since I first met him; his muscles were more defined, not as soft-looking. He leaned against the bedroom door and folded his arms over his chest, flexing his biceps as he did. His eyes were yellow as they looked me over, and my breath caught in my throat. The man was perfect and completely flawed, and I loved it all. I wasn't sure if that made me stupid or crazy, but either way, right then, I knew I needed serious help. *Was this how all werewolves felt when they were in the presence of an alpha?* I wondered as my eyes drifted over him. I tried reminding myself that he had let this happen to me, but it was useless. Each time the thought passed through my mind, my inner-wolf growled as if it were trying to banish it.

"Jade, let's go." His voice was sharp, and I jumped to my feet without an ounce of hesitation, my tangled mess of blankets falling to the floor.

I couldn't pull my eyes away from him, and right then, I was glad for it. I watched as he took a step toward me. His eyes traveled down my neck, along the strap of my tank top, and then they paused on my cleavage for far too long before he glanced down at my skimpy pajama bottoms and took in my bare legs. If I hadn't been watching him so closely, I probably wouldn't have even noticed it. His nearness, his scent, it all screamed power and authority, and it was fogging my brain.

I snapped out of it in a rush, grabbed a pillow, and whipped it at him. "Get out!" I shouted as he batted the pillow away, and it dropped to the floor.

He frowned. "I'm not asking, Jade."

"I don't give a shit," I snapped. I grabbed the pile of blankets and dropped back into bed, pulling them around me.

Aidan took up his post again, leaning against the door. "It's Tuesday. You have school."

His scent thickened, and a soft glow, an outline of what looked to be the letter 'A,' lit up on his chest, shining white through his shirt. My skin buzzed, my inner-wolf pressed against my chest, and my throat tightened.

I got up. I couldn't stop myself. I needed to get closer to him. That power. It was unbelievable. It rolled off him in waves of delirious heat. It was as if I floated across my room. I barely felt my feet touch the floor. I stood in front of him for a second before I couldn't hold back any longer. I lifted my hand and traced the glowing 'A' on his chest.

The sensation was like nothing I had ever felt before. My finger lit up as soon as it connected with what felt like a raised scar beneath his shirt, glowing with the same white light. It sparked and heated my entire body. I shuddered with pleasure. The unbelievable power ... authority ... command ... I wanted it. It called to me. It was like a little whisper in my ear telling me to take it. Claim it — *him* — as my own.

Aidan's hand snaked around my wrist and pulled my hand away from his chest. "Jade, focus. You need to get dressed. We're going to be late."

"Seriously?" I asked a little breathlessly, still staring at his chest. I lifted my other hand, wanting to touch it again, and he quickly snagged it. "You're worried about my education, but you'll let one of your wolves attack me. What's wrong with you?"

"You missed yesterday," he said dryly, pushing me back a step and holding me at arm's length. "I promised your parents you wouldn't miss anymore. Get dressed. You're going."

"My parents ..." I licked my dry lips. "You know where my parents are?"

"Yep, your dad went out of town for a few days, and your mom's at work. Get dressed." He dropped my wrist then, and his scent all but vanished into a thin and ultra-light film in the air.

I sucked in a deep, fresh breath and my insides shuddered with a deep-seated longing. I glanced up at him, meeting his golden eyes, and asked, "You going to let me change?"

He chuckled and crossed his arms over his chest, making his broad shoulders look even bigger. "I'm not stopping you. Go ahead."

I blushed from head to toe. He couldn't actually think I would give him a strip show, could he? He leaned back on the door casually as if that was exactly what he intended. "God, Aidan, get out."

He smirked. "How cute. A modest werewolf. You worried I won't like what I see, sweetheart?"

"I couldn't give two shits what you like," I lied, spun on my heels, and stalked toward my closet.

He chuckled, and it was positively infuriating.

CHAPTER 24

JADE

Aidan really made me go to school.

After a few minutes of shuffling through my clothes stalling, I heard the soft click of the door as he left. I let out a pent-up breath, thankful he wasn't actually going to make me change in front of him. He hadn't gone far. He was standing right outside my bedroom door when I emerged after tugging on blue jeans and my favorite plum hoodie.

When we got into his black Mustang, I tried to ask him about the mark on his chest, but all he'd say was that it was none of my business. He pulled up to the coffee shop and left me in the car, with a firm warning not to move an inch, while he bought coffee and donuts. He shoved them at me without a word.

Aidan escorted me to my locker, and he hovered over me in my classes, making people move so we could sit beside each other. Things had ... changed. Something had shifted in him. For the past few weeks, he had been approachable. Now, not so much. He was testy. His eyes flashed a lot. And he was seriously turning into a jackass. He was snapping at everyone, including the pack.

He wouldn't let me sit with Ben and Ann at lunch, and he wouldn't let Marcy sit with the pack or Trevor. He dragged me — literally dragged me — around, his hand always gripping on my wrist, or his arm looped around my waist, everywhere he went.

I had never been so happy to hear the bell ring at the end of the day. News had already traveled about my new *status,* and between the cautious looks from the student body, and Aidan's retardedly possessive behavior, I couldn't wait to get out of there. I left the computer lab, very aware that Aidan was right behind me, and I turned left, heading for my locker.

"Jade, come," Aidan snapped. I stiffened and spun around. I didn't want to, but that tone ... I just couldn't ignore it. I whimpered, and my inner-wolf stirred in my stomach. He gave me a stern glare and pointed to the floor in front of him.

My jaw dropped, and I put my hands on my hips, attempting to glare, and fighting the urge to run at his command, although I was sure I failed miserably because he didn't even flinch. Thankfully, though, my feet stayed firmly in place. "Did you just beckon me like a dog?"

His eyes flared, and he pointed again to the floor in front of him. "Jade," he growled.

At the sound of his growl, all of the *end of the day* chatter died, and tension rose all around us. Students rushed by so quickly it was as if they were running for cover from a bomb that was about to explode.

We stared off for a few long minutes. *He's serious,* my inner-wolf reminded me over and over, and it was a struggle not to run to him. But dammit, I'd had enough. Since I had been bitten, he had been acting like a complete jackass. But the worst part about it was that this new attitude made my body sing. The way he looked at me with those wide eyes, the tone of authority in his voice ... it spoke to me in a whole new way.

I wanted to walk away and turn my back on him, but I couldn't. His glare pinned me to the floor. My knees were shaking, my hands started to tremble, and damn him, but he grinned as if he had just won a battle. He paced toward me, never once looking away from my eyes, and he leaned in so close that I felt his warm breath push against my lips as he whispered, "Do you know what the penalty is for defying your alpha?" I shook my head, just a small side-to-side bob. My mouth and throat were too dry to answer. He chuckled softly. "Death, Jade."

He locked his hand around my wrist. The touch of his hand on my skin sent a rush of sparks and chills through me, and he pulled me to his car. And I hated myself for following along like an obedient little dog.

AIDAN

Jade locked me out of the house.

She didn't say a word to me as I drove her home, and she even smiled that sweet smile she used to give me before she knew who I was when we got out of the car. I figured she was coming around. I thought that my little threat had done the trick. For half a second, I was sure she was going to fall in line and accept me as her alpha. But clearly, I was wrong.

I didn't have time for this crap. Not with the werecougars and the constant issues with the pack. Not to mention the fact that if she didn't submit soon, I was sure we'd have more than one pack running around town. Jade was putting out more signals of her dominance than I was able to mask, and I was pretty sure that she didn't even know she was doing it.

All through our classes, I had rolled Dominic's words around in my mind, but the problem with his solution was that I just couldn't submit to her until she was officially my mate. She needed to first claim her place in the alpha pair and be recognized as my equal. I might not have been able to submit to her like he had suggested, but I had figured out a loophole. A small gap in the laws allowed me to take her under my guidance even as a challenging female, and what did she do? She locked me out of the damn house!

"Open the door, Jade," I growled for what had to be the twentieth time. I was starting to think I'd have to break a window. The top of her head was just visible through the small window in the door as she leaned against it.

"Looks like I'm smarter than you," she said through hysterical giggles. She must have rolled up on tiptoes then. Instead of seeing just the top of her forehead, her big brown eyes and wide grin peeked through the window.

"Jade, open the damn door!" I shouted again and banged my fist against the wood.

She jumped back quickly and called, "Don't think so," still giggling like a crazy person.

I had always liked to think of myself as a calm man. Patient, caring, rational, but all I saw was red at that moment. Her scent was stirring something in me that I had never felt before, and her *screw you* attitude was driving me mad. My inner-wolf clawed in my chest. That part of me, my animal side, had already accepted her. It didn't care about the rules or the laws or the challenges. It saw her as my equal — my mate.

The image of her wrapped in the thin towel the other day and the one from this morning in those skimpy little shorts and tank top flooded my mind. My skin heated, burning hot. I wanted her more than I wanted to breathe.

"Jade, you are going to be mine," I growled without thought. I slammed my palm against the door so hard it shook. "Fighting me will only delay it, but it won't stop the inevitable. I know you feel it."

That stopped her laughter abruptly, and I chuckled under my breath. "I'm not a piece of property, you jackass," she retorted.

"Yeah, you are," I said and sighed loudly. *You are as much my property as I am yours.*

I felt as if I were standing in quicksand, sinking deeper and deeper. What the hell was wrong with me? I hated this feeling of helplessness. I'd been a werewolf all my life. I knew how to control my inner cravings and the erratic behavior. But Jade ... her inner-wolf ... the wanting ... I shook my head, pushing the thoughts away.

She let out a strangled laugh. "Yeah, and that's the way to get me to open the door. Have a good night under the stars or go home."

I listened to the soft pat of her footsteps as she made her way through the house, and then I heard the whoosh of air as she sat, most likely on the couch.

I had to stop going easy on her. I'd been trying to tame my scent for her. The last thing I wanted was to cripple her under the full force of the alpha power. I wanted her to want me willingly. I wanted to see that lust in her eyes again without forcing it out of her. But I was running out of time. I could see it, her, slipping away. She wasn't mine yet, I didn't have to hold back, and maybe I shouldn't be, at least until she won.

I don't know how long I stood there staring at the door before I took a seat on the porch steps. I was starting to wonder if alphas were banned from the games not because of the interference issue but for their own sanity. I felt as if mine were teetering on a cliff, ready to tumble and shatter in the rocky cove below. Watching Jade beat the last two challengers had been amazing. She was amazing. And each time she pinned someone in place, a challenger or not, by just her glare ... it sent my inner-wolf crazy with want.

I scrubbed at my face roughly and then raked my hand through my hair. I didn't need this kind of distraction. Not now. Jeff claimed that he could distract the cougars and give me more time, but I wasn't so sure. Even now, I could smell them. The cougars were coming closer and closer to town, marking my woods as their own.

And there was just something about Jeff that wasn't sitting well with me. It turned out that the incident Dominic had been referring to when he had punched him was the moment he had caught Jeff cheating on his wife. That kind of thing happened, I knew that, but after finding out what the women were used for in his pack, and with the way, he could hide his scent ...

"You're breaking the laws," a voice said, yanking me from my tortured thoughts. "You cannot hide her."

"I'm not breaking any laws, Trisha," I said, not bothering to look up. I scrubbed at my face. "She's a new wolf, and with that status, I'm allowed to train her." Couldn't I just get five minutes alone? Five minutes with my thoughts. I really didn't think that was too much to ask for, but it was as if my pack could sense when I wasn't doing anything.

"You're interfering in the games," she said coolly. "We have a right to fight her."

I would have been lying if I tried to say I wasn't stunned at the aggression I smelled pulsing from Trisha. I was floored that the woman even wanted a shot at Jade after this morning. A part of me had hoped that the last two standing would drop out now when they saw what she could do and save us all the hassle. But I figured that just would have been too easy. I looked up at her then and said with a chuckle, "I'm not stopping you from challenging her."

Trisha crouched in front of me, leveling herself to my gaze. She was the oldest challenger, in her mid-forties, I guessed. She was lean and long like a dancer, wearing yoga pants and a long-sleeved, bright pink T-shirt. Her blond hair was pulled back in a severe ponytail.

"You're playing favorites, Aidan," she said. "You want her. I can smell your desire." She laughed cruelly and reached out, running a long fingernail along my chin. "When you're mine, the first thing I'm going to do is mate her to another. Trevor maybe. She despises him, and it will break her little friend's heart. Or Jared. He'll keep her in line."

Jealousy rushed through me at the idea of anyone else touching Jade. My eyes flashed. "You're walking on dangerous ground, Trisha," I snarled. I had never felt jealousy like this before, and it scared the crap out of me. Right then, I knew I'd rather be dead than see Jade mated with someone else.

The deadbolt on the door clicked open, and I swiveled to see Jade standing in the doorway. She looked furious. Her nose was scrunched, her cheeks were red, and her body was trembling as she stepped over the threshold and onto the porch.

"Jade, get inside," I said. Her inner-wolf was on the verge of breaking out. Her skin looked as if it were slithering over her bones and the hair on her arms was coarser, darker. She didn't have the restraint yet. I didn't want her to fight again. Not so soon. Not until I worked with her a bit. This morning I had been certain that she would have killed her opponent. If it hadn't been for Dominic drawing her attention ...

"Shut up, Aidan," she growled, not even glancing my way, and she pointed at Trisha. "You touch him again, and I'll rip you apart."

"Oh, is the little puppy coming out to play?" Trisha said with a snicker as she rose from her crouching position in front of me. She backed up a step and then flicked her hands as if to say, *Bring it on.*

I stood up and stifled a groan. Seriously ... all I wanted was five minutes of peace. I turned to Jade and folded my arms over my chest, giving her a look that I hoped would make her turn around and run back into the house. I could feel the warm burn of my alpha imprint, and I let my scent grow and grow.

She didn't even notice.

"How old are you?" Jade snapped and moved to the railing, leaning on it. "Like forty? Don't you think he's a bit young for you?"

"He's going to be mine, Jade." Trisha's voice was strained, and her face turned paperwhite. She gave me a leery look, and it looked as if she were struggling to stay on her feet. "Aidan, you can't interfere like this!"

At least my scent was working on one of them, I thought before I pulled it back. She was right, even if I didn't want her to be. My interference could render anything that happened between them void. I moved to the side, leaning up against the railing, and folded my arms.

"I'll give you a chance," Jade said, a smirk spreading across her lips. "Submit now, and I'll let you walk away without a scratch."

Holy shit! Did she really just say that? I almost laughed. She was falling into her new life faster than I would have thought possible. Jade's eyes flashed and then settled into a golden glow. Her scent ramped up and more dark hair sprouted along her neck. My skin felt like it was on fire. It was a fight not to move from my spot. The sweet smell of power was intoxicating, and all I wanted to do was pull her into my arms.

Trisha looked ... nervous. She was jittery, hopping from one foot to the other. She sucked in a deep breath. Her knees were starting to shake, and her shoulders were beginning to sag. "Submit to a pup?" she asked, her voice quivering. "A big demand for someone so young." Trisha looked at me, just a quick glance before focusing on Jade. "Time for you to leave, alpha."

"Nope," I said, holding in my laugh. Trisha looked as if she could barely keep Jade's gaze, yet she still seemed determined to go through with the challenge. Jade's scent rocketed up another notch, and my heart quickened. "Not going anywhere. I've put her under my training." I shrugged my shoulders, making it clear that there was nothing she could do about my presence. "Besides, you need a witness."

Jade didn't wait for me to finish my sentence before she leaped over the rails on the porch and landed on the balls of her feet in front of Trisha. She growled, a lethal sound, and her skin started to shudder. "Last chance, old hag," she said, snarling the last word. "He's mine."

Trisha sucked in a noisy breath. She held Jade's gaze for half a second before she turned and ran down the driveway as quickly as she could.

"What the hell was that about, Aidan?" Jade asked. She tried to sound tough, but I heard the laughter in her voice as she watched Trisha run down the street.

"I'm yours, am I?" I said, feeling a little cocky. I raised an eyebrow and chuckled.

Jade gave me an adorable dirty look. "Don't let it go to your head, jackass."

"Of course not," I said with mock sincerity. She rolled her eyes dramatically, spun away from me, and marched into the house, leaving the door wide open. *Three down, one to go, and then ... you'll be mine*, I thought and smiled as I followed her inside.

CHAPTER 25

JADE

My veins pulsed from his scent. Its power pressed against my bones and toyed with my muscles as I fought the urge to turn back to him and pull him to me. I had never really believed the stories about alphas or about the imprint that helped channel their scent. Obviously, I should have, but how was I to know that an alpha's scent would have such a powerful effect on me. Why would I care when joining the pack was the most ridiculous and inane suggestion anyone could ever make to me.

I had heard these stories all my life, but really, I honestly never thought a scent could do this to me. I should have figured it out this morning when I saw that soft glow under his shirt. He was trying to manipulate me then, and by the pressure, I felt on my skin now, he was doing it again. And the thing that freaked me out about it was the feeling that he was still holding back, and part of me wanted to feel the full extent of his control.

But according to the stories, this was not the sensation I should have felt. It should have been piercing and shuddering, forcing me to bow to him.

Painful even if I tried to fight it. But Aidan's scent didn't make me feel like that at all. It was a wild feeling. Full of desire and overwhelming confusion. It centered me and tore me apart. It spoke to the beast inside me like a song. Slow and sensual, and then fast and out of control.

I wasn't sure what was happening to me or what had come over me when I stepped outside. When I'd heard that woman talk to him as if they were lovers, something inside me just snapped. And when I opened the door to see her looking at Aidan as if she wanted to jump him right then and there, I lost it. I had never felt jealous of anyone before. Not like this. I might have felt a bit jealous when Dominic left me for the pack, but that had been like a mosquito bite compared to the blinding anger that had spiked within me when I saw her touching his face.

I was shaking from the inside out, and my skin was moving, sliding over my bones in a fast rhythm. My inner-wolf was begging me to let go of my restraint and shift. It felt as if that was the only thing that could give me an ounce of relief from the torture of seeing that woman so close to *my* alpha and from his invasive, mouthwatering scent, which was demanding that I make him mine. I was changing. I could feel it in my bones. I was no longer the prey but the predator, and he was what my inner-wolf wanted to hunt.

It's natural. Trevor's reassurance played through my thoughts. *He's an unclaimed alpha.* But this ... this wasn't natural. I was losing control. A control that I had fought so hard to keep. It was the only thing that kept me safe from the wolves. I had let it slip once with Erika, and look at where that got me. But right at that moment, I wanted to let it all go. It was as if something else was taking over. Something deep within me knew, without a doubt, that Aidan was mine. My mate. And I'd kill anyone who stood in my way of getting him.

They are your wolves now, a small voice in my head whispered. My skin heated, burning like wildfire.

My wolves. My pack. My alpha. It scared the hell out of me how possessive I felt of the things that I had spent so long hating. Of the pack that I would have been happy to see vanish from this earth only a few days ago.

I focused on my slow steps, making my way down the airy hallway. The hardwood floors felt cold and unforgiving with each step I took. I could feel him behind me, following me into the house, and I cursed myself silently for not locking the door. I passed by the arched doorway leading to the kitchen and kept my gaze firmly on the staircase in front of me that would take me to the sanctuary of my bedroom. His scent wrapped around me. It was sexy as hell. It fogged my brain and made my skin buzz.

"You need to shift?" Aidan asked, shutting the door behind him. "We could go for a run. That will take the edge off."

I took a deep breath, trying to clear my head. It didn't work. Aidan and his stupid scent worked its way over and through me. I turned slowly, backed up a few steps until my heels hit the staircase, and then I dropped down, taking a hard seat.

I looked at him. His expression was full of humor, and he looked way too cocky as if he knew exactly what he was doing to me. A morsel of my sense came back to me, and I gave him the dirtiest look I could muster up. "That's the third wolf that wanted to fight me in three days, and she was also the second one that made it clear you were the reason for it."

He chuckled, still wearing that cocky grin. "Your point?" He stood in the hallway, looking pleased with himself, his grin stretching further, and the corners of his eyes crinkled softly.

"I'm not buying this jackass thing you're trying to pull," I said with a groan. I tried to look away from him, but I couldn't. His laugh and his chocolaty eyes captured me, making my skin grow warmer. "I know you, Aidan. This isn't you."

A strong wave of his scent hit me, and his grin faltered for a second. "You've known me for two weeks. You have no clue who I am." There was bitterness and challenge in his voice, coated with authority, that made me want to crawl across the floor to him and beg at his feet not to be mad at me. My body trembled with a need that I didn't understand, or maybe it was one that I didn't want to understand.

"I swear if you don't tell me what's going on, I'll walk away. I'll leave town without another thought of you or your stupid pack." I tried to stand up then to prove a point that I knew I wouldn't be able to follow through on. I failed miserably, my knees shook too much to hold my weight, and I plopped right back down. I was lost to him. Completely and irrevocably lost.

That shook him. His jaw dropped a little as he looked me over. His nostrils flared as he sucked in deep breaths, searching for what I didn't know, but on the fourth one, his smile returned. "Mmmm, I love a challenge," he said. His voice turned deep and husky. "You're making this so much more fun, sweetheart. You and I both know you'll submit to me. You'll be mine."

"Excuse me?" I snapped, trying to hide the surge of pleasure that unraveled in my stomach. *Submit to him! Be his!* My body came alive, and my inner-wolf stirred. But just as quickly as the pleasure came, fiery rage burned it away. "You're just digging a bigger hole, jackass."

He chuckled and took a slow, teasing step toward me. "I can smell it, Jade. Your inner-wolf is practically salivating for me. And you've had your eye on me since the first day we met."

"A little full of yourself?" I scoffed, hating how right he was. I managed to stand up and step closer to him. He was only a few feet away, but the distance felt like miles.

"I could put you on trial for your disobedience," he said. "But I'm feeling a little generous. Submit now, and I'll consider letting you off the hook, and maybe I'll even pretend I didn't notice that Dominic and Marcy helped you defy me."

"You're threatening me with my friends?" I asked as the spark of anger from before reignited within me. My muscles stiffened, and my face burned with heat.

"Submit to me or let them fry." Fire flared in his eyes. It was dangerous and intense, and it suddenly hit me that I knew nothing of the man that stood before me. I was also certain that he meant exactly what he said. I had been right. He had been holding back. He'd been keeping the alpha authority at bay with me, but what I saw in him now scared me to death. My anger froze. He moved closer, backing me into the wall, and released a trickle of his scent, enough to make me want to throw myself at him and run from him at the same time. "I have them in custody as we speak."

I said nothing, not wanting to provoke him and knowing that it would only make things worse if I opened my mouth. His scent was fogging my brain and blurring my vision. I wanted to melt against him and run away as fast as I could. He smiled faintly. It was clear that he knew the effect he had on me. He started to move away, receding toward the door, and as he did, I felt stripped to the core.

"Aidan, wait," I said a little desperately. I didn't want him to leave, and I hated myself for it. The further he got from me, the more I shook. That man was mine. Every part of me knew it, wanted it. "Let them go. I'll do what you want. Just leave them out of this." After the words were out of my mouth, I felt sick. I didn't know whether I was saying it to get him to stay or for my friends.

He stopped and gave me a sexy half-smile. "Will you submit, Jade?"

Yes! I wanted to scream it, but the word wouldn't come out. I didn't know what to do. It was as if he were speaking in another language. My body shook as my inner-wolf, and my human side battled against each other. One wanted me to stay strong and claim him as mine, and the other wanted me to drop at his feet. And I couldn't figure out which one wanted what or which one to listen to.

He must have taken my silence as a rejection because he started to turn from me again. "Aidan, please don't go," I whispered.

"Submit to me." His husky voice wrapped around me, demanding and gentle, a confusing mix, and for a second, I couldn't breathe. My lungs just ... stopped working. His eyes were full of desire and longing. If I had to guess, he and his inner-wolf wanted me just as much as I wanted him.

"But Dominic told me not to back down to you." I didn't know what else to say. I'd had boyfriends before, but not one of them did this to me. Not that he was my boyfriend ... yet, but every part of me wanted him to be. It felt as if I were being torn down the middle. His intense gaze was as if he could see through me, into my head, my soul.

He laughed. It was a cool sound, one that held little humor but no malice. "It's your choice, Jade. You will give in sooner or later." He held my stare for another long minute as if he were waiting for me to say something, and when I didn't, he shook his head with clear disappointment. "I'm going out. Do not leave this house without permission. My number is on the fridge. And by the way, you're not smarter than me."

CHAPTER 26

AIDAN

Damn, but that girl could really push my buttons. I seriously wasn't looking forward to going back and seeing her. She was weak to me for a moment. I hadn't held back this time, letting every ounce of my scent wrap around her and merge with her. It was the most incredible thing I had ever felt. For a split second, we had been one. Her scent mingled with mine, teasing me in a way that made me want to forget the rules and claim her. And I was pretty sure that if she actually knew that there were rules, she would have felt the same. I had never thought I'd find a mate that would fill me the way she did. Not in this town.

But without my scent taming her, I was sure that when I went back, there would be hell to pay. She'd shake it off, and when she realized I had the house surrounded, keeping her locked up tight ... I shuddered at the thought. My only saving grace so far had been the fact that she was new ... unstable. She didn't know how to manipulate her scent yet. Every time she let it out, it was random, not really directed at anything or anyone in particular. But when she figured it out, and when she claimed her imprint, I knew I'd be just as lost to her as she was to me. But then again, I was pretty sure I was already lost. Jade was the only thing I was sure of — my clarity — when everything else around me was a jumbled mess.

There had already been moments where she had made me want to submit to her. She was the strongest female I had ever met. She would be mine. Maybe, possibly, that is if she didn't kill me first. And after the crap I just pulled, I thought she just might try when she figured it all out.

I was so close to telling her about the games. So close to ruining my chance at having her. She lusted for me now, but lust was far from love, and the hatred that burned behind it was just as fierce. She wouldn't fight if she knew it was for me. I was sure of it. And I needed her to fight. She was my perfect match in every way. She was my home.

When did I start thinking that I could have love? The thought shook me. Love didn't, and shouldn't, matter to me. Not as an alpha. But the idea of being with Jade had my heart pounding. I could ... no, I did love her. I loved her fire and her lippy responses. The way she challenged me and kept me on my toes. I loved everything about her.

I sat in my new living room, not really listening to Dominic and Trevor as they went over the plan to deal with the werecougars. The house had been vacant for a while now. It had belonged to the alpha before Ray, and as pack property, it was now mine. It wasn't much. Two bedrooms, two bathrooms, a tiny kitchen, and a living room were better than the motel. The paint was peeling on the walls, and the carpet needed to be ripped out. But the furniture was still good. A black leather sectional couch and a matching armchair pretty much filled the room.

Dominic had gathered my few things earlier while I

was with Jade, and he had been here when the bed was finally delivered. And right then, I would have killed to be able to go lay down on it. Marcy had even picked up and washed a new set of sheets for me, and she had also cleaned and stocked the fridge. Trevor had been right when he said Marcy didn't know how to stay mad. I didn't think she'd ever forgive me after her little flip-out this morning, but as Trevor promised, it was as if it never happened.

Their kindness was ... weird. I got the feeling that they hadn't done all this because I was the alpha, but because they actually wanted to. I hadn't expected it, not after the way I had been treating them since Jade had been bitten, but I figured it was Marcy's doing. After watching her for the last few weeks with Trevor, I knew she thrived on making the people around her happy. And for a human, it was pretty impressive that she had Dominic and Trevor wrapped around her finger.

After Jeff had woken up from the Dominic-induced nap, he had divulged Bruce's sick obsession with recruiting females. The women were never changed. As Jeff had said, they were community property, used only to breed males to be changed. When a female was born, they raised her until she was old enough to be used. Ray had had an agreement with Bruce. He'd ignore the twisted use of the women as long as the werecougars stayed away from his town. I couldn't ignore it, though. Dominic swore he hadn't known, so did the pack enforcers, and each one of them was behind me, eager to put an end to the sick use of the women.

Right now, we were waiting for a full count from Jeff. We had sent him back to his pack to investigate how much Bruce knew about me and report back with exactly what we were up against. At the last check-in, he had reported that Bruce had him tied up, and he would let us know once he had something we could use.

Dominic's phone buzzed on the coffee table, and the voice caller display chirped, *Jade Shaw*, in a mechanical female tone.

"Don't answer that," I said and grabbed his reaching hand before he could get the phone. "She kind of thinks I locked you up."

"What?" Dominic asked, and he gave me a look that clearly said he thought I'd lost it. He glanced at the phone again and then leaned back, settling into the couch, with a raised eyebrow, waiting for me to explain.

The oven door slammed, and the scent of hot pizza filled the room. "Jesus, Aidan, what the hell did you do this time?" Marcy yelled from the kitchen. She clattered around, slamming cupboards and banging plates against the counter.

I groaned and watched the phone until it stopped skittering across the table. "She wouldn't submit. She also thinks I have you locked up, Mac. Oh, and I kind of left the enforcers with her to make sure she doesn't leave the house." Saying it out loud made it worse, and dread pooled in my stomach. *Yep, she's going to kill me.* And I knew I'd let her if she really wanted to. I'd welcome it. I deserved it. *I really am a jackass.*

"Really, Aidan? Really?" Marcy said, aghast. She came through the small doorway juggling two pizzas and a stack of plates and stomped over to us.

"I want her to win," I said lamely. Trevor and Dominic were both chuckling, and Marcy rolled her eyes.

"Dumbass," Dominic said and shook his head. "I didn't think you were this stupid."

Marcy giggled. "She's going to kill you when she

finds out you've lied to her again." She placed the pizzas on the coffee table and started filling the plates, handing them out before taking a seat next to Trevor.

I gave them all a dirty look, biting back the urge to tell them off. The only thing that stopped me was the fact that they were right. I certainly felt like a dumbass. So I leaned back on the couch, propping my feet up on the edge of the coffee table, and let them laugh.

"Aidan, do you really want her to submit?" Trevor asked curiously. "I thought alpha pairs aren't supposed to submit to each other. You know, to keep them both in control."

I hadn't expected the question, and I took a large bite of pizza as I thought it over. The spicy sausage and pepperoni made my stomach growl with hunger, and I devoured the slice before I finally said, "She's being impossible. She needs to learn some respect." *And she is not an alpha ... yet,* I said silently. There was no point in reminding them. The two werewolves in the room had made it clear on more than one occasion that they had already considered her their alpha female. I just wished that I could ignore the rules, too.

Marcy shot me a stern glare. "Lying to her and manipulating her isn't going to get her to respect you."

I scrubbed at my face roughly, attempting to rub away all the confusion that that girl had brought into my life. "I thought she wanted me. I thought ... I thought ... dammit. After she beat Trisha today ..." I let my words fall short, and I glanced at Dominic, waiting for the lecture that I knew was on the tip of his tongue. I almost wanted to hear it. Dominic watched me, chewing on his pizza. I'd never seen him so quiet. He was pissed off, that much I could tell, but the rest was hidden under his carefully placed mask. "Look, I didn't have much of a choice," I said to Dominic. "Her scent was overpowering me. My inner-wolf has already accepted her as my mate. Whenever I get near her, all I can think about is claiming her. I had to let my alpha out."

"You haven't been using it with her?" Trevor asked and laughed again.

"Not fully, well, at least not until today," I admitted guiltily. I knew I should have been. Dominic had even advised me to do it. We had all hoped that it would encourage the alpha in her out, but every time I thought about doing it before today, I felt like an ass. "Call me crazy, but I was kind of hoping she'd feel the same thing for me as I do for her. I didn't want to force her inner-wolf to realize she's meant to be my mate. And I didn't really lie to her completely. You both have violated laws."

"Dude, not part of the pack," Marcy said around a mouthful of pizza.

"Dude," I said, mimicking her snark. "Trevor claimed you. He did two nights ago. Even if you haven't been changed, a mate is considered part of the pack. You're bound by my laws."

I instantly knew I'd said something stupid. Marcy turned ten different shades of red before she shrieked at Trevor, "You told him!"

I held back a laugh, but Dominic didn't. He let out a deep belting roar, and he started to cough, choking on his pizza. Trevor turned white as a sheet, and his eyes widened. It was more than a little obvious he didn't tell Marcy what would happen after they hooked up.

"It's a scent thing, Mac," Trevor said in a rush. "I can't hide it. Our scents have synced together since we ..."

"Don't you dare say it!" she said, jumping up from the couch. "God, isn't anything private with you guys?" She spun on me then and snapped, "Jade does want you, but she'll never bow down to you. She's not going to fight for someone who is trying to force her either."

"Okay, I get it," I said, throwing my hands up in the air, and all my pent-up laughter fizzled away. "I'm a moron. How the hell do I fix it?"

"You let the people that know her best out of jail," Dominic said with a chuckle. "She'll win the games tomorrow." He laughed again and focused on Marcy, "Mac, you up for it?"

Marcy considered it for a second before a grin inched its way on her lips. "She's going to kill us. But I'm in."

CHAPTER 27

JADE

My heart dropped when I heard the engine of a car pull into my driveway. It was a rumbling, clunking sound instead of the purr of Aidan's Mustang.

I stood at the fridge, cell phone in hand, staring at the sharp scrawl of his handwritten number. Last night after he left me, I had realized four things. One: He might have been smarter than me. Two: He was hiding something from me. Three: I needed to play nice and get Dominic and Marcy out of jail. Four: I was falling for him — hard.

His alpha wolf spoke to my inner-wolf in a personal way. It took the control that my inner-wolf craved. But it wasn't just his alpha that spoke to me. It was him. This jackass thing was an act. I knew it without a doubt, and I was determined to break through it.

As soon as Aidan left, I had snuck out the back door. He had been right; I needed to shift. I had too much energy coursing through me, burning me up from the inside out. I hadn't noticed the wolves until I walked out the door, and they surrounded me. But Aidan hadn't just left some wolves at my house. No. He had stationed the pack enforcers to make sure I didn't go. The enforcers were a team of five. And they were ruthless. Their sole purpose was to enforce the alpha's commands. I had seen them in action before, and when Jared shifted and stood nose to nose with me, stark naked, demanding to know where I thought I was going, I almost threw up from the sudden fear of facing them.

The enforcers were the only wolves that I never had, and would never, pick a fight with. No one walked out of that alive. They had no compassion. They didn't ask questions. They didn't have to follow the normal rules of the pack. In a sense, when they were called upon, they held just as much power over the pack as the alpha did, except they always executed that power with death and violence.

But Jared had given me a choice, which had shocked the hell out of me. Jared wasn't known for his patience or for giving options. Kill first, ask questions later. That was pretty much his motto. But instead of attacking me, he let me decide: call Aidan or go back inside. In the end, my stupid pride had won ... again. Jared made it clear that I wasn't allowed out unless I spoke to the alpha, and since I refused to call him, I was escorted back into the house. But before Jared closed the door on me, he had looked me up and down and said, *'We're going to have a lot of fun once you lose the alpha games, little girl.'* There had been no mistaking his meaning. The gleam in his eyes when they settled on my breasts told me everything I needed to know. He planned to take me as his mate. I wanted to ask Jared what he was talking about. What were the alpha games? But instead, I slammed the door and locked it.

That was when I decided that Aidan just might have been smarter than me and when I realized that he was hiding something from me. It was also that moment that I knew I was falling for him. The idea of anyone else touching me other than him was something I didn't want to think about, and it made me feel a little queasy for more than one reason. I was supposed to hate him. I was supposed to hate the pack.

I'd been trying to call him for the last hour, but my inner-wolf had been fighting me. For reasons that I couldn't begin to understand, it didn't want me to submit. *Not yet*, a voice chanted over and over in the back of my mind. *You need to win him first*. It just sucked that I really didn't understand what that meant.

"Jade?" Mom called from the hallway. "Honey, are you home?"

"In here, Mom," I said, bracing myself for what I was sure was going to be a lot of tears. I hadn't seen her since I was bitten, and knowing my mom, I knew that wasn't by her choice.

"Oh, honey," she said as she came into the kitchen. She looked exhausted, but she tried to hide it with an overly bright smile. Her pink scrubs were all wrinkly, and her hair was a mess, falling out of her ponytail. She set her bag on the counter and rushed over to me, wrapping me in a hug. "I've been so worried about you. How are you feeling?"

"I'm fine, Mom," I said, squeezing her back. She sniffled in my ear and swallowed loudly as if she were trying to choke down her tears. "I'm good, really," I said softly, trying to sound reassuring. "I shifted. Everything's fine."

"If everything's fine, then why are there wolves surrounding our house, Jade?" she asked as she released me and folded her arms over her chest, waiting for my response.

"Because the alpha is trying to show me how smart he is," I said with more than a little bite to my tone. I was on edge, fighting with everything I had not to shift. My skin was crawling, and quick bursts of adrenaline shot through me every few minutes.

Mom laughed and sniffled as she wiped at her misty eyes. "You should be happy that the alpha is showing interest in you." She looked me over from head to toe, taking her time as she searched my body as if she needed to see every part of me to make sure that I really was okay.

"The alpha is being a jackass, and those wolves outside are the enforcers," I said. I grabbed my steaming mug off the counter, took a seat at the table, and drank a deep gulp of my coffee.

A spike of tangy fear flitted through the air, reaching my nostrils, and Mom lost a little color to her cheeks. "Let me guess, you haven't submitted to him and recognized him as your alpha yet." She made her way through the kitchen and sat down at the table, giving me a stern look. "You really should do it before he loses patience with you. The pack has always been about the rules."

She was serious. I could see it on her face. But there was something else there. A small knowing smile. A slight twinkle in her eyes. Pride that her only daughter had joined the pack and caught the alpha's attention. And right then, I was sure she knew exactly what Aidan was hiding from me.

"Don't you have an issue with the fact that your daughter is a werewolf?" I snapped. This was the first time I had seen her since I was bitten, and she looked ... happy about it. Freakin' happy! I started to shake with hot anger, and I glared at her. "You want me to give myself to some guy to use me as he chooses? Seriously, Mom, I think you and Dad need therapy or parenting classes or something. This is not something to be happy about."

I might as well have slapped her across the face. She

certainly looked like my words had hurt her just as much, and a rush of guilt washed over me. Her eyes misted up, and she took a few breaths before she was able to look at me again.

"Jade, Aidan is not Ray," she said in a shaky voice. "I won't have you speaking about him that way in my house. Use you as he chooses." She shook her head and made a *tsk* sound, clearly disappointed. "He's not a monster. It's just the way of the pack. He's the leader. You need to show your respect. And besides, once the games ..."

The front door opened and slammed shut. Mom looked up, and I watched as the blood drained from her face and her complexion turned to a sickly gray. I didn't need to look to see who it was; his scent hit me hard and fast.

"What games?" I asked, fighting to ignore his presence. "What were you going to say?" I may have been too freaked out to ask Jared, but Mom was a totally different story.

"Nothing, honey," she said in a rush, still looking over me at Aidan. "Better hurry. You'll be late for school."

I jumped up, and my chair rocked back, crashing to the floor. "School! Really? I'm not going. It's not like I need an education now. I'm never getting out of this stupid hick town."

"Jade!" Aidan barked from the doorway. I spun around; anger sparked over my skin, and I met him straight on. *There goes playing nice,* I thought. What was it about him that made my blood boil and my heart melt at the same time?

His eyes flared with that dangerous warning that shook me to my core. The sweet Aidan was gone, replaced by the alpha that scared me to death. I tried to hold his stare. I fought for the control and the authority I had had only days before. The command that had made this man trembled under my stare.

His scent hit me again, strong and sweet and powerful. It pulled at me, making my body convulse with the effort to stay standing. His gaze hardened, and he nodded in my mother's direction. "Apologize."

It wasn't a request. There was no mistaking the tone. I wanted to tell him off and kick him out of the house just as much as I wanted to tell him that I was his if he still wanted me. But I couldn't do either. The words lodged in my throat. "Now, Jade," he said tightly, and he closed the distance between us. He took my chin in his hand with surprising gentleness and forced me to meet his eyes.

"Aidan, please ..." My bottom lip trembled as I spoke. His eyes were wide, glowing yellow, and his scent thickened in the air until I could hardly catch my breath.

"You need to learn," he said, and I was sure I heard a hint of regret in his voice.

"I'm sorry," I whispered. I didn't want to whisper, but my voice just wouldn't work. I was lost in his eyes, in his scent, and my world was crashing down around me.

Aidan held me in place for another long moment before he dropped his hand from my face. I sagged against him almost instantly. Without his hand supporting me, my knees began to shake, and they refused to hold me upright. His arm snaked around my waist, holding me close, and my heart hammered in my chest, thrilled and terrified of the man that I was falling for. He spoke to my mom, but I felt as if I were drunk with his scent so strong. His voice was garbled and slurred in my ears.

Aidan took my hand in his and led me out of the house. I vaguely registered the smirk on Jared's face and his team of enforcers standing behind him, watching me as I got into the car. A moment later, Aidan jumped in and backed out of the driveway. He didn't say anything to me, and his brain-numbing scent was hardly noticeable now. His jaw was tight, twitching as he clenched and unclenched it.

"I don't mean to be so, um, difficult ..." I started. He snorted and gave me a quick sideways look that made me want to giggle. "Okay, maybe I do mean to be. But really, you've been a bit of a jerk."

His hand clenched the steering wheel, and his knuckles turned white. "Jade, when you walked out that door and shifted with us, you chose the pack. With that choice comes rules. You may not care about the rules, but I don't have that luxury."

I was certain I heard the regret return to his voice. Silence stretched awkwardly between us. This was a side of Aidan that I had never imagined. He'd always seemed so carefree. So confident. I had never pegged him for a *rules* kind of guy.

"I need a freakin' handbook," I muttered under my breath, breaking the silence.

He chuckled softly, and the velvety sound made my heart flutter. "Did you have a nice time sneaking out last night?"

"I ... I ... needed to shift," I said softly. "You were right."

He grinned. "I told you I was smarter, Jade," he said with a confident-sounding chuckle. "I told you not to leave the house without asking me. Did you really think the enforcers weren't going to tell me?"

CHAPTER 28

JADE

Aidan didn't take me to school.

He left me sitting in the pack's headquarters' sterile-looking, white waiting room. The smell of bleach and various lemon-scented cleaners was overwhelming, and they were seriously making my head hurt. I would have preferred school.

I'd never been inside their headquarters before. But then, I hadn't even known they had one until today. Really, what could a bunch of werewolves need with a headquarters? It seemed ... stupid, and it also reminded me again that I had so much to learn about the pack. Number one on my list was to figure out the rules that Aidan had been talking about. Again, I found myself seriously wishing for a handbook.

For the last three and a half hours, I'd been sitting there watching the door to Aidan's office. After he had deposited me in an uncomfortable, bright orange plastic chair, he gave me a stern warning not to move, and then he went into his office and closed the door. About ten minutes after that, Beck, one of the enforcers, escorted a sobbing Marcy and a furious Dominic into the room.

They didn't even look at me as they went by, and I wasn't sure if they didn't notice me or they didn't want to see me. I wouldn't have blamed them if that were the case. It was my fault that they were in this mess, but the idea of them hating me burned anyway. I had started to get up to talk to them when Beck focused his golden gaze on me and mouthed, 'Not a word,' and I froze.

Beck was about Aidan's height with the same kind of thick and muscular build, but unlike Aidan, he was kind of scary. He was a lot like Jared in the no patience department, and since I had pissed him off more than a few times before, I didn't want to risk pushing it. Not with the vicious warning that burned in his eyes. Damn, I hated the enforcers.

About thirty minutes after the three of them went in, and Beck never came out, I thought I was going to lose my mind from nerves. If Aidan kept one of the enforcers with him, it probably wasn't a good thing. I snuck over to the door, and I pressed my ear against it, trying to hear the conversation. The door must have been reinforced with something because I couldn't make out anything even with my enhanced hearing. Not even a second later, the door flew open, and I tumbled into the room.

Before Beck scooped me up, I didn't even get a peek at Marcy or Dominic. He carried me back over to the waiting room and set me down. "If I catch you moving again, I won't be this gentle," he growled, and then he vanished back into Aidan's office, slamming the door behind him.

I hadn't moved an inch since. My butt was tingly, my feet were pins and needles, and my back was throbbing, but I refused to move. I could deal with Aidan — kind of. I was pretty sure he wouldn't actually follow through on his threats, but Beck … there wasn't a doubt in my mind that Beck would.

The sound of shoe-clad feet slapping against the white ceramic tiles down the hall drew my attention. As soon as my eyes found the source, I shuddered. Jared was coming toward me.

Jared was shirtless, and his gray track pants hung low on his hips. He had a small white towel wrapped around his neck, and his sculpted abs and chest glistened with sweat. Even though they were resting at his sides, the roped muscles in his forearms and thick biceps seemed as if they were flexed. His short black hair was messy and damp, and when his eyes, which were such a dark brown that they looked black, met mine, a one-sided grin twitched at his lips.

"Hey, little girl," Jared said, closing the distance between us and taking a seat beside me. "You in shit again?"

I shrugged my shoulders because I really didn't know if I was or not. "How many times do I have to ask you to stop calling me *little girl*," I said and rolled my eyes in an attempt to make him think that his closeness wasn't at all nerve-racking. He had started calling me *little girl* back when I was in seventh grade. He had been in grade nine then, and I had a horribly stupid crush on him. Right then, I wished I was back in seventh grade when he didn't scare the crap out of me.

He chuckled. "Will you relax," he said. "I'm not here for you. I was at the gym." He nudged me in the ribs playfully and winked.

I tried to relax, but it wasn't an easy task with him beside me. I hadn't really spoken to him since seventh grade, and I had avoided him at all costs when he became the head of the enforcers. Just like when Dominic had joined the pack, Jared had turned cold. Heartless. Ruthless. But then, Jared had always been a little cold.

"Who's he with?" Jared asked, nodding toward the

closed door. He stretched his long legs out in front of him and draped an arm around the back of my chair.

"Dom and Mac," I said, leaning forward a little, so it didn't feel like his arm was actually around me. After last night, I didn't want to give him a single reason to think I was interested. "They're in shit for helping me."

My palms were starting to sweat, and I roughly wiped them on my jeans. A pulse of sugary sweet power hit me, not like Aidan's scent, which made me think of nothing else but ripping off his clothes, but it was strong enough to make my heart hammer against my ribs. My breath caught. I heard it, and so did he. His chuckle gave it away. The pulse turned into a trickle and then to a stream. "He's not the only one who can speak to your inner-wolf, little girl," Jared said. "You're strong. What you crave is the power, not him. I can give you what you need."

I sucked in breath after sweet, sweet breath. My inner-wolf clawed at my stomach like a crazed lunatic. It was a weird feeling, nothing like the passion that Aidan brought out in me. This was vicious. It filled me with something that resembled anger and made me feel like a savage beast. I fought against it. Hated it. Needed it. Wanted it. And really, really feared it.

My own scent changed, ramping up and swirling around us. The stronger it got, the more stable I felt, and after a moment, my inner-beast settled — a little. "Jared, can I ask you something?" My voice was a throaty whisper. I looked over at him, meeting his glowing yellow eyes.

He arched an eyebrow, looking at me as if he were waiting for me to do something. When I didn't do whatever he had expected, his scent slowly dissipated, and his expression turned stony. "Shoot," he said, coating the word with a growl.

I shivered. I didn't know if it was his growl or the lack of the mouthwatering smell that made my insides freeze, but whichever it was, I didn't like it. I opened my mouth, then closed it, and cleared the prickly lump in my throat before I asked, "Why did you give me a choice last night? I didn't think you guys did that. Like ever."

His hand clasped my arm, and he pulled me back into the chair, draping his arm securely and a little possessively around my shoulder. I fought the urge to jump away from him, terrified of what he might do if I did. "You'll be more fun to me alive," he said, his voice husky. "You ready to give up yet?"

"Give up what?" I asked, and a chill ran up my back, forcing my spine to jolt and straighten. *He knows,* a voice in my head hissed. He knew what Aidan was hiding. Everyone knew. My mom, Jared ... Right then, I bet the whole freakin' pack knew. I didn't know whether to freak out or feel hurt. Both seemed like a viable option right then.

He chuckled and pulled me closer. "Step down from the games, little girl. I'll be more entertaining than the alpha. Promise."

"What games?" I asked. He ignored my question, leaned into me, and nuzzled at my neck. "Keep your hands off me," I snarled. It burst out of my mouth before I could stop it. His touch felt wrong and cold and forceful. It made my skin crawl and heat up at the same time. My inner-wolf stirred again, and a low growl rumbled from my throat, and I tried to wiggle free of his arms.

He didn't let go. His arm wrapped tighter around me, pulling me closer. "Mmmm, love that fire, but I'll have you purring like a kitten in no time," he whispered in my ear, and his hot breath played with the fine hairs on my neck. "Give up. Let Tiff be his mate."

All the hints and warnings that I had received over the last few days played through my mind in a blast, fighting over each other to be heard. *Stay away from him. She's treating you like an alpha. Don't back down from him. I can't live with my alpha hating me. Packs have alpha pairs. Two alphas. One male and one female. He'll be mine. When you lose the alpha games ...*

"Tiff's the last one fighting for him?" I asked. The frost I heard in my voice was bittersweet. *He really is a jackass,* I thought, as all the pieces slid together. My body began to shake, and I hardly felt Jared's arm around me anymore. Red-hot fury blazed through me. The bastard had me fighting for him! He'd been playing me all along. Was I a werewolf because of him? Was it his idea to ruin my life and then sic his wolves on me? Would he have even cared if they killed me? I'd seen the murder in that dirty-gray wolf's eyes. And because of a stupid crush, I had walked right into his games. At that moment, I thought I hated myself even more than I did him for letting myself care about a stupid dog.

Jared's arm slipped to my waist, and he yanked, pulling me onto his lap. I gasped, and my hands flew to his chest, pushing him away. "Hands off, Jared," I snapped, but he didn't let go. He pulled me against his chest, placing a trail of hot kisses down my neck.

"Mmmhmm, it's just you and Tiff," he said against my neck. "You don't want to be an alpha. With your fire, you'd make a great enforcer. We don't have to play by the rules." I pushed at him harder, and he pulled me closer, pinning my arms between our chests. "Jade," he murmured into my ear, "I know you want me. I can smell it." He flicked his tongue against my earlobe.

I gasped, and every muscle in my body went rigid.

Tight knots twisted in my stomach and a nervous laugh slipped out. I tilted my head back, trying to move away from his kisses. "This is not happening," I snarled, pushing away as hard as I could.

CHAPTER 29

AIDAN

"Answer my question," I said with a lethal note in my tone. I was on edge. Even with the door closed, I could smell her. That sweet scent slid through the crack under the door and wafted around me. Her inner-wolf was calling me, seeking me out, and begging me to claim her. I needed this to end. Now. Before I completely lost my mind.

And Beck wasn't making it any easier. It had been just over three hours now since I had him drag Marcy and Dominic in, more than enough time to make Jade believe that they were actually in deep shit. But for the last three hours, Beck had lounged in one of my leather chairs with his feet up, and eyes closed, making comments about what pack member we should stick Jade with when she lost.

"Yeah, he called," Beck said, keeping his eyes closed. "Talked to him last night while Jared was playing with your newbie." He cracked one eye open and smirked at me.

"Beck," I growled a clear warning. I leaned forward, placing my palms on the oak desk. Dominic gripped my shoulder before I could stand up, holding me in my chair. The enforcers had their own set of rules they played by. It was supposed to keep some balance in the pack and gave them the authority to deal with alphas that didn't follow the rules or punish those who needed it. And Beck seemed to be intent on reminding me at every turn.

He chuckled softly. "Easy alpha, I'm not your enemy." He clasped his hands, lacing his fingers together, and stretched his arms over his head. "If she doesn't win, Jared would be a good match for her. He'll tame her. Or we could always do what we do best. Jade's broken more than a few rules."

I growled. It ripped out of me before I could stop it, and Beck laughed. He was toying with me. He had been since he came into the room, seeing how far he could push me before I snapped. I knew they had no plans to take Jade down for the rules she'd broken. While she was in the games, she had a free pass for most of them.

Beck was about my height and build, maybe slightly bulkier, but not by much. And he carried himself just like the enforcers from my father's pack. They all had the same air about them. Confident. Cocky. They knew they could get away with pretty much anything. Without them to carry out and enforce the rules, most packs would crumble. They didn't just keep the wolves in check, but they kept alphas from abusing their power.

"Beck cut the shit," Dominic snapped. He gave my shoulder another squeeze before letting go. "What did Jeff say?"

Beck chuckled, and I let my alpha scent trickle into the air. Enforcer or not, he still had to obey me to some extent, and right then, I was out of patience. As soon as I did, his eyes hardened, and he fixed a burning glare on me. "Bruce is sending him out on a recruiting mission," he said through gritted teeth. "There was an *accident*, and they lost the last of their females. He says Bruce doesn't know about you, and the cougars Trevor ran across were a fluke."

"What kind of accident?" Marcy asked. She'd been sleeping, curled up on the leather couch for the past hour. I wished she had stayed asleep. She yawned loudly and then propped her head up with her elbow, looking at Beck groggily.

"You know what they're used for," Beck said coolly before I had a chance to come up with a lie. "Do you really need to ask how they died?"

Marcy jolted upright, and her hands flew to her mouth. She gasped. "Oh my God." Her eyes widened, and she started to shake.

Dominic squeezed my shoulder again, most likely trying to warn me not to flip out, and then he went to Marcy, pulling her into a tight hug. Heat rushed up to my neck, and my muscles tensed as she started to sob into Dominic's sweater.

"Were you planning on telling me?" I growled, settling my glare back on the enforcer.

He raised an eyebrow and shrugged. "Just did."

"How many?" I demanded. My imprint started to heat up, and my scent rolled off me like a tidal wave. I gripped the armrests of the chair, feeling the plastic snap within my hands. If Beck wanted to push me, I'd push back.

He winced, and he let out a mix between a growl and whimper before he said with a slight tremble in his voice, "Two. Jeff is trying to stall things so you can claim your mate. He says that's why he took the mission to bring in the women they want. With them dead, we've got time."

"Beck, you're a heartless bastard," Marcy shrieked. Her face was tear-stained, and her shoulders were shaking. She pushed out of Dominic's arms and stomped over to him, balled her tiny fist, and swung at him.

Beck caught her fist easily, closing his hand around it, and his eyes flared. "Maybe, but it is my job to kill people." He squeezed her hand, and Marcy yelped and tried to tug out of his grip. "You've been claimed," he said to Marcy, letting his voice drop to a growl. "You're part of this pack now. Learn the rules. I'm not going to warn you again."

"Let her go, Beck," I said and scrubbed at my face in an attempt to cover up my simmering rage. Things just weren't adding up. No one seemed to know why Ray would have made a deal with the cougars. Something was missing; I was sure of it, and I just couldn't figure out what it was. What could Bruce offer that Ray wanted?

Beck cut me a look and let Marcy go. She jumped back from him a few steps as he dropped his feet from the table. A yellow ring glowed around his blue eyes, and his jaw twitched with tension. He growled, letting his inner-wolf come out in his voice. He flexed his hands, balling and un-balling them, as he glared at me with a silent challenge. "Tone the scent down, alpha," he said. "The enforcers are behind you now, but that can change."

I laughed, a cruel kind of laugh that didn't sound right coming from me. I pushed my chair back, and as I did, Dominic skirted around my desk and leaned on it, blocking my view of Beck. "Has your team picked up anything?" he asked with an edge. He shot me a quick pleading look, and I reluctantly pulled the scent back ... a little.

"Not yet, but we will," Beck said tightly, and I smiled, more than a little glad that I was affecting him so much. "And now that we don't have to worry about the humans, we can clean them out when we find them."

A sick feeling rushed over me as I listened to the enforcer. I didn't want to admit it, but he had a point, and I actually agreed with him. Without any humans left to worry about, we had time to track them down. We could watch them. Figure out their weaknesses. It would give us more of an edge against them. And with Jeff stalling and feeding us information, we could hit them and clear them out in one shot. I hated to admit it, but overall, the deaths would make everything ... easier.

The tension slowly started to break and fizzled away as I pulled back the last of my scent. Dominic's rigid shoulders sagged, and he let out a loud puff of a breath. "I think we've freaked her out enough," he said, turning back to me.

"Yeah, probably," I agreed. "You sure you guys want to do this?"

Marcy was all splotchy, but her tears had dried up, and she gave me what I thought was supposed to be a reassuring smile. "Jade will forgive us later. She always does. Besides, Jade is an act first ask second kind of person. If she thinks she's losing you, she'll finish this off."

"You're really going to tell her you're taking Tiff as your mate?" Beck asked, leaning back in his chair, the smug and cocky smile back on his face.

"Yep, that's the plan," I said, pulling myself up to my feet. My legs felt like they were tied down as I made my way over to the door. I still wasn't sure that Dominic and Marcy were right about this little idea, but everything I tried had failed epically, and I was out of options. I just hoped Jade didn't try to kill me after telling her.

"You've got guts," Beck said and chuckled. "That girl has bite to her."

I glared at Beck hard. His commentary was not helping, and he damn well knew it. He grinned and got up, joining me at the door. I took a deep, steadying breath and then stoned my expression, forging cold remoteness into my body, and I pulled the door open.

As soon as I opened it, I froze. Jared had Jade on his lap, his face buried in her neck. And Jade … Jade was giggling. Her hands were on his bare chest, and her head was tilting to the side as if she were trying to give him better access.

My inner-wolf went wild, clawing at my stomach and tearing at my heart. Raw heat pulsed through me, and my chest started to hurt. A cold sweat broke out on my back, and the plan to tell her that I was picking someone else vanished from my mind. "Jared," I growled. "She's off-limits. This is one rule you can't break."

Jared chuckled and looked up. His golden eyes met mine, burning with a silent challenge. "I think she's ready to give up, alpha," he said. He took his time untangling himself from Jade, stood up slowly, and pulled her to him. "She's free game."

Jade looked at me a little desperately as she tried to wiggle out of Jared's arms. Jared leaned into her, whispering something so softly in her ear that I couldn't make it out, and she stopped moving. She held my eyes, and as Jared spoke, something passed across her face. It was cold and hateful and vile, and her scent pulsed into the air. Jared smirked and let his arms drop from her waist, but Jade didn't move. She kept her back pressed firmly against his chest, and his smirk turned into a wide grin.

I started toward her, slowly, carefully, wishing I knew what was going through her mind. She'd looked at me with hatred before, but it was nothing like this. I was halfway across the waiting room, only about fifteen steps from her, when she snarled, "You had me competing for you. When did you plan on telling me?"

"Jade ..." I said, and dammit, but my voice cracked on her name. The hatred in her eyes ... it was just too much. My heart crumbled like a piece of dried bread.

"Did you think I wouldn't find out? That I'd just ... just ... become an alpha, be your mate ..." She was visibly shaking, and her skin flushed cherry red. Her scent burst from her wildly, hitting me with a deadly force, and I stopped instantly, unable to move. My throat closed up as if someone cinched a rope around it and started to choke me.

"Jade," Marcy snapped, stepping toward her.

Jade's eyes flared, and a shudder rushed over her skin. "Shut up, Mac," she growled, and her canines sharpened. "Let me guess. You weren't really in jail with Dom. You two have known all along."

"Jade," Dominic said, with the stern tone he always used with her, and he groaned long and loud. "You're overreacting."

"I think I hate you guys," she said. There was so much heartbreak in her voice. Her invasive scent receded, and I sucked in a breath. She looked at me then; her golden eyes shimmered with what I was sure were tears. "How many more things are there, Aidan? What else have you lied to me about?"

I took a step toward her. I wanted to pull her into my arms and comfort her as she cried. She was breaking; I could see it in her shivers as her inner-wolf tried to take over and in the small tears that slid down her cheeks. I wanted to tell her it was all going to be okay. I wanted to hold her and tell her how sorry I was, but as I moved toward her, she put her hands up and leaned further into Jared.

He grinned over her head and snaked an arm around her waist possessively, and she let him. She didn't wiggle or try to move out of his arm. She sagged against him a little as if she were taking comfort in his presence. My inner-wolf stirred restlessly, and my scent ramped up.

Now was my chance to tell her everything. I knew that. I could tell her about her father. About the cougars. About the humans that died. But the only thing that came out of my mouth was, "I graduated high school last year."

Jade stiffened, and another shudder rushed over her skin. She clenched her fists and sucked in a few noisy breaths. She met me straight on, her expression an emotionless mask, and said, "I won't fight for you, alpha." She grabbed Jared's wrist, pulling his arm from her waist, and she started for the door.

Jared chuckled and went after her, slinging an arm over her shoulder. She shrugged it off and turned into him, "Jared, I need space," she said, putting a hand on his chest.

"Sure thing, little girl," he said and leaned into her, brushing a light kiss on her lips, and dammit, but she let him. She even smiled at him a little before she dropped her hand and walked out the door.

I lost her. I really lost her. I deserved it. I knew that, but it didn't make it hurt any less.

"Looks like the games are over," Jared said, snapping me back to the room as the door slammed behind Jade. He folded his arms over his chest and leaned against the wall. I crossed the room, feeling oddly calm, and when I was directly in front of him, I pulled my arm back and punched him. His nose crunched and snapped under my fist. Too bad it didn't make my shredded heart feel any less broken.

CHAPTER 30

JADE

I ran through the woods. I couldn't stop. I didn't want to stop. My heart was pounding in my ears, and my breath was coming fast and ragged. Branches whipped at my face, and the underbrush ripped at my ankles, but I didn't care.

The trees around me were covered in fall. Oranges and reds, deep and rich. Leaves scattered the ground and crunched under my feet. The fall leaves used to be soothing, but right then, the fiery colors only added to my rage. Betrayal hurt more than I had thought it would. It was like an icy pick jabbing and twisting into my heart. I'd watched Dominic turn his back on me before, and Marcy, well, Marcy pulled crap like this all the time, but this ... this was too much. They were playing with my life. I could have been killed. Erika could have ...

All of this for a stupid crush, I thought bitterly. I should have listened to Dominic from the start. I should have stayed away. Found someone else. But I walked willingly right into Aidan's game. I had never felt as utterly stupid as I did right then.

I felt stripped to the core. And vulnerable. And

225

stupid. Really, really stupid. Each step I took, my inner-wolf fought me. It wanted Aidan. It wanted the power. It wanted its mate. Aidan felt like ... home. But that home was gone. Ruined with lies and deceit. It just sucked that my inner-wolf didn't care about that. She wanted out. The bursts of raw adrenaline were only seconds apart now, but I fought against it. I knew with every part of me that if I shifted, I'd end up right back at his feet.

My stomach rolled, and I swallowed the bile. I felt dirty. I shouldn't have let Jared touch me. I shouldn't have let him kiss me, but when he had, all I could think about was hurting Aidan as much as he'd hurt me. How could he endorse women fighting over him? It was sick ... twisted ... *What did you expect from an alpha?* My heart twisted and split down the center. He was no different from the rest of the pack, using and manipulating people to get what he wanted.

My legs burned, and my skin was numb from the beating of the tree branches as I ran. I didn't want to stop, terrified that if I did, I'd run back to him. What was wrong with me? Even with the cold truth, a part of me still wanted him. *He's your perfect mate,* a voice in my head whispered.

Suddenly someone grabbed my arm and yanked me to a stop. I spun and snarled viciously. My skin felt like it was on fire, and my blood was boiling. "Back off, Erika," I snapped in a voice that did not sound like my own. It was like gravel, rough and jagged and sharp.

She jumped back, dropping her hand from my arm, and averted her eyes from mine. "I tried to see you last night," she said softly. "The enforcers wouldn't let me in. I've been worried about you." She looked at me then and smiled a little. "I heard what happened with Aidan."

"Leave me alone," I growled and turned my back on

her. I needed to keep moving, keep fighting my inner-wolf from breaking free.

"Tiff's been searching for you," she said as I started walking away. "She wants to end this. You need to get ready."

Another shudder rushed over my skin, and my ankle buckled and snapped. I sucked in a breath and waited, willing my body to relax and stay human. "Let her have that lying piece of crap," I said, gritting my teeth against the rush of power and adrenaline as my ankle began to piece back together. She grabbed me again, spinning me around to face her. "Erika, back the hell off!"

Her fear was thick in the air, tangy mixed with salty sweat. It was so thick that I could taste it. "She's made a deal with your dad, Jade. I'm the first female she's going to send to the cougars." She was shaking, her hand trembled against my wrist, but she squeezed harder.

I forced myself to relax. She was terrified, and the urge to hug her and tell her everything would be fine was overwhelming. My inner-wolf calmed slightly, and I asked, "What cougars? What are you talking about?"

"Jade, please," she begged. She dropped to her knees before me, grabbing at my jeans. "They'll kill me. Your dad ... he's ..." A gasping sob fell from her, and she jammed her hand into her pocket. "Here, just watch this." Erika pulled her iPhone out of her pocket and tapped the screen, bringing up a video.

"So we have a deal then?" my dad's voice crackled through the speaker, and my heart stopped. The image was fuzzy and dark, but I knew the voice well, even if I couldn't make out the face.

"Yeah, I'll send you some females, but why wolves?" a female asked, that I assumed was Tiffany. The image zoomed in a little, and her carrot hair came into focus, confirming my assumption. She was the only person I knew with hair like that.

"They'll heal faster," Dad said, his voice cold and impossibly cruel. "These humans break too easily, and my boys like some fight in their women."

"And your daughter?"

There was silence for a second, and then my dad laughed. "She's Aidan's weakness. The boy is lovesick. Give her to one of the enforcers. We'll use her when we're ready, but someone might as well have a little fun with her in the meantime."

The video stopped, and the play icon appeared in the center of the screen. My body temperature dropped to ice cold. I snatched the phone from Erika and played it again. I couldn't believe it. I didn't want to understand what was being said. I'd never seen anything like this in my father before. He sounded twisted, cruel, wrong. *They heal faster. My boys like some fight. Give her to one of the enforcers.*

My inner-wolf stirred again, restlessly. My chest felt tight, and the adrenaline rush hit me again. "Did you show this to Aidan?" I asked harshly, trying to hide how much I was hurting. My father, Aidan, Marcy, Dominic ... I couldn't handle much more. How many more people were going to betray me? "Shouldn't you bring this up to the enforcers or to him?" I glared down at her, trying to stay strong. I never thought for a second Erika, of all people, would come to me before her pack. She hated me, attacked me, and changed me into a monster only days ago. She'd done everything she could since she had become a werewolf to make my life hell. *She's treating you like an alpha,* Dominic's voice clouded my brain.

"Challenging females don't have to follow pack rules," Erika said. "As long as they don't kill an opponent after they've submitted ..." she let her voice trail off for a second, and a flash of guilt passed across her face, but she shook it off fast. "Once the alpha female steps up, Aidan has no control of what happens to the rest of us. Alpha female rules the females, alpha male handles the males. The enforcers could do something, but they scare the hell out of me. I tried to show Jared, but he was all 'get out of my face, and he wouldn't listen. And Aidan hates me because I'm following you." Her voice was getting higher and higher as she spoke. She was desperate. I could see it in her eyes, and it scared me to death. "Jade, you can't let her win. This pack is screwed up enough. I need you. We all need you. We need a strong alpha pair. You'll stand up to him. I know you can stop this."

My brain was spinning, and my stomach rolled. I paced a few steps away from Erika. What the hell was I supposed to do? Mate with Aidan and try to fix this screwed-up pack? Walk away and keep the little bit of self-decency I had left? I didn't want to do either. *I should have just stayed away from the pack!* Did I want the responsibility of the females? Could I handle it? Could I actually walk away knowing what would happen to them and leave them in the clutches of Tiffany? If I walked away now, I could leave town and never see that lying jackass again, and that idea wreaked havoc on me. I couldn't imagine not having Aidan around, even if I did want to kill him at that very moment. But if I took alpha female, it's as if I've condoned what he's done.

An idea began to form, slow and a little sketchy, but it was something. Something that I thought I could live with ... maybe. I turned back to Erika. "I've got an idea. Do you have Jared's number?"

CHAPTER 31

AIDAN

My office felt empty. It wasn't, but it felt it. The average-sized, beige room felt huge and dull and vacant. Jared sat on the edge of my oak desk with a smug grin, and Beck stood nearby fighting back a laugh. They were playing with her, I was sure of it, just as they were toying with me, and they were enjoying every second of it. What I didn't get was why? Why did the enforcers give a shit about Jade? And what were they getting out of ripping us apart? I couldn't bring myself to believe that Jared actually wanted her or that she was attracted to him. I knew it was possible; I'd seen them all over each other, but the thought of her with him, or anyone else, made me feel sick.

Jade had been gone for twenty-eight minutes and forty-two seconds. Each minute that passed by and she didn't walk back through the door, my heart died a little more. I thought about all the lies, about the way I manipulated her and used her, and I figured I deserved the gut-wrenching pain that spread through me with every beat of my heart.

"Aidan, it's going to be okay," Marcy said. Except she didn't sound too sure about it. "She'll be back once she calms down." She offered up a shaky-looking smile as she pulled her knees to her chest and rocked slowly, back and forth, on the couch.

"Mac's right. Jade always comes back," Dominic said. It sounded like he was trying to convince himself just as much as he was trying to convince me. He paced the room restlessly, glancing at the door every few seconds. I didn't need to ask what he was thinking; I was sure it was the same thoughts going through my head. There was no way to cover up that she stepped down. Too many people had heard her say it. The games were ... over.

"I can track her if you want," Beck offered. I glared at him and gritted my teeth. He was enjoying this. Enjoying every second of watching me crumble as I lost the only thing that mattered, the only person that brought an ounce of good into this screwed-up pack.

"No," Dominic and Marcy shouted in unison before I answered, which was probably a good thing because I wanted to say yes.

"Dude, don't drag her back before she's ready," Marcy said frantically. "If you force her to fight now, she'll never forgive you." She flushed and cut Jared a dirty look. "Dammit, Jared! What were you thinking?"

Jared shrugged his shoulders in a bad attempt to look innocent. "Figured she knew what was going on. She did take down three of them."

"You damn well know she didn't," Marcy snapped.

"Enough!" I yelled, glaring at Marcy. I knew she was only trying to help, but I couldn't take the constant bickering anymore. She started to cry and hugged her legs tighter to her chest. "Mac, you should go," I said and scrubbed at my face roughly. "Trevor's probably waiting for you, and Jade already stepped down. Doesn't matter anymore. Tiffany won."

"Aidan, she's going to come back," she said, her voice hitched on her tears. "I promise."

I tried to smile at her, but I was sure it fell flat. The reality was it didn't matter if she came back or not. I couldn't restart the games. I didn't have a choice. Tiffany had won by default when Jade walked away. My fate had been sealed the second she said she wouldn't fight.

A phone rang, breaking the silence, and Jared groped in his pocket, digging out his phone. He looked at the screen and chuckled before tapping it and bringing the phone to his ear. "Miss me already, little girl?" Jared said and smirked at me. "Your house or mine?" he asked and then paused. "Be right there, kitten." He chuckled softly, "Get used to it, Jade." He hung up and slid his phone back into his pocket. Looking at Beck, he said, "See you in a bit," and then he pushed off my desk.

"You're not going anywhere," I growled, pushing my chair back and standing up. My hands were shaking with rage, and I pushed them down on the desk to keep them steady. I couldn't believe she had called him. She wasn't wasting any time replacing me. Not that I was really hers to start with, but right then, whether I had been hers or not didn't matter. Jared chuckled, obviously enjoying my reaction, and white-hot fury flooded over me.

"Enforcer business," he replied coolly and padded over to the door, pulling it open.

"Screwing my mate isn't enforcer business," I snarled. I shouldn't have said it, and I really didn't mean to, but it just came out. As far as my inner-wolf was concerned, Jade was mine. She always would be, and the lust-filled scent that Jared gave off right then sent the beast inside me over the edge.

"Jade's not your mate, alpha. Tiff is. Beck, track

down Tiffany and bring her in," he said, keeping his eyes on me. There was a warning in his voice, and his muscles visibly coiled, as if he were just waiting for me to step over the line and break a rule.

Beck chuckled. "Sure thing, boss," he said, and right then, I felt as if I were dead.

CHAPTER 32

JADE

I waited impatiently as Jared made the call. He had been waiting for us on my porch when Erika and I had emerged from the forest. For the last hour, I'd sat in my bedroom and listened as they filled me in on everything they knew about the cougars and the alpha female games. The gist was that the cougars were sick bastards and had been tormenting the town for more than a hundred years. Jared said that the wolves started to fight back about forty years ago, which was when the pack decided not to hide their presence in Dog Mountain.

As for the alpha female games, well, it all sounded stupid. I found it hard to believe that all these girls would fight for a guy just to become the alpha female. Erika said it had nothing to do with the guy. She claimed that love didn't matter. Alphas were paired together because of dominance, leadership, and strength. She said that she didn't even really like Aidan, and she had been fighting for the pack, not for him. I hated to admit it, but I thought she was crazy. How could she not like Aidan? And why did I still want him?

When Jared walked out of my bedroom to make the call, I told Erika about the scent. I told her what Jared had done to me and what Aidan did. I was hoping for some kind of explanation from her, anything to make my cravings for the two men make an ounce of sense, but all she said was that my inner-wolf had an alpha in its scent. When dominant wolves of the opposite sex meet, it causes a different reaction. She figured my inner-wolf was recognizing them as potential mates. She explained that for most of them, the scent was crippling, basically telling me things I'd already (somewhat) figured out and not really helping with the things I hadn't.

Needless to say, the last hour had been ... tense. I had a few meltdowns, learned more about the pack than my brain could really absorb, and overall, came up with a plan that would probably get me killed. The whole time I tried to tell myself that this near-suicidal idea had nothing to do with Aidan. It was for the pack. That was it. But my heart (and my inner-wolf) wouldn't believe me.

Jared rubbed his sandpaper-looking jaw as he strode back into my bedroom, his cell phone still in hand. "It's done. Tiffany has just accepted the position."

"And even without the games, I can still challenge her, right?" I asked. I was more than a little glad that my voice was strong and not showing the nerves that were jumping around as if I had a circus of juggling acrobats in my belly.

He considered it for a moment and then nodded. "Yep, at any point, an alpha can be challenged. It's just harder to beat them once they're branded, which, by the way, is happening to Tiff right now."

I threw my hands up in the air, frustrated, annoyed, and more than a little confused. "What the hell is the point of the games if she can be challenged at any time?"

"It's entertaining," Jared offered dryly. I could have smacked him. Entertaining? Really? I'd been put through hell for the last few days to entertain them? He started to chuckle as he padded across the room and sat beside me on my bed. "I'm just kidding. The games happen when more than one female wants to be alpha." He ran his hand up my leg and winked at me.

"Cut the crap, Jared," I said, slapping his hand away from my knee. "Will the plan work?"

"Don't know. Never heard of a female winning and then not taking the alpha male as her mate." He leaned back on my bed, propping himself up with his elbows. He hadn't bothered to put on a shirt before he came over, and his abs flexed and rippled as he got comfortable.

"But is there a rule against it?" I asked, forcing myself to look away from him. He may be a complete dick, but he was hot, and the last thing I needed was more temptation. His scent was more than enough to drive my inner-wolf crazy, and the visual seriously wasn't helping.

"Number three?" Erika asked meekly from the other side of the room.

"She can't screw him over if she doesn't claim her rights to him," Jared snapped, glaring at her, and she pressed herself further into the corner, hiding behind my dresser.

"Stop freaking her out," I hissed, giving him a dirty look. "If I win today, she's going to be my beta, so be nice."

He rolled his eyes and rubbed his jaw as he looked me over. "I really don't know about you joining my team, little girl. No offense, but you don't have what it takes."

I stood up, spun around, and put my hands on my hips, glaring down at him. "No offense? Really, that was an offense. I'm seriously offended. Did you miss me taking down three challengers, one of which when I was still human?" *And hadn't he just told me that I'd be good at it?*

It felt weird admitting it out loud and even weirder knowing what I had done. But I'd be lying if I said it wasn't all a little amazing, though. I'd beaten three werewolves that I hadn't even known why I was fighting in the first place. And right then, as I glared down at the enforcer, who only a few hours ago had me sweating with fear, I was pretty sure it was going to my head — a little.

Jared didn't move. He stayed on my bed and grinned at me. "The enforcers go up against alphas, too, not just pack members."

"Tiff is the alpha right now," I scoffed, "and I'm going up against her."

"You're too soft, Jade," he said with a chuckle. "You care too much." He glanced over at Erika then, and I had a pretty good idea what he was talking about. Maybe I was too soft. Erika had put me through hell and back, but even with that, I hadn't been able to walk away when she needed help. Did that make me soft or just a good person? I wasn't entirely sure. I didn't really feel like a good person right then. Not while I planned to attack someone and fight until only one of us was left alive.

I narrowed my eyes. I wasn't going to back down on this. As far as I was concerned, the enforcers needed just as much work as the rest of the pack. They were all screwed up, and I figured the best way to try to fix them was by becoming one of them. Well, that, and if I actually won, working with them would give me a distraction, and I was pretty sure it was a distraction I'd need if I wanted any chance at staying away from the alpha male. "If I win, you take me on your team and train me."

"If you lose and survive it, I'm taking you as my mate," he countered. "You will not compete in the next round of games after we take her out."

I didn't think about it because I knew if I did, I'd back out of the deal. I nodded, a stiff bob of my head, and said, "Fine," as quickly as I could.

"Jade, don't make a deal with him," Erika said, still cowering in her little corner by my dresser. "Rule number four: You can't screw over an enforcer. You won't be able to back out of this."

"Rule number one: Always obey your alpha. When I win, he won't be able to back out either." I shrugged and cut her a straight-faced look. "It's a fair deal."

"But he can just deal with this himself," she said, her voice rising and pitching. "We have proof. The enforcers can handle it. You don't have to challenge Tiff."

"Erika, stop," I said, forging calm into my tone. "If I don't, then it leaves the door open for the games to start again." I sighed and shook out my trembling hands. "I want this to end."

CHAPTER 33

AIDAN

Tiffany screamed when she received her imprint, and I had to hold her in place while the metal seared her skin. If she moved too soon, it would just heal, and we'd have to do it again. It was painful to watch and even more painful to listen to. I thought what made it hurt the most was that the girl screaming in my arms wasn't Jade. But then, I couldn't really see Jade screaming. She'd have put on a brave face and hid the pain, just as I had when it was done to me.

I reminded myself that it had nothing to do with love as Tiffany sobbed against my chest. I held her loosely, like I was supposed to, and rubbed her back gently. It was better this way. Love was an unneeded distraction. Jade would be better off, and so would I, definitely, maybe.

It had been ten minutes since the branding was done, and she still sobbed against me. I didn't feel the need, nor did I want to comfort the girl. I knew she had already healed, and there was no pain, and knowing that made it all so much harder to stand still and hold her. I did it solely out of duty. To keep up the appearance of us united. *Detachment is better,* I thought and rubbed another circle on her back. This was what I needed to take back the pack. A partner, not a lover, not someone I would worry about every second. At least, that's what I tried to convince myself.

Marcy pulled Tiffany's dress back up over her shoulders. "Come on, sweetie, let's get you cleaned up," she said, taking Tiffany's hand and pulling her off my chest. It should have sounded sweet and comforting. Marcy always did, but right then, she sounded hollow. She sounded how I felt.

"Don't think I've ever seen an alpha cry before," Jared said, strolling into my office. "What did you do to her?" He took up a post beside Beck, leaning against the wall, and folded his arms over his chest.

"She took her imprint," I said and dropped down onto the couch. I hadn't expected Jared back, not this soon, and I was more than a little stunned that I didn't really care that he was. It was done. I lost her. I had a mate now. And even though I wanted to tear him apart, I figured there wasn't much point, and it would take a lot of energy that I just didn't have.

"You should have heard her scream," Beck said with a snicker. "Where've you been?"

"Jade's," he said, watching me closely as if he were expecting some kind of reaction. When I didn't give it, he said, "Sorry I missed it all."

I looked him over, taking in breath after breath, looking for any difference in his scent. I didn't find any, and I didn't know whether to be happy about that or not. He hadn't claimed Jade ... yet. I sighed. "I'm not giving her to you, Jared," I said, after a moment, keeping my voice even. "I'm not going to force her to mate."

"My little kitten doesn't need to be forced," he said and winked suggestively. "She'll come to me willingly soon enough." He looked toward the door and called, "Jade, anytime now."

My stomach dropped at the sound of her name. I should have figured he'd drag her back here just to rub it in my face, but honestly, I had never thought he could be that cruel. Clearly, I was wrong.

Jade stormed into the room and growled, "Shut it, Jared." She swiveled around, looking everyone over, and then snarled, "Where is she?"

She looked wired. Her brown eyes were rimmed with gold, and her fists were clenching and unclenching rapidly. She was fighting her inner-wolf; its scent was thick in the air, and by the looks of her, if she relaxed at all, she'd shift instantly. I'd never seen a newbie with so much restraint before. But then, I'd never seen one as strong as she was either.

"Jade, tread carefully," I warned, looking her straight on. What the hell was she doing? I could have strangled Jared right then. How could he have let her walk in here like this? Didn't any of them give a shit about what happened to her?

"Tiffany broke pack rule number five," she said, marching up to me. Her skin was twitching, and dark hair had already started to litter her cheekbones. She put her hands on her hips and stared down at me, scrunching her nose.

I sighed. Why did she have to be so damn cute when she was mad? "Jade, stop. She's your Alpha now."

"Are you even listening to me!" she yelled and stomped her foot. "She's not my Alpha. She's turned her back on this pack."

"Jade!" I stood up and stepped closer to her. I was vibrating with anger. Wasn't it enough that she walked away? Even if it was completely my fault, she ripped out my heart without a second thought, and now she was on a one-way path to getting herself killed.

"Dominic," I barked. "Take her and teach her the rules before she gets herself killed."

Right then, I hated myself even more. I should have forced her to submit. I should have taken control. Jared and Beck were watching her closely as if they were just waiting for her to do something stupid now that her free pass was over, and I couldn't do anything to help her. It was hard enough standing here, seeing her in so much pain, and not being able to pull her into my arms. *Dammit! What was she thinking, throwing out random accusations about an alpha?*

"Let her speak, Aidan," Beck said. He pushed off the wall and strode over to her, a glimmer of curiosity shining in his eyes. "Do you have proof?" he asked when he was standing in front of her.

"Erika, show them the video," she said, with more gentleness than I expected her to have with the girl that changed her life.

CHAPTER 34

Aidan watched the video. Twice. And as he did, I started to lose control. Jared tried to help. He rubbed my back each time a bone snapped and whispered random nonsense into my ear as if he were trying to talk over my father's betrayal, but it didn't help. My inner-wolf had been trying to break out for hours now, and I didn't know how much longer I could hold her in.

"I want to challenge her," I said, pacing back and forth before they could watch the clip again. "Where the hell is she?" My voice didn't sound like my own anymore. Each word that I said was slurred and growled. But if Aidan noticed, he didn't care, or if he did, he hid it well.

"Jade, you don't need to," Aidan said coolly. "She'll be killed for this." He looked at me with cold detachment, and I hated how much it hurt. I wasn't supposed to care about him. He was a lying jackass. I was the one who walked away. But I just couldn't help it. Everything about him made my body sing.

"Not good enough," I snarled, using the pain he'd

caused me to fuel my determination. "The games aren't starting again. I want to end this."

Aidan cocked his head and looked me over, and as he did, I knew I had picked the wrong words. He started to smile, a soft smile, and for a split second, his desire burned brightly in his eyes. I was about to take it back and try to rephrase it when Tiffany's nasally voice pierced my ears. "I won't submit to you."

I pivoted, following the earsplitting sound. She stood in the doorway, grinning at me. Her carrot-colored hair was pulled back in a ponytail, and her light blue dress was dotted with what looked like dried blood on the right side of her chest. She was shorter than me by a few inches and thinner, too. Instead of my soft muscles, she was skin and bone.

I grinned as I took in my opponent. "Yeah, you will, or I'll kill you. You pick," I said. I stripped out of my clothes quickly as the first snaps of my bones rang out around me. I let my body remold in a rush of steamy heat, and my fur sprouted from my skin. Shifting felt like a high, a fast-acting drug, one that I would never get enough of. Energy pulsed through me, hot and cold and blissful.

I growled, and my lips curled back over my gums as I stalked toward her. She had her eyes closed, and her nose was scrunched. The outline of her mark flickered to life with that soft white glow that I had seen on Aidan's chest. Her bones started to break, and her dress fell to the floor.

Tiffany's wolf was a deep brown with scattered flecks of white. She backed out of the office, growling, and I followed her into the gleaming white waiting room. My claws clicked against the tiles, echoing around me.

I didn't wait. I didn't want to give her a chance to make the first move. As soon as I was through the doorway, I lunged at her, and my teeth found purchase in her hip before she could fully jump out of my way. I held on tightly, throwing my head back and forth until a chunk of her flesh gave way.

Maybe I should have waited. She spun on me as soon as she was free, and I felt her teeth tear into my side and then into my shoulder. She danced back, snarling, and then came at me again, biting into my hip. Her movements were fast, and her bites were clean and effective. In seconds, a sharp pain shot from all over my body.

I twisted, biting out at her. She was fast, dodging out of the way before I could get my teeth into her. I snarled. The coppery scent of blood wafted around me, mixing with an overwhelming scent that was spicy and bitter and strong and near-crippling. I backed up a step, confused. I didn't know what it was or where it was coming from. It made my throat constrict and my knees shake.

She circled around me, growling and snarling, and I shook my head, trying to clear the pain that coursed through me. Between her bites and that scent, my body was screaming with agonizing, burning pain.

I focused on her, swiveling with her slow circles. Her chest was glowing, the white light pulsing through her fur, and I was certain the scent was coming from her alpha's imprint. Right then, I knew I needed to end this before it consumed me.

I crouched down and pushed off with my hind legs. Sharp, hot pain slid through my joints and muscles, and I collided with her side. We smashed breathtakingly hard into the tiles, snarling and rolling together in a jumbled ball. I bit her, tearing through her flesh over and over, as we tumbled across the waiting room, a trail of crimson laying the path behind us.

We hit the wall, and suddenly she was on top of me. Her razor-sharp canines flew at my neck, and I bucked under her, trying to throw her off. Blood sprayed across the floor as her teeth sank into the hollow side of my neck just above my shoulder, and she tore out a chunk of skin and fur. I kicked and clawed at her, tossing her off before her teeth could find me again and finish me off.

I scrambled to my feet. Blood dripped off me, pooling at my paws. I tried to growl, but it didn't sound right. My breath shortened, wheezing and gasping, and I trembled as I tried to keep my feet under me.

Tiffany stood in front of me, her scent thickening in the air and blood dripping down her muzzle and hindquarters. I felt my scent pulse from me in a warm, hazy burst, trying to mask hers. She staggered slightly to the side before letting out a menacing growl, and my body convulsed with a shiver.

"Jade!" Aidan yelled, and out of the corner of my eye, I saw him struggle to get to me. Jared and Beck held him by the arms, pulling him back.

I'm going to die, I realized, as my legs gave out from under me. I could barely breathe, and dizziness was consuming me, turning the world gray around the edges of my vision. I'd known it was a possibility, but I'd never really believed it would happen. I fell to the floor. I heard the thud, but I didn't feel it.

"Jade, don't give up!" Aidan shouted again. There was pain in his voice and desperation that I had never thought I'd hear in him, and it made my heart quicken in painfully fast beats.

Tiffany landed on top of me, snarling down at me. I tried to roll out from under her, but she pinned me, holding me on my back. Her lips curled back, and some of my own blood fell from her mouth, splattering on my face.

"Jade!" Aidan yelled desperately as Tiffany's muzzle came down at me with bared teeth. It was all happening so slowly. I could feel her breath ruffling my fur, see her teeth closing in on my neck, feel the cold of her wet nose as it got closer and closer.

Someone let out a guttural cry, and heat rushed through me. My scent ramped up, and my body burned, fever hot. I bucked again, rising up to meet her attack, and then my teeth were in her neck, and I ripped out her throat.

The limp body of the brown wolf fell against me, and a whimper burst out of me.

The silence was loud as I kicked the wolf off me and shifted back to my human form. I looked down at the wolf, hardly believing that the mangled body at my feet was dead because of me. My mouth tasted of blood, and it chilled me when I realized that I didn't mind the taste. Someone put a sweater over my shoulders, and I was vaguely aware of my arms being pulled into the sleeves and the zipper tugging up to my chin.

I looked around, following the sprays and splatter of blood that covered the walls and floor. My body hurt, and warm blood trickled down my neck, soaking into the sweater. My skin began to tingle as it slowly pieced back together, and I found myself wondering if I would have scars. I knew it was a stupid and irrational thought, and I almost laughed. Almost.

"I am yours now," Aidan whispered. He placed a hand under my chin, tilting my head and giving me a look that said, *Accept it and deal with it.* "And whether you meant to or not, you made yourself mine."

"I'm not a possession, you big jerk," I growled, still sounding more wolf than human.

He chuckled a deep velvety sound that made my knees go weak. "Actually, yeah, you are. You're my possession. Mine. To protect and love and have.

Mine." He grabbed me then, coiling his arm around my waist, and pulled me tightly against the length of his body.

"Get your hands off me, Aidan!" I shrieked, but I couldn't make myself move out of his arms. I breathed in his scent, and I felt the smile spread upon my lips.

He smirked down at me, and my heart pounded loudly in my ears. "Is that what you want? For me to let you go?" His voice was just a whisper, his warm breath brushing against my lips as he spoke.

I stared up at him, feeling some multicolored emotion of guilt and desire and self-loathing all rolled into one and tied with a neat little bow, keeping the confused emotions clustered together. "Yes," I murmured.

He didn't let go, and dammit, I was furious at myself for being glad about that. But then his lips crushed against mine, roughly, greedily, and it was intoxicating. And for that moment, I simply forgot that I wasn't supposed to want him anymore.

CHAPTER 35

JADE

They branded me. Freakin' branded me! After I had cleaned myself up, Dominic heated what looked like a cattle prod until the metal 'A' on the end glowed red, and he stuck me with it in the chest. It hurt like hell, and it took everything I had in me not to scream out. Half the pack was right outside the door dealing with the mess in the waiting room, and the last thing I wanted was for any of them to think I was weak. I was having a hard enough time hiding how wrecked I was over killing someone. I knew she had to die. I knew she would have died whether it was by my hand or one of the enforcers, but knowing it, and dealing with the fact that I had actually done it, was an entirely different story.

Jared stood in front of me, glaring at me for the entire five minutes it took for the imprint to stick without my skin completely healing the scar. Disappointed didn't even come close to describing the look he gave me, which made me feel sick. Was I really that weak? Maybe he was right when he had called me soft. It was clear that he sure thought I was. The first chance I got, I flew back into Aidan's arms like a lovesick fool.

When Dominic pulled the burning metal away, Aidan leaned in to kiss me, and I forced myself to move my head, letting his lips brush my cheek instead of his intended target. Aidan didn't seem to notice, and I was glad for it. I backed up a step, putting some distance between us, and said, "Tell me what you know about the cougars."

It was a long conversation. Aidan relayed every bit of information he had, which turned out to be not much more than what I had already known. The part I found most interesting was that no one had ever met Bruce. Dominic said that Ray had handled everything when it came to them, and Jared and the enforcers had never had a need to seek them out. For the most part, the cougars stayed away. And it was that piece of information that made me wonder if Bruce was even real. The way my dad had spoken in the video, it was as if the cougars were his.

I did a lot of pacing, mainly to keep myself away from Aidan. I was pretty sure that what I was planning to do would hurt me more than him. Even so, I knew I'd spend every minute I had regretting it if I let him think I was okay with everything that had happened between us.

I wondered how I didn't know that my father was a werecougar. The thought of living with the enemy my whole life made me feel sick. And then I spent some time thinking about how the enemy had changed. Only a week ago, I would have sworn that it was the pack, and now, everything in me wanted to protect them. They were mine. My wolves. My life.

When an idea hit me, I almost laughed. It was more from nerves than anything else, but I managed to hold it in as I divulged my thoughts to our little group. The idea was simple: let Dad think Tiffany won. We had all come to the same consensus. We needed to buy some time to track the cougars. We knew Dad wanted to use me, but we didn't have a clue for what. And I didn't really think he was actually out *recruiting.* Not when he thought Tiffany would send some wolves to him if she won.

Aidan and I took turns calling him. Although it wasn't that hard, I put on a big show of being heartbroken. My heart was, after all, completely shattered. And when Aidan called him, he even agreed to mate me with one of the enforcers. When it was all said and done, Dad promised to try and stall, giving Aidan a few days to settle in with his new mate, and Aidan swore he'd call as soon as he had a plan to deal with the pack of cougars.

Aidan leaned back in his chair, folding his arms across his chest. His forehead scrunched a little as he thought, and he scrubbed at his face. "Okay, we've bought ourselves a few days. You guys can go," he said, waving a dismissive hand. "Jade and I need to discuss this, and we'll call a meeting when we have a plan together."

Crap! That was the last thing I needed. One on one time with Aidan. I wasn't strong enough, not yet, not when every part of me wanted to pretend as if nothing had happened. "Wait," I said before anyone had a chance to leave. Everyone froze, and I glanced back at Aidan. "Aidan?" I said cautiously, stepping back from him, and I met him straight on, squaring my shoulders and stoning my face. I took a deep breath, and then another and another, trying to calm my nerves. It wasn't working. My inner-wolf fought me, and my heart started to crack again. My palms were sweating, and my stomach twisted into painfully tight knots.

"We need to find them before we can do anything else," I said in a rush.

Aidan watched me with confusion marring his gorgeous face. He arched a questioning brow, folded his arms over his chest, and leaned further back in his chair.

I shook out my trembling arms, and before I lost every bit of my nerve, I blurted, "Aidan, I'll be the alpha female of this pack, but I can't be your mate."

The silence was thick in the air. No one moved. No one breathed. I glanced back at Jared. I didn't mean to, and I was sure it would give everyone the wrong impression, especially him, but as I met his eyes, I was glad I had. He gave me an encouraging smile and nodded his silent approval, and I hated how much that approval steadied me. "And I'm going to join the enforcers," I said, looking back at Aidan, focusing on his chest, so I didn't have to see if I was hurting him or not. Either way, I knew I couldn't handle it. "I want to help find the bastards."

"Jade," Aidan said, uncertainty in his voice. He pushed back his chair and stood up, taking a few steps toward me. I stupidly looked up then and wished I hadn't. A swarm of emotions flew across his eyes, devastation being the most prominent. But he also looked ... scared ... no, more than scared ... terrified. "Jade, what are you doing?"

"You were right," I said, putting my hands up in a desperate plea for him not to come any closer. "I know nothing about you, and what I do know, I don't really like."

"Jade, have you lost your mind?" Dominic barked. He was furious. His fists clenched, and his neck tensed. He started toward me, red streaking his face and settling in his cheeks.

"Careful, beta," Jared said with a laugh. He grabbed

Dominic's shoulders, pulling him to a stop. "My little kitten has claws. You don't want to get too close."

I shot Jared a murderous look. *Kitten* was seriously worse than *little girl*. And really, this wasn't the time for his stupid pet names.

"Jade, please ..." Aidan whispered, ignoring them and bringing my attention back to him. I almost cracked. Walking away from him was by far the hardest thing I'd ever done. Everything in me wanted him ... needed him. My inner-wolf stirred in my stomach and tears bit at my eyelids. I quickly blinked them away, but by the broken look on Aidan's face, I didn't do it fast enough. The problem was I knew I couldn't live with letting him think that I was okay with all the bullshit he had put me through. I wasn't okay with it, and I really didn't know if I ever would be.

I turned away from him then. I had to. If I didn't, I knew I would have caved, but caving wasn't an option right then. "Beck, can you organize the team and start tracking them?" I asked. "I know Jared should be doing it, and I'm sorry to dump this on you, but I want him to take me home for appearances, just in case my mom's in on this. Maybe we can get someone watching her?"

Beck grinned and cut me a knowing kind of look, and the blood rushed from my cheeks. I hadn't meant to give any of them the impression that I wanted it to be Jared because I really didn't care which one of the enforcers it was. He just seemed like the most logical option, or at least that's what I tried to tell myself. In a rush, trying to cover it up, I said to Beck, "Or Jared could do it, and you could take me home."

Beck didn't get a chance to answer. "I'm taking you," Jared growled with a possessive edge.

I glanced back at Aidan then, hoping to see anything other than the pain I was causing. I did, but what was on his face now was far worse. His eyes were lined with gold, and his glare was fixed on Jared. Hot jealousy spiked through the air, suffocating and thick. His fingertips were clawed, and he ground his teeth so hard that I could hear the enamel grating together. God, I hated being able to smell their emotions. It was as if nothing was secret anymore. Could he smell my heartbreak just as I could his?

"I'll get the team together," Beck said, stepping in front of me. He gave me a warm smile that looked completely out of place on him and then wrapped me in a hug. "Welcome to the team." And then, for my ears only, he whispered, "You're doing great. I can barely smell your nerves or anything else coming off you."

I froze, stunned at what he'd said. He let me go and winked at me. I smiled a little, wondering if he had any idea how much his reassurance meant to me. Maybe the enforcers weren't as completely heartless as I thought. He chuckled then, and I groaned. "Beck, don't you dare get all mushy on me."

He elbowed me playfully and then turned to Aidan. "You have any issues with the order?"

"Go ahead," Aidan snapped through clenched teeth. Marcy jumped, and Erika grimaced. But Dominic ... Dominic just stared at me with fierce disappointment and clear disapproval. I knew he was just itching for everyone to leave so he could give me one of his lectures. And I realized something. I didn't want to hear it. I didn't care if I ever talked to him or Marcy again. This was the last time I was going to let the two of them play me to get what they thought was best for me. This time, they'd gone too far.

"As for you two," I said, pointing at Marcy and Dominic, "stay away. I don't want to see you guys for a while."

Marcy started to cry and garbled something that

sounded like an apology, but Dominic didn't show an ounce of emotion. He was a mask of cold indifference as he went to Marcy and looped his arm around her, dragging her out the door.

I started to follow. I needed to get out of there, away from Aidan, and I desperately wanted a nice hot shower. I didn't even get halfway across the office when Aidan asked, "Jade, can we talk? Alone?"

I gave him what I was sure was a sad smile and shook my head. "I can't do this right now, Aidan. With my dad and the cougars and everything ... I just can't. I've appointed Erika as my beta. She'll spread the word about what happened, or you can get Dom to do it. But please, work through her for now. I need some space."

He let his scent trickle out, just a soft brush, and I stood stiff, wishing he would stop. He must have noticed my effort not to throw myself at him because he smiled ... a little, and he pulled it back instantly. Jared took my hand, and Beck took the other, and I let them, thankful for the support, and as I left, I couldn't stop the tears from finally breaking through and trailing down my cheeks.

CHAPTER 36

AIDAN

I followed the scent of almonds and fruit punch and mouthwatering power around the large log house and into the backyard. The air was brisk, but I didn't mind it. It was refreshing and helped alleviate some of the nervous sweat that beaded along my forehead. I jammed my hands in my front pockets and kept my head down as I made my way across the grass to where she lay, staring up at the sky.

I hadn't seen Jade in two days. She needed space, and I'd been determined to give her that, but two days ... it felt more like a year. She wouldn't even accept my phone calls. Text messages were all I got, and they were only status updates on the progress of tracking the cougars.

I pulled in another deep breath, and my heart thudded wildly in my chest. I hadn't been sure what to expect, but I had figured her scent would have changed by now. From what Beck had relayed back to me, Jared had moved in, or maybe not officially moved in, but he hadn't gone home since she claimed alpha status. But her scent was the same, unclaimed and perfect.

I stopped a few feet away, watching her for a

moment. Her dark hair covered the grass like a fan around her head, and her chest rose and fell rapidly as she pulled in deep breaths. She knew I was there, she was breathing me in, and it killed me that she forced herself to pretend I wasn't.

You did this, and you deserve it. I knew it was true. I'd driven her away. I'd caused this, but it didn't change how much I still wanted her. She was my mate or should be. My perfect match in every way, and I'd ruined it.

Her muscles had toned up. The black yoga pants that clung to her hips and thighs revealed the firm skin underneath. She had the sleeves of her plum hoodie pushed up to her elbows, showing the tight and lean muscles of her forearms. She was breathtaking. The most beautiful creature I had ever laid eyes on.

The wind picked up, bringing her scent right to me, and my skin heated and tingled. I drank it in, savoring every breath. My inner-wolf scrambled in my stomach, begging me to move closer. It wanted her just as much as I did, and it was torture staying away. I pulled in another deep, calming breath and closed the last few feet between us, lying down beside her in the cool grass.

"That one looks like an ice-cream cone." I pointed up to the sky, letting my finger trail along the sharpened point of the cloudy cone and the rounded top.

"Go away," she said, tensing but not moving from her place beside me. I probably should have just gotten up and left her alone, but I decided to take her not moving as an invitation to stay.

"I used to spend hours watching the clouds," I said. "Always found it calming." I pointed up to a thick gray cloud that looked like a ball of dirty fluff more than anything and said, "Cheeseburger."

She sighed a deep-bellied sigh. "What do you want, Aidan?" She sounded ... tired. But I figured she probably was. From her short text messages, I knew she'd been training with Jared a lot, learning how to fight and use her scent as an advantage.

"That one's spaghetti and meatballs. And that one there, it looks like a loaf of bread," I said, ignoring her question, not because I didn't want to answer, but because I didn't know how to.

"They all look like food?" she asked with a laugh. It was a musical sound, and it made my heart leap and my inner-wolf stir in my chest. My breath caught, and I swallowed hard.

"It's subliminal messaging," I said. My voice hitched, and I cleared my throat. "I figure if they all look like food, you'll get hungry and won't be able to say no when I ask you to come with me for dinner."

She was quiet for a long moment, and I tilted my head to look at her. Her typically soft features were tense, her jaw tight and clenched. "Not happening," she finally said.

I'd expected the rejection, but even knowing it would happen, it didn't hurt any less. "Is Jared really living here?" I asked.

"Yeah," she said, her voice was a bit airy as she let her pent-up breath out with the word.

I rolled onto my side, resting upon my elbow, and I traced the twitching line of her jaw. She glanced at me, her eyes shimmering with tears, and she leaned into my hand. "You deserve better than him, Jade."

"Aidan, don't do this," she whispered as she rubbed her cheek against my palm.

Her inner-wolf was craving me, I thought, surprised that she was rubbing against me. It gave me a small ounce of hope, but there was also a pleading note to her voice that crushed my heart all at once.

"Hey, little girl, you ready?" Jared said, and she jumped away from my touch.

Jade flushed bright red. "Just give me a sec," she said, looking up at Jared with what could only be guilt. She sat up, glancing back at the house, and then quickly locked her eyes on him. She smiled the kind of bright sunshine smile she used to give me.

"Sure, kitten," Jared said in a husky voice. He crouched down in front of her. His hand snaked out, wrapping around the back of her neck, and he pulled her into him. And she let him. She even looked ... happy about it ... eager. I wanted to look away, but I couldn't, and I watched as he crushed his lips against hers. It was a possessive kind of kiss, one that made my blood boil and adrenaline rush through my veins. There was nothing sensual about it. But then, I was sure it wasn't meant to be. Jared was marking his territory, attempting to give me a clear sign that she was no longer on the market, and it took every ounce of willpower I had to not pull him off her and snap his neck.

He broke the kiss as abruptly as he started it and stood back up. His eyes flared as they settled on her, and then he smirked at me. I fought the urge to growl and let my scent loose on him. I wanted to see him crumble at my feet and inflict as much pain on him as I could. Jared chuckled and gave me a knowing kind of look as if he knew exactly what I wanted to do before he glanced back at Jade. "Don't be long," he said, and then he turned and walked away.

Jade watched him walk with a soft smile on her face, and that smile hurt more than watching the kiss. It was ... contentment. She looked happy. I should have been okay with that. She deserved happy after what I put her through, but I figured I wasn't that good of a person because the last thing I felt was okay with it.

"Jade?" I said, pulling her attention away from Jared's backside.

She looked at me, and her smile disappeared almost instantly. "Yeah?"

"Would you have fought?" I asked. I dreaded the answer. I wasn't really sure if I could handle it, but I had to know. "Did I ever have a chance?" *Do I still have a chance to make this right?* I wondered, unable to voice the last question.

She smiled a little. "Yeah, I think I would have." She rolled up to her feet then and glanced at Jared leaning against a tree at the edge of the forest. "I've got to go."

"Jade," I called, a little desperately, as she started to walk away. This wasn't going as I had hoped, although I had to admit, it was better than I expected. She turned back; her face was blank — emotionless — as she waited to hear what I had to say. "I know it doesn't mean much, but I'm really sorry."

"I know, Aidan," she said with a smile that didn't even come close to reaching her eyes, and then she turned away from me. She took a few steps and then glanced over her shoulder. "My dad called this morning. He'll be home in two days."

JADE

Jared watched me cross the backyard, and it took everything I had not to lash out at him. What the hell did he think he was doing kissing me like that? Or better yet, kissing me at all? It was degrading and overly wrong. What was it with these stupid dogs that made them feel the need to treat everything like a possession? I'd be damned if I was going to be part of a pissing contest between the two of them.

Sure, my mom had been watching from the window,

but a smile or a peck on the cheek would have been more than enough to keep her thinking we were together. The fact that he'd been sleeping in my room (on the floor) for the last two days was more than enough as it was.

I could feel Aidan watching me and his eyes trailing along my back was the only thing that kept me from attacking Jared. I desperately wanted to turn back and tell Aidan that none of this was what it looked like. I wanted to beg him to believe that it was all an act for my mother's benefit and tell him it was all part of the plan to deal with my father. But I couldn't. No matter how much I wanted to fall into his arms and tell him everything, I couldn't. Not yet. He had to believe the act as much as everyone else did. It was the only way we'd be able to beat my dad at his own game. The less people that knew, the less likely my dad would be to pick up on it. As he said in the video, I was Aidan's weakness, and I was beginning to believe it. Right now, Aidan needed to be strong, and when he was near me, he wasn't. He was lost and confused and hopeful when he was with me, focusing on fixing us instead of dealing with my dad and the cougars. And right now, I needed him to be strong. But not just me. The pack needed him to be strong.

Seeing him again was harder than I thought it would be. I had trained with Jared every waking minute for the last two days, just to avoid him. My body ached everywhere, and I was exhausted, but having Aidan lying beside me for those few minutes, gave me more energy than I knew what to do with. My body was alive, my skin sparking, and my inner-wolf did summersaults in my stomach, begging me to go back to him.

I stopped in front of Jared and glared at him fiercely with my hands on my hips. He chuckled and reached out a hand, caressing my face. "You okay?" he asked and then dropped his voice to a whisper, "We still have an audience."

"Nope, not really," I said through gritted teeth, but I forced myself to lean into his touch. The hardest part about letting Jared touch me was the simple fact that my inner-wolf responded to him just as much as it responded to Aidan.

It was a different feeling with Jared, though. Wilder. Reckless. It made my heart thump and my body come alive in an entirely different way, and I hated it. I despised how he made me feel. I loathed the way he spoke to me. And it made me sick that, at times, I wondered what it would be like to just let myself go and become his mate. However, the thing that stopped me was the lack of birds in my belly. Jared only spoke to my inner-wolf, but Aidan ... Aidan spoke to my human heart as well. He made me feel ... alive. Alive in a complete and utterly perfect kind of way.

He chuckled. It was infuriating, and I bit back a slew of nasty words I wanted to spit at him. "Wow, I never thought I'd see the day that a werewolf would make your heart go thumpaty-thump."

"Me neither," I snapped with a frustrated huff, banishing the thoughts from my mind. I glanced over my shoulder then, seeking out the person that had put me in this position. Aidan still sat on the grass, watching, with an utterly blank look on his face.

"Come on, kitten," Jared said and pushed off from the tree. He slung an arm over my shoulder, and he led me into the forest.

I let him. I didn't have much choice until we figured out how deep my mom was in all of this. So, I snuggled into him, wrapping my arm around his waist as we walked the trail.

As soon as we rounded the bend in the trail and

were out of sight, I said, "Seriously, you have to stop calling me kitten, and news flash — you and I are never going to happen." I shrugged off his arm and cut him a sideways glare. "And if you pull that kissing crap again, I'll kill you myself. It's bad enough that I have to lie to him and make him think we're together. You don't need to rub it in his face."

"I don't know about that," he said with a wink. "I think you're warming up to me. Oh, and it's not just us today. Beck and I thought it'd be fun to see if you could stand up to both of us."

"Bring it on," I said, stifling the groan. My whole body ached from yesterday, but I'd be damned if I was going to admit it. And in all honesty, I knew it would be a good distraction. It would give me something to think about other than Aidan and Jared and how crazy they were making me and my inner-wolf. I smirked. "I can't wait to kick your asses."

Note from the Author

Thank you for reading *Deadly Crush*. If you enjoyed this book (or even if you didn't) please consider leaving a review on the site where you purchased it. Word-of-mouth is crucial for any author to succeed and your review, even if it's only a sentence or two, makes a huge difference in helping new readers make the decision to read my books. Many thanks for your support.
XOXO,
Ashley Stoyanoff

Acknowledgments

Deadly Crush owes a lot to my editor, Kathryn Calvert, so thank you, Kathryn, for having such a great eye, and for being so invaluable to me and my work.

To my mom, Jo-Anne, and sister, Jonel, thank you for all your support and for keeping me sane through the writing process.

A quick shout out to all my awesome coworkers. Thank you so much for acting as my trusted sounding boards, and for vetoing the twists and turns that made no sense. You all are the best!

And to my husband, Jordan, thank you. You are my inspiration.

But most of all, I would like to thank the readers, reviewers, and bloggers for your support and for sharing your love of books. You all are the reason I keep writing.

About the Author

Romance author Ashley Stoyanoff is the recipient of two Royal Dragonfly Book Awards for young adult and newbie fiction. Her first book, *The Soul's Mark: FOUND*, came out in 2012. Her other passions include reading and shopping for the latest fashions. Learn more about Ashley and her work at ashleystoyanoff.com.

Further Reading: Deadly Mates

Did you love *Deadly Crush*? Then you should read *Deadly Mates* by Ashley Stoyanoff!

Jade never thought she'd embrace being a werewolf, but after having accepted her new role as alpha female of Dog Mountain's pack, she finds herself doing just that. She's training with the enforcers and learning to use the alpha within her to her advantage. And for the most part, Jade is content, well at least with her training she is.

But Dog Mountain is a small town with big problems. The new alpha pair is divided, splitting the already unstable pack with them, and to make matters worse, Jade's father is on his way home. Except Jade's father and his twisted pack of werecourgars aren't the only threat.

When Aidan brings in a new set of enforcers to weed out the problems within the pack, Jade is forced to delve into the center of the issue. She soon realizes that she is the indirect cause of the uneasiness within the pack, and if Jade doesn't fix it, she'll lose everything, even Aidan.